Praise for the Books of Devon Delaney

"The Cook-Off Mystery series by Devon Delaney is a very tasty treat of a series. Readers will be glued to their seats wrestling with continuing reading the story or getting up to get a tasty treat to eat . . . I highly recommend getting something to eat before you sit down to indulge yourself in the story . . ."

—*Cozy Mystery book Reviews*

"This is a very fun and rollicking mystery that stays light-hearted even as the case gets more complicated, building toward a get-all-of-the-suspects-together-in-a-room conclusion. Cooking, holiday celebrations, and moving family drama all make for the perfect end-of-the-year escape."

—*Kings River Life*

"I've read several in the series and enjoyed them all. It was interesting to see Sherry acting as a judge rather than a competitor. The book kept my interest from the beginning but any book that combines cookies and murder has to be interesting. The characters are varied and seem like a lot of fun. I look forward to more in this series."

—Alicia F.

Books by Devon Delaney

Cook-Off Mysteries

Expiration Date
Final Roasting Place
Guilty as Charred
Eat, Drink and Be Wary
Double Chocolate Cookie Murder
A Half-Baked Alibi
Murder for Good Measure
Serving Up Spite
A Holiday for Homicide

A Holiday for Homicide

A Cook-Off Mystery

Devon Delaney

BEYOND THE PAGE
PUBLISHING

A Holiday for Homicide
Devon Delaney
Copyright © 2024 by Devon Delaney
Cover design and illustration by Dar Albert, Wicked Smart Designs

Beyond the Page Books
are published by
Beyond the Page Publishing
www.beyondthepagepub.com

ISBN: 978-1-960511-86-7

Chapter 1

Juicy Bites

Augustin will celebrate two Labor Days. One traditional, one for entertainment TV. Stay tuned.

"What are you reading?" Kat asked. "Is that a napkin?"

Sherry handed her tennis opponent the folded paper square she'd discovered that doubled as a napkin and a source of news.

"Is this something new Pep's adding to the food truck menu?" Kat asked. After examining both sides, she returned the napkin to Sherry. "A *Juicy Bites* napkin? What is *Juicy Bites*?"

"He said someone left a stack of these printed napkins on his truck windshield this morning. He received fifty. That means first come, first served. Get 'em while they last."

"I'd say they're some sort of puzzle," Kat said with a casual tone.

"The napkin has me guessing why Augustin would have two Labor Days. One for television is interesting. I will stay tuned."

"Ladies, your Gold Coast Avocado Toast is ready," Pep called out from the Toasts of the Town's service window.

Kat's blonde ponytail, wet at the hairline from her recent shower, bobbed with her youthful vigor as she raced Sherry to pick up their post-match breakfast. Kat was the victor in their tennis match, and because of their standing wager, the loser paid the bill. That was happening way too often for Sherry's liking.

Pep's sous chef, Angel, stood alongside Sherry's brother and waved.

"*Hola, señoritas,*" Angel greeted.

Sherry and Kat returned the greeting. "*Hola,* Angel, *gracias por el desayuno.*"

"*De nada, chicas.* See you next time. Pep, take good care of *mis amigas.*" Angel wiped his hands on his apron and picked up an order slip on his way back to the truck's kitchen.

"I love when we can catch a glimpse of Angel, Pep He makes the best toasts in New England. I can't repeat enough, the concept of your food truck is brilliant. Are customers liking the *Juicy Bites* napkins?" Kat asked.

"This is something new. The napkins only started today, but I bet they do. They're cryptic and a curiosity all in one. The message is an unfinished puzzle, so there's got to be more. Clever. That'll keep customers coming back to see if any more information is provided. I don't mind that at all," Pep said. "If the delivery was a one-and-done, they'll be disappointed."

"I do like a good puzzle. And a bonus, whoever the supplier is, they've followed Pep's mandate that everything must be made from recycled material," Sherry said. She reached up and handed her brother her credit card. "Kat and I had a nice match today. The weather has been so lovely this August. Just enough rain to keep my garden happy but not enough to interfere with my outdoor activities. Playing tennis before work is the best way to start the day. A shower in the park's locker room afterward and we're ready to get to work."

"You two have become my best customers, always stopping by for your breakfast after your tennis match," Pep said.

"Give thanks to the mayor for introducing us. Sherry edits his newsletter and I get to see her smiling face at town hall when she stops by to meet with him," Kat said. "Credit also goes to my mom. She knew Sherry was a tennis enthusiast and nudged me to ask her to play. My mom won't admit it, but she makes it her job to keep me active outside work."

Pep leaned forward across the service counter. He pushed the two paper containers toward Sherry and Kat. "Are you liking your job as the mayor's assistant?"

They stepped aside as the next customer gave Pep her order. He jotted down the order and passed the slip of paper over his shoulder to Angel.

"Very much," Kat said. "Mayor Drew has some great ideas for the town. And don't think he won't have a dozen more by the end of the day. He has more energy than anyone I've ever known."

"He's about thirty years younger than his predecessor, who was getting a little long in the tooth," Pep said.

"Same with the ex-mayor's assistant," Sherry said. "Tia was wonderful. She was a quirky character, to say the least, but she loved her job. Kat, you have some hefty shoes to fill."

"I know. It's not a bad thing to bring some fresh blood into town hall. The mayor's a go-getter. I love the idea of working for an overachiever. He doesn't mind that I come in at nine on the dot in the morning after a game of tennis either. He never asks me to skip a match in favor of an early start to the workday. Now that's a good boss."

"We better move along, Pep. The line is growing behind us," Sherry said. She scanned the people helping themselves to the napkins as they waited their turn to place an order. "See you soon."

Sherry and Kat carried their breakfast a short distance to the landscaped green in front of town hall. They took a seat on one of the many wooden benches.

"The town hall location is such a win for the food truck," Sherry said. "Pep parks the truck here around seven thirty and by one he's sold out. Couldn't be more perfect for folks coming into town for the day."

"Awarding Pep the location was a no-brainer for this administration. Mayor Drew is a big fan of the Oliveri family. He'd bend over backward to showcase your father's artisan rugs, your cook-off successes, or Pep's popular food truck."

"It was nice of him to grant a permit for Pep to sell here," Sherry said as she surveyed her breakfast. "And the fact he wrote a note introducing Toasts of the Town's menu in the newsletter was a bonus." As she leaned in to take her first bite, a stretch limousine turning into the lot caught her eye. The car slowly circled the area.

"A celebrity?" Sherry asked. Her gaze followed the car until it turned onto Main Street. She checked her phone. "Town hall doesn't open until nine, right?"

"That's right. Ten more minutes." Kat swallowed a bite of the crunchy whole-grain toast topped with avocado mash, chopped egg, sun-dried tomatoes, lemon, honey, and fresh herbs. "They're back." She tilted her head in the direction of the car.

The car was so long the trunk extended beyond the parking space limits. The engine was cut and the driver's-side door opened. A man in a gray suit stepped out. He walked to the rear door and pulled the handle. A casually dressed man who Sherry estimated to be in his forties left the car and made his way toward the food truck.

"Do you know him?" Sherry asked.

"I know who that is. He's been in the mayor's office multiple times over the last couple of months," Kat said. "He's usually in a suit and tie."

Sherry waited for Kat to elaborate. When no further details came, she probed. "Is he a celebrity of some sort?"

"I'm not at liberty to say until I get the go-ahead permission from the mayor. You understand, don't you?" Kat pinched up her forehead.

Sherry had known Kat for about four months. The look on Kat's face suggested Sherry hadn't cracked the level of friendship where her tennis opponent felt comfortable confiding sensitive information to her. "No problem," Sherry fibbed. "I completely understand."

The ladies ate in silence until Kat introduced a new topic. "I'm organizing an event to raise money for a children's community garden. One tract of land with multiple plots, solely dedicated to gardeners fourteen years old and under. I'm hoping to attract kids who come from the surrounding underserved neighborhoods. The well-kept secret is there are plenty of pockets of poverty in and around Augustin and the kids are the most vulnerable. A garden to tend would provide a community-minded after-school mission."

"What a wonderful concept," Sherry said.

"Don't worry, I know how busy you are with the Augustin Community Garden, and I won't ask you to spearhead the project, as I really ought to." Kat laughed.

"Ask away. I might not volunteer to spearhead the project, but I'd love to help if I'm available."

"What I could use is some advice on how to organize a kids' cook-off. That's my fundraiser idea," Kat said.

"Of course. That's right up my alley. I think I can reduce the steps that go into an adult cook-off down to a kid-sized event for you. I'll start brainstorming right away."

Kat closed her empty food container and stood. "Thanks so much. I should get going. Work time. Want me to bring your container to the recycle bin?" Kat reached out her hand. Her gym bag was balanced precariously on her shoulder, and she struggled to keep from dropping her container.

"You've got your hands full. Let me take them. I'm heading in that direction. I want to say goodbye to Pep too," Sherry said. "You go on. Thanks again for the game. Text me when you want to schedule the next."

Kat handed Sherry her container. "Will do. Might even be tomorrow. Have a great day."

As Sherry neared the truck, she spotted the man from the limo engaged in conversation with her brother. She took her time closing in on the pair, checking her phone every few seconds to appear preoccupied.

"Sure. You must step on a few toes to get anywhere in the television industry. Dog eat dog. I haven't earned that reputation, as far as I know, but the nice guy finishes last, unfortunately."

"I couldn't work in such a cutthroat environment," Pep said.

"Don't kid yourself, son." The man shrugged before rubbing the four-leaf-clover pendant on a leather bracelet between two fingers. "Success is hard to come by. You must play the game, pay your dues, and rise through the ranks." He pointed to the truck. "Take your situation, for example. You don't think you've taken someone else's coveted parking spot here? Someone who maybe needed the location exposure more than you, just to survive another day?"

"I never thought about my luck in that way," Pep said. He peered down from his window perch at his sister. "Sherry, back for seconds?"

Her cheeks warmed when the man leaning on the side of the truck shifted his sights in her direction. Sherry shook her head. "Not today, thanks. Just wanted to say goodbye."

Pep glanced from his sister to the handsome man with the wavy brown hair and back again. Pep gestured for Sherry to come closer. She pinched her brows together and darted her gaze toward the mystery customer.

"He's a television producer if that's what you wanted to know," he whispered. "He's been here a few times recently. He's negotiating with town hall. He needs permits and police presence and stuff like that for an upcoming shoot. Pretty exciting."

"His car is as subtle as a punch in the nose." Sherry laughed.

"Mr. Sturges, your four Parisian Prosciutto Scramble Toasts and four smoothies are ready," Pep called out.

"Thanks," the man said as he handed Pep his shiny platinum credit card. The card caught the rays of the late summer sun and the reflection blinded Sherry for a second.

"This is my sister, Sherry," Pep said. He ran the card through the card reader.

"Another Oliveri. Pleasure to meet you. I'm Basil Sturges. Your brother has kept me well-fed on my trips to Augustin. Are you as good a cook as him?"

Pep couldn't contain his amusement. "Sherry is one of the country's best amateur cooks. She's won more cooking competitions than anyone can count. I wish I was half as good as her. As a matter of fact, several of the recipes I serve are her brainchildren."

"My goodness," Basil said. "It's an honor to meet you." Something in his tone didn't ring true to Sherry. Or maybe she was being judgmental and should accept his compliment word for word.

"Nice to meet you, too," Sherry said.

Sherry's gaze drifted from Basil's face to the large bag of food he received from Pep.

"If you're thinking I'm a huge eater, this isn't all for me. Not to say I'd have any trouble at all polishing this delicious food off all by myself. I have a hungry driver and two co-producers in the car editing my notes for this morning's meeting with the mayor and chief of police. Speaking of which, I'm going to be late if I don't get going."

"That's not what I was thinking at all. I'm always happy when Pep fills a large order, whether it's for one person or many. I'm his biggest fan."

"Need any forks or napkins?" Pep asked.

"I'll take a few napkins. The ones that aren't printed, please. Thanks. Nice to meet you, Sherry. Thanks again, Pep." He lifted his bag and tipped his head before returning to his car.

"Nice guy," Pep said.

"Kat couldn't fill me in on what he's working on, exactly. She's sworn to secrecy," Sherry said. "Putting two and two together, he may be behind the entertainment television the *Juicy Bites* napkins allude to."

"We'll know more soon, I'm sure," Pep said. "News in Augustin spreads like wildfire and it seems we have someone fanning the flames." He tilted his head toward the dwindling pile of printed napkins.

Chapter 2

"Did you have a nice tennis game, dear?" Eileen called to Sherry from her driveway across the street.

"Yes. I wasn't triumphant today. Next time I'll get her." Her neighbor was within arm's length before Sherry closed her car's tailgate lift.

"I'm sure you will. Think positively. That young lady from the mayor's office is sweet. Only yesterday she was a little girl squealing *trick or treat* at my front door. As I recall, she always dressed as some variation of a famous athlete. A soccer player, a football player, a tennis player. She was quite a little tomboy. Now she's all grown up with a very important job."

"Time marches on," Sherry said. She hoisted her tennis gear over her shoulder as she listened for Eileen's response.

"She and Mayor Drew are a breath of fresh air. I've been over to town hall to see what they're all about and I like what I see."

"If they can pass the Eileen test, they receive the highest score," Sherry said. She smiled at her friend, who made most of the town's business hers as well.

"Did Kat mention any word of a television show being filmed in town?" Eileen asked. "It's no secret a production crew has been scouring the town for filming sites."

"I think it's more of a secret than you know," Sherry said. "At least Kat said it was."

"If they wanted to keep it under wraps, the crew shouldn't travel in such a high-profile vehicle," Eileen said. She set her lips in a straight line to reinforce her point. "I've spotted the limo at the beach, at the Community Garden, and even in the grocery store parking lot."

"Any word on what the show is about?" Sherry asked. Her tennis bag slipped off her shoulder and dropped to the pavement with a clatter. Sherry could hear Chutney's muffled bark, a warning he expected Sherry to hustle inside, or else.

"Oh dear, I don't know everything," Eileen said with a wink. "Give me time."

"My fur baby is calling me," Sherry said. "I'll see you soon."

"Your number-one priority." Eileen turned and headed home.

Once inside, Sherry gathered the coffee mugs left on the kitchen table hours earlier. She didn't often get up at the crack of dawn with her fiancé,

Don, but her pre-work tennis game was becoming a regular feature of her summer schedule and a good excuse to start the day bright and early. He didn't always stay the night, as they weren't officially living together, but when he did, she enjoyed seeing him off for his day of running his commuter boat, the *Current Sea*.

After the table was cleared, Sherry opened her laptop and checked her calendar. The articles for this week's Augustin newsletter were due to her by six p.m. Only one had arrived in her inbox and the word count was low. The summer slowdown was in full swing. Editing and formatting the town newsletter would be a breeze with less content. The day was looking relaxed. She had no hours to put in at the Ruggery until tomorrow, despite that her father, Erno, was taking a much-deserved vacation with his girlfriend, Ruth. Amber was capably manning the Ruggery solo and had waved off Sherry's offer to come in. There wasn't even a pending cook-off deadline to prepare a recipe idea for. This might be the day to formulate her fall project, running a children's rug-hooking workshop. She had presented the idea to Erno, and he was ecstatic. Teaching the future generation the heirloom artistry of rug hooking would contribute to keeping the Oliveris' craft thriving and Erno's business relevant. She could also factor in time to give Kat's idea for a children's cook-off some thought.

After an hour of alternating between note-taking and birdwatching a pair of goldfinches harvesting echinacea seeds from her flower garden, Sherry's me-time ended when her phone buzzed. The words *Feral Creations* flashed on the screen.

"I have no idea what or who that is," Sherry said to her dog. Common sense told her the call was a scam. After the fourth buzz her curiosity got the better of her.

"Hello?"

"Good morning. Am I speaking to Sherry Oliveri?"

"Yes, hi, this is Sherry."

"Hello, Sherry. This is Mick Snider. I'm a producer with Feral Creations Productions. Do you have time to speak about a cooking competition?"

"Hi. Yes. Sure." Sherry recognized the introduction as being like so many she'd received from the organizers of cook-offs. The strange thing was, she wasn't currently vying for a spot in a contest, so this couldn't be the reason for the call.

"Great. Sherry, our production company is beginning a new series filming a cooking competition. We have it on the best of authorities that you are one of the country's most talented amateur cooks. An online search of 'Sherry Oliveri' has produced an impressive number of cooking wins all over the country. You've been doing cook-offs for over ten years. Is that correct?"

Sherry's heart skipped a beat. "Yes, that's me."

"We hope you would accept our invitation to be a contestant in our cooking competition. To give you an idea how the process would work, imagine a cook-off that involves various cooking challenges, pits you against other talented cooks, and as the three filming days pass, ongoing contestant eliminations would produce an eventual overall winner. The last cook standing. We're filming in Augustin, over three days, as I said, beginning next week. Monday."

"Monday? Next Monday?" Sherry asked. That was just a week from today.

"Yes. First, you would need an interview with our team and, if that goes as planned, you'd need to clear your calendar for next Monday through Wednesday. Does that sound like something you'd be interested in? If so, I will email you the paperwork to read, sign, and notarize and we will go from there."

"Wow. I'm in shock. This is amazing. Of course. Please send me the documents. When do you need them back?"

"Immediately. As soon as possible. Whichever comes first. Television moves quickly," Mick said. "Do you have time this afternoon for the team to video conference with you? We run an interview session with our potential contestants. We ask questions, get to the bottom of who Sherry Oliveri is, give you a chance to shine on camera, that sort of thing."

"This afternoon. Wow," Sherry said.

"You'll be fine. Don't do any prep. Be yourself. Your personality is what we want to capture."

"That's what I'm afraid of," Sherry mumbled to herself. If all she could utter was "wow," they might reconsider her for the project.

"If you can manage the papers by tomorrow, we can keep the ball rolling. They should be in your inbox within the hour."

"Okay. That all sounds fine. Not the direction I thought today would go in and I'm still processing it."

Sherry's gaze drifted toward the nearest window, where the sun shone brightly on her backyard. The goldfinches were still canvassing echinacea flowers for seeds. She'd thought they were the busiest creatures she'd see today. She was wrong. Her day began with the promise of a light schedule and all that went out the window in five minutes.

"One last request," Mick said. "Please keep our conversation to yourself until details are set in stone. There will be a confidentiality agreement among the paperwork you'll receive today and that's very important for the integrity of the production."

"Okay, yes." Sherry provided Mick with her email address and wished him a good afternoon with the promise of hearing from her soon. "Bye now."

Something startled the goldfinches and they scattered.

Sherry ruffled Chutney's neck fur and shared the news with her Jack Russell. The little dog reacted in terrier style, only displaying a subtle tail wag. "You're the only one I can tell. You could at least show some enthusiasm. How about we choose something nice to wear on camera."

By the time Sherry finished considering clothing choices for her video interview, the documents had arrived in her inbox. She googled Feral Creations Productions before she opened the email. Her eyes widened as she read Basil Sturges was the creative director and senior executive producer with the company. His photo was prominently displayed on the home page of the website. She clicked over to her inbox.

"He was putting on an act when he pretended to be impressed by hearing of my cooking accomplishments. He already knew," Sherry said to her dog. His ears pricked up before relaxing again.

Sherry wasn't surprised at the number of pages of cook-off documents she received. Cooking competitions were strictly regulated affairs involving law firms, big corporations, and a publicity circus covering all aspects of the event. There were often large sums of money at stake for the winner, and the consequences of not understanding the legal repercussions, including tax obligations, were big. She read the papers thoroughly.

Sherry electronically signed her name on seven out of the fourteen pages and initialed an additional five. The final page required agreeing to the confidentiality of the project until notified otherwise by Basil Sturges, who was named project creator/director/producer. She was required to print out the page and sign it in front of a notary. That was a task Sherry knew well. Her friend Vivian, vice president at the Bank of Augustin, was always at the ready to notarize her cook-off documents when necessary.

The phone buzzed as she hit the print key on her laptop.

"Hi, sweetie. How's your day going?"

"It's taken a bit of an unusual turn, but a good one," Sherry said. Don's phone broadcast the background sounds of the marina. She identified a horn bellowing, seagulls squabbling, and the crackle of wind brushing the phone's speaker.

"Mine, too. I have time for a quick lunch. Are you available? Down my way, if possible. I'm doing a special pickup and delivery at four and that's jamming up my regular schedule. Then I'm on call to pick the passengers back up and ferry them someplace else."

"That sounds intriguing. Am I allowed to ask about the special pickup and delivery?" Sherry asked. Her curiosity was on high alert since the morning chat with Kat. And her chat with Basil Sturges. And the napkin puzzle.

Don hesitated. "Some industries have secrecy requests. This trip involves one of those. I can say that it's television-related."

"I met a television producer today at Pep's truck. His name is Basil Sturges. Might the secret voyage be ferrying him around to look at shoot sites? Is he taking some footage for the show he's filming here in Augustin?"

"Hard to keep a secret in this town," Don said with a chuckle. "Do me a favor and sit on the news. He asked me to keep this quiet."

"I completely understand," Sherry said.

"You do?" Don asked. "You don't need any more information? Not that I have any."

"Nope. I'm perfectly happy with just what you told me." Holding on to her own information made Don's reluctance to share easier to take.

"If you're happy, I'm happy. Now, how about lunch? Does the Clam Shack sound okay for a few minutes of loving conversation with my fiancée? Say around twelve fifteen?"

"Perfect."

"See you soon. Can't wait," Don said.

"You don't have long to wait," Sherry said. "See you in twenty minutes."

• • •

Sherry's lunch choice was a lobster roll splurge for her. She considered it her time to celebrate the upcoming chance to be on television, despite the fact she couldn't share the news. Don had a Reuben sandwich, one of his favorites.

"Any plans for the afternoon?" Don asked.

"I didn't until the phone rang this morning. Now I have an interview for a cooking contest. A video interview on my computer," Sherry said. "Not the usual way to choose the contestants. I didn't even have to submit a recipe."

"That means the contest is on television, if I'm not mistaken. You did a computer interview once before when you were in contention to be on one of the cutthroat cooking game shows."

"You've been paying attention to my favorite hobby," Sherry said with a wry smile. "The important thing is, I didn't tell you. You assumed. That way, I'm not in trouble. You know, some industries have secrecy requests." Sherry winked.

"Bonus points for me," Don said. He winked back.

"I didn't get chosen for the show you're talking about, and I might not get chosen for this one. But it's fun to try."

"Good luck," Don said. He leaned across the table and kissed Sherry. "You'll be great." He flipped his phone over. "Time to get going. I'll be late tonight, so I'll stay at my place." He rose from his seat and gathered the empty plates.

"I'll miss you," Sherry said. Don's townhouse lease was up in early fall, a subject that was looming with each discussion of the overnight logistics between the two. She packed away the thought knowing it would resurface again soon.

• • •

The video interview was an hour away by the time Sherry returned home from her lunch with Don. That gave her plenty of time to prep. Only her shoulders and head would be captured on screen, making for a minimal wardrobe change. She already had a floral shirt picked out and resting on her bed. She glanced at her reflection in the bathroom mirror. After an application of eyeliner, mascara, and blush, her look was nearly complete. The last personal detail she had to conquer was her hair. The front locks had a mind of their own after receiving fresh highlights days ago. The plan of attack was to do her best to tame the fly-aways moments before the interview.

Her next task was choosing a location to set up her laptop. The lighting in the kitchen was tricky in the early afternoon. Side light streaming through the window onto her face could be too honest. Not even a supermodel looked good in the revealing, harsh light. She tested turning the laptop camera and rotating her chair ninety degrees to where the indirect light painted her face. She wasn't happy with the angle; too many shadows were cast. An alternative was her bedroom.

Sherry carried her computer upstairs and parked it a distance from the window for more control of the light filtering through the adjustable shades. She tested the shot and quickly realized her en suite bathroom door was wide open and made for a distracting backdrop. She had her location after closing the door and pushing aside all the items on the dresser showing up in the background of the video frame. She sprayed her hair into place and her appearance was complete. Minutes later, the computer rang, announcing her incoming call.

.

Chapter 3

A voice welcomed Sherry before any video was available. "Good afternoon, Sherry. Thank you for meeting with us."

The screen lit up with a vision of Basil Sturges and two others, who introduced themselves as Mick Snider, the assistant to the producer, and Rachel Yaro, a second assistant to Basil.

"As I mentioned to you both, Sherry and I had an impromptu meeting at her brother's food truck this morning," Basil said to the others. "I did a fine job of acting as if she were a stranger who we hadn't spent hours researching. Sherry, you and your brother underplayed your cooking contest accomplishments to the point I almost couldn't contain my laughter. I have never met such a humble talent. The fact that you're not advertising your wins from a rooftop is beyond me."

Sherry's cheeks tingled with pride as Basil painted a glowing portrait of her. "You're too kind."

"Let's put your accolades aside for the time being. We have some questions for you," Basil said. "Be your most fun, bubbly self as you respond to the questions. Whenever possible, use our question in your reply for a fully understandable response. That assists our casting group in matching the answers with the questions when they review the video. You'll know whether you made the cut by the end of the day."

"Television production moves at lightning speed," Mick added.

"Okay," Sherry said. "I'll do my best."

With the preface out of the way, the interview began. Mick posed a question.

"Have I been interviewed for any other cooking shows?" Sherry repeated the question as instructed. "Yes, I have been interviewed for a cooking show once before." She didn't feel the need to elaborate, especially since the previous attempt to get on TV didn't go as well as she'd like.

It was Rachel's turn.

"How long have I been competing in cooking competitions?" Sherry repeated. "I have been competing for ten years, give or take a year. It's my favorite hobby. I fell into it when one day I saw an advertisement in a magazine promoting a recipe contest using a piece of bread. I invented my Orange Dusted French Toast Fingers with Maple Dipping Sauce recipe, typed it up and sent it to the National Wheat Council. Amazingly, a few months later I was notified I won the two-thousand-dollar grand prize. I was hooked after that."

Mick whistled his approval of Sherry's accomplishment. Basil added a question.

"No, I don't know anyone working at the Feral Creations Production Company. And I have no relatives working there. To be honest, I've never heard of Feral Creations."

Sherry answered questions pertaining to her culinary background for close to an hour. Among her favorite questions was being asked to come up with an impromptu recipe using mango chutney, black beans and salmon. This was an easy one. Chutney was a favored cupboard staple in her kitchen, so much so she named her dog after the condiment. Don loved black bean salsa and Sherry made it from scratch at least twice a month. Salmon could be flavored every which way to please any palate. Her answer jumped off her tongue so quickly she forgot to repeat the question back to the interviewers before answering.

"Cooking brings me the greatest joy when I'm challenged to be creative. I play a game with myself most evenings to come up with the most inventive meal I can, for myself and my fiancé, with the ingredients on hand, in the least amount of time. The fewer ingredients I use, the higher the score I award myself."

The interviewers laughed at Sherry's candor.

"He's a lucky guy," Basil said.

"I hope you can meet him one day," Sherry said. She observed Basil's brow flinch at her comment. If Don was captaining the Feral Creations team on board his boat later in the day, he didn't tip his hand.

"Your recipe?" Mick added.

"Oh, yes. I'd rub the salmon fillets with a blend of mango chutney and mayonnaise before sprinkling the fish with ancho chili powder, sea salt and black pepper. Bake until done, time depending on fillet thickness. Meanwhile, I'd combine the black beans, chopped tomato, fresh cilantro, lime juice, chopped red onion, salt and pepper for a black bean salsa topping to the bronzed salmon. Bronzed salmon with sweet heat black bean salsa."

"Three orders, please," Mick said.

"Sounds fabulous," Rachel said. "My mouth is watering."

Sherry raised her hand to the interviewers. "Wait, I have one more ingredient to add. If you're lucky enough to have a firm ripe mango on hand, dice up some and stir it into the salsa. That way there is a nice connection between the salsa and the salmon rub. That's it."

Basil's head bobbed up and down as he considered Sherry's amendment.

Sherry was questioned about her love of recipe innovation, her inspirations for recipes and her favorite ingredients. She'd answered variations of these questions in past interviews but never in such a continuous barrage. Sherry's energy level began to waiver when, mercifully, Basil asked the question that required little thought. The question had been asked many times in various interviews she'd taken part in.

She was happy to repeat the question. "What is my signature Sherry Oliveri recipe? My signature recipe would have to be Grilled Ranch Steak Bruschetta. I won forty thousand dollars in a contest with that recipe. It put me on the culinary map."

The three interviewers huddled together and exchanged quiet remarks, providing her with a brief respite. It wasn't long before the give-and-take resumed. Sherry's replies to their questions kept the panel engaged with nodding heads and constant note-taking. She kept the process running smoothly and everyone was impressed. As the end of the hour approached, she was tapped out.

"Sherry, when the production team began research on the country's finest home cooks, your name rose to the top, along with a few others. That's how we chose you to interview. What we also discovered was you're quite a presence in your community when it comes to volunteering your time for those less fortunate, especially the youngest generation. Is there a volunteer project you're especially passionate about that you'd like to share with us?"

Sherry straightened her sagging posture. Her mouth was dry, and her shoulders were heavy. The question injected some adrenaline into her system. "I volunteer at our town's community garden. I'm also about to coordinate a children's workshop to teach kids the art of rug hooking. All the proceeds will go to a new children's community garden." The idea for the proceeds of her hooking class benefitting Kat's garden popped out of her mouth so quickly she had no chance to reconsider. She made a mental note to pass the notion on to Kat.

"Lovely," Basil said. "I think we have what we need from you. Right, team?"

Mick and Rachel nodded and thanked Sherry for her time before logging off. Sherry blew out a deep exhale. "I think that went pretty well."

After the interview Sherry changed out of her floral shirt and back into her multipurpose short-sleeve polo shirt. She made herself a mug of tea and sat on the couch enjoying the caffeine lift. When the mug was empty and she'd flipped through three end-of-summer sale catalogues, she gathered the document needing to be notarized and headed downtown to the bank, Chutney in tow.

Her phone read nearly four, the time Don was performing his "special pickup and delivery." If she drove her car following the Dock Street route instead of Park Street, she might catch a glimpse of Don's passengers boarding the boat. She wasn't spying on Don and his passengers; rather, she considered it a reconnaissance mission to get a better picture of the people she may be filming with.

Sherry parked her car in the newly revamped visitor lot at the marina, where she'd have a chance of not being spotted. The plan was on point until she saw the expansive limousine parked at an odd angle between the old lot and the new lot. Once again, if the cook-off crew was operating undercover, they chose the most conspicuous location to hide themselves at. Sherry stopped her car just inside the marina entrance as she watched Basil exit the car. Rachel stepped out of the limo dressed in black leggings, brilliant white running shoes, and a dark windbreaker. The driver's door opened, and a block of a man stepped out.

"Oh, to be a fly on the boat deck as the group motors around the town's waters," she muttered to herself.

Basil and Rachel stood alongside the car as the limo driver ducked his head inside the car's trunk. Bracing his legs in a wide stance, he wrestled to remove something cumbersome. The driver then assembled a collapsed mass of steel, canvas, and wheels into a wheelchair. Basil lent a hand assisting Mick as he wriggled out of the backseat and into the chair. Rachel adjusted the leg supports. Mick settled in before giving Rachel a high five.

"That's teamwork," Sherry remarked from her vantage point. She watched Rachel push Mick's wheelchair over the gravel driveway, which wasn't an easy journey. "Don must know Mick's situation and has made special accommodations." She considered texting him to give a heads-up. She reconsidered and decided to let Don handle what was coming his way on his own. Sherry lost sight of them when the group reached the launch dock. That was her signal to get over to the bank and finish her paperwork.

• • •

Vivian made fast work of notarizing the cook-off document. She never asked many questions about the specifics of whatever contest Sherry was involved in, which Sherry appreciated. She could always count on Vivian offering well-wishes for a win and that was the most acknowledgment she wanted. There were no guarantees of a win and Sherry was superstitious about too much fuss being made prematurely. The next steps were to return home, scan the signed document, and email it back to Feral Creations. Sherry would snail mail the original paperwork to them for backup. She was left to wait for word of her acceptance or rejection when all was signed, sealed, and mailed.

Sherry took advantage of the free time to give her rug-hooking workshop more thought. A chocolate chip cookie and another cup of tea were the perfect motivators to drum up some ideas. Not long into the undertaking, Kat texted and asked for a tennis rematch the following morning. The challenge was immediately accepted. Sherry wasn't expected at the Ruggery the next day until ten o'clock, leaving her plenty of time to play, eat, shower, and get to work on time.

Happy to play. Bring money! I feel lucky.

Sure thing.

I met Basil Sturges today. The guy in the limo. He told me about the project he's working on here in town. Your secret-keeping isn't necessary anymore. Juicy Bites is a tattler.

Minutes later Kat replied, *See you at 7:30 sharp tomorrow. I don't think all the secrets are out.*

"What does she mean by that?" Sherry set her phone down and pulled her computer forward. She checked her email. Her inbox contained six out of the seven newsletter articles she was waiting on. No sense formatting the documents into the word processing template until she received the final article, Mayor Drew's address to the town. That was the article the entire body of the newsletter was built around. It would be the last article he submits before his Labor Day vacation.

Sherry put the workshop notes aside and spent the next hour proofreading the newsletter material she collected. When she was done, she moved the mouse arrow back to unread mail and took a deep breath. She clicked on the message she was waiting on. Feral Creations had sent her a response. There was one word on the subject line, "Competition." That was a good indication she was still in the running. Her squeal woke Chutney from a sound sleep. He grumbled and relocated from below her feet to the front door. She opened the email and read the word that always preceded the body of an acceptance email.

"Congratulations."

The details of the cooking competition were limited. She had to show up at the Augustin Public Library next Monday morning, dressed for kitchen success. She was asked to prepare for three days of competition. The length of stay was dependent on the cook's success or failure. All filming would take place in the immediate area and, being a local, she needn't worry about overnight lodging. She was instructed to keep the information to herself, which was frustrating but doable, as she'd had to use discretion during the early stages of cooking contests many times before. The organizers control the publicity under their terms. It was going to take all her willpower not to blurt out the exciting news to anyone who'd listen. Chutney was the only living being she could tell. He was indifferent when she yelled, "Yay!"

Chapter 4

Juicy Bites

Filming 3-day cook-off. Begins Monday at the library. Come cheer on Augustin's finest.

"How did the napkin author know those details?" Kat asked. "Everyone privy to the production schedule has signed a nondisclosure agreement."

"I told you it wasn't much of a secret," Sherry said as she passed Kat a napkin.

Pep slid two orders across the Toasts of the Town's service counter. Eggs Benedict-tini Toast was the day's breakfast choice. "It's fun the way you have to unfold the napkin to get the full message."

"Thanks, Pep," Sherry said. "I'm burning a hole in my credit card paying for Kat's breakfasts."

"You'll get her next time," Pep said. His forced smile didn't lend Sherry much confidence. "See you both soon."

"I hope this information isn't leaking from the mayor's office," Kat said as she followed Sherry to a picnic table. "The mayor has had many meetings with the production team. All hush-hush. And I certainly hope no one thinks I'm the source of the leak. I'd be fired on the spot. Pep has no idea where the napkin stack is coming from?" Her gaze dropped to the brown paper squares. "Could Pep be the author?"

"I also thought for a split second the author could be Pep. Then I came to my senses. Obviously, the author has access to a good printer. That leaves Pep out for sure. His printer is about as efficient as my dad's Rolodex. That's not true. Dad's Rolodex is much more efficient." Sherry envisioned Erno studying the index cards to read comments he'd made on Ruggery customers' preferences. He began accumulating information on color choices, rug design suggestions and pertinent customer milestones on his first day of work over forty years ago. The idea of transferring the Erno-speak data to a computer was an ongoing debate Sherry and her siblings were on the losing end of.

"Pep says he has no idea who the author is," Sherry continued. "He isn't too concerned, either. He says the newsy napkins aren't hurting anyone or anything. He's enjoying the author's anonymity and the entire mystery of where the news is headed. If it continues, that is. It's only been two days."

"I guess no harm, no foul," Kat said. "The mayor hasn't said anything about it, but he might get bent out of shape if too many details are leaked. He's not permitted to speak about the production. Why is someone else spilling the beans?"

"Pep mentioned the mayor took an extra napkin this morning."

Kat threw up her arms. "Ugh, hope that's a good thing."

"Do you think yesterday's message about Augustin having two Labor Days is related to Basil Sturges's production?" Sherry asked.

"Makes sense," Kat said.

"Don ferried the Feral Creations group around to some locations yesterday afternoon. He said one of the sites the production team visited was the town beach. Augustin puts on a good show for Labor Day down there. Food, a mini fireworks display, music. The beach would make a festive venue for a cook-off."

"Being the cooking contester you are, you of all people would know," Kat said. "Sounds like you know as much as me. I admit to being the person that recommended Don for the job."

"You sneaky devil," Sherry said with a laugh.

"The town is small. There aren't even six degrees of separation between most citizens here. You, especially, are a hard one to keep a secret from. You know everyone in Augustin. I figured whether I commissioned your fiancé or a total stranger to take the crew around, you'd find out. Might as well be the one who's best at what he does."

Sherry beamed a grin. "Don said Mick and their driver stayed aboard the boat while Basil and Rachel surveyed the beach's pavilion. When the others returned, they talked about celebrations, grilling, and the end of summer. What do you think?"

"Their driver? Limo driver? Lucky him. He got to go for a boat ride. His name is Yonny. I met him a week or two ago," Kat said. "He seldom comes inside the office. Says he prefers the fresh air while waiting for his charges."

"I'm sure Don was appreciative of having an extra hand on the boat considering Mick's state of immobility, especially if there was a safety incident."

"Absolutely," Kat said.

"My guess is the mayor's office knows the full schedule of the cook-off. It sure would be interesting to know where they're filming each day. Monday is the library. Do you know any other sites they've decided on?" Sherry asked.

Kat shrugged and continued munching her topped toast. After savoring the bite, she swallowed and stared into Sherry's eyes. "Anyone employed in the mayor's office can't say one way or the other. I'm sorry, Sherry." She did a double take when Sherry put on a wry smile. "Wait a minute. You know something and you're not sharing. You're trying to pry information out of me when I should be the one doing the prying."

Sherry gave Kat a sneaky glance. "I have no idea what you're talking about."

"Are you involved in the production?" Kat asked. "I may know the shoot locations, but I honestly am not privy to who is competing. That's the most closely guarded secret of all. I'm asked to leave the room every time they need to discuss the potential contestants."

Sherry took a bite of her toast. She took her time savoring her breakfast. "Anyone involved in the casting end of the production can't say one way or another. I'm sorry, Kat." Laughter erupted from the women.

"Would make a ton of sense, as it's a cooking competition. That much I can say since *Juicy Bites* has blabbed the theme all over town. Oh, I'm so dumb." Kat whacked her forehead with her free hand.

"We're both under a cloak of silence, I guess. Let's agree to share when we can."

"Perfect. I don't want to be fired and neither do you," Kat said.

"Speaking of cook-offs, have you made any progress on the kids' cook-off you're spearheading? I'm mulling over some ideas for you," Sherry said. "At the end of next week, I'll have some extra time to lend a hand in planning."

"Next week? That's about the time Feral Creations should be done with filming. Coincidence?" Kat asked.

"Have you ever heard the saying there are no coincidences?"

"Yes. I take the saying with a grain of salt," Kat said.

"You are wise beyond your years."

"Can you play tennis tomorrow morning? Sounds like you might be busy next week and can't play," Kat said.

"I won't be available Monday through Wednesday, as far as I know. I'd love to play tomorrow morning. I won't be doing much in the way of exercise for a few days after that, if all goes well."

"I don't think cooking is considered exercise, but it's probably more competitive than our tennis games, the way you perform in the kitchen." Kat giggled at her joke. "I'd have no chance against you."

Sherry stood. "I have a better winning record in the kitchen than on the court. Just ask my worn-out credit card. Time to get home, change, and get to work at the Ruggery."

"Time for me to get to work, too," Kat said as she peered at the town hall building.

"Kat," Sherry said. "You won't mention my involvement in the television shoot, will you? I have a gag order until Basil Sturges gives me the okay to talk about it."

"I wasn't told the names of the cooks. And technically, you didn't tell me either. You have my word."

"Thanks. Have a good day. I'll see you tomorrow." Kat made a motion to be on her way but came to a stop mid-stride.

"Sherry? Kat? Hi, I'm so glad you're here. I have a big problem." A voice Sherry heard often rang in her ears.

"Hi, Eileen. And Elvis. Fancy meeting you both down here. Are you trying out Pep's breakfast menu?" Sherry asked. The cat wrapped his tail around Sherry's ankle while his leash lassoed her leg.

"I will, after I visit town hall. It opens in five minutes, doesn't it, Kat?" Eileen asked with a hint of "you better hurry to your office, if you don't want to be late" flavoring the tone. "I want to be first in line for a license tag for Elvis. I want him to be a legal resident of Augustin."

"Eileen, in Connecticut cats don't need licenses. Only dogs. Elvis is legal as is," Kat said with a warm smile.

"I'm going in anyway. I need a copy of my property survey. My neighbors, the Donaldsons, are building a fence and I'll be darned if they aren't claiming four more feet for their border than I'm willing to agree is theirs." Eileen held her gaze on Kat. "Are you finished eating? I'll walk you inside."

"I am, thanks," Kat said.

"Oh, and Sherry. I have a big problem. I forgot my dang reading glasses. Would you have a minute to come with me and look at whatever land records are filed for my property? I'll be darned if I'm forced to pay a surveyor five hundred dollars to confirm my suspicions. Akin to highway robbery, if you ask me."

"I have about fifteen minutes to spare," Sherry said. "I'm coming."

"Careful, you're all tangled in Elvis's leash," Kat said. She knelt and unraveled the leash from Sherry's leg.

The three ladies and a leashed cat paraded across the parking lot. They had trouble keeping up with Elvis as he bounded up the marble steps of town hall. They passed the fluted columns supporting the massive overhanging roof and yanked open the cumbersome wooden doors. The cavernous reception hall was a vision in white marble. The echo of their tapping shoe soles on the expansive porcelain floor tiles announced their arrival. As they neared the mayor's office, the hallway's grandfather clock displayed the fact Kat was one minute late to work. She didn't mention the fact so neither did Sherry. Sherry and Eileen walked Kat to her office.

"Stop by when you're done," Kat said as she settled in a rolling seat behind her desk. She was the first line of defense outside the mayor's closed door. A desktop copper-trimmed nameplate affirmed as much.

Kat Coleman—Special Assistant to the Mayor

Sherry admired the air of confidence Kat displayed when she shored up the papers on her desk and clicked on her desktop computer. Sherry spotted a man seated in one of the chairs feet from her desk.

"You're early," Kat said.

"You're late. The mayor let me in," the man said.

"One minute. First time ever. I had an emergency to attend to. One of our constituents had a land dispute to settle, requiring intense scrutiny and research." Kat tipped her head toward her shoulder playfully. "And she's a good friend of my mother."

"Family first," he said with a smile.

Eileen sent an enthusiastic wave in the man's direction.

"See you soon," Sherry said. "Land records this way, Eileen." Sherry pointed to a door farther down the hall.

Before the women reached their destination, a couple crossed their path.

"Morning, ladies."

Sherry's gaze tracked the greeting to a woman pushing a wheelchair. Sherry was taken aback by the unhappy frown on the woman's face. "Rachel. Mick. This is a surprise." With Eileen at her side, Sherry was at a loss for what to say next. Any follow-up may contain a hint of the upcoming work they were collaborating on and jeopardize her chances at participating. She needn't have worried as the duo continued on their way toward the mayor's office without more than a smile.

"Do you know those two?" Eileen asked. "I saw them downtown a day or two ago. They were having quite an argument. Another man was with them. Dapper-looking gent with expensive taste in clothes."

"All three were arguing?" Sherry asked. "Or was it just a spirited conversation?"

A Holiday for Homicide

"I could make out some choice words from walking about ten feet behind them. Made my hair curl so I ducked into the dry goods store. Do you know them or don't you?"

"I think I do," Sherry said.

"You think, but don't know for sure? Sherry, you're talking in riddles." Eileen led Sherry into the room that housed land records. Not long after, Eileen had the information she needed. They went their separate ways, as Eileen wanted to double-check Elvis' legal status at the license bureau, despite the fact she was told he was on the up-and-up. Sherry continued down the hall to give Kat a departing wave. Since the office didn't appear busy, she stepped inside.

"Mission accomplished. Eileen has her ammunition and is ready to take on her neighbors and the case of the alleged offending fence line." Sherry dusted her hands together.

"She stops in here so often I'm beginning to think she's spying on me," Kat said with a laugh. "If I didn't know any better, I'd suspect my mother of putting her up to the task." Kat's glance lingered on the man still seated in her office.

"I wouldn't worry about that. Eileen has a keen interest in knowing all aspects of Augustin's goings-on. Short of dumpster diving through the building's trash, patrolling the halls may be how she stays current."

"To each her own," Kat said with a sigh. "I'm sure she appreciated your help." She squared up some paperwork before raising her gaze to meet Sherry's. Kat lowered her voice.

As she began to speak, Sherry needed to lean in to catch the words.

"Were you ever harassed at work to the point you were running out of options?" In a beat, she continued. "Never mind, what am I saying? You work with your wonderful family. You'd never have that problem."

"Kat, what do you mean? Who are you talking about? Is someone bothering you?"

The man seated opposite Kat's desk cleared his throat. "Excuse me, but aren't you Sherry Oliveri, the famous cook?"

Sherry straightened up. She glanced behind her. "Yes, I'm Sherry. Famous? I don't know about that. Do I know you?"

The man stood and took a step forward.

"Everyone knows you, Sherry," Kat said. "This is Garrett Stein. He's a writer for *Absolute Entertainment*. He's working here on an assignment."

Sherry tracked Kat's expression as the man spoke. She showed no

25

outward signs he was the harasser. Then again, from what Sherry read in some of her favorite suspense novels, when someone is being pressured by an aggressor, they're programmed to not let on. That's part of the control the bully has over the victim. On the other hand, he had an angelic face and a peaceful demeanor. She'd reserve judgment.

"Nice to meet you," Sherry said. Garrett shook Sherry's hand.

"The pleasure is mine."

He sat down and returned to reading a book. It was hard to reserve further judgment when she read the title of his book, *Script for Murder*.

"Kat, I'm heading to work. Keep me posted on our next game," Sherry said. "And on all fronts."

"It's you who needs to keep me posted," Kat said.

As Sherry turned to leave, the door to Mayor Drew's office swung open. Rachel skirted the edge of the paneled door as it came to rest with a screech, halfway open. "Oops, I hope I didn't scratch the floor. Now the door's stuck."

"That door swells up if we have humidity in the air, which basically happens all of August. The door's over one hundred and fifty years old," Kat said.

"I'm running to the ladies' room. Too much coffee. And I left something in the car. I keep doing that. Car's way too big. I keep losing track of my stuff. I hope Yonny's still parked here. And I've been relegated to get a glass of water for Mick." Rachel shifted her attention from Kat to Garrett. The scowl on her face disappeared. In its place grew a broad smile. "Hello again, Garrett. Can I get you something to drink?" The teasing lilt in her voice left Sherry wondering about the nature of their familiarity.

"No, thanks," he said.

"We're almost done with the legal issues, then you're welcome in the meeting," Rachel said.

"Yup. Thanks," he said.

"You know where to find the ladies' room and the water cooler," Kat said, her tone chilled. "If you need a hand or the cooler's dry, let me know."

Rachel attempted to squeeze past Sherry at the doorway. When they were shoulder to shoulder, she turned on her heels. "I didn't have a chance to buy breakfast at Toasts of the Town and I miss it. Your brother has a good gig going."

"Thanks, Rachel. I'm proud of him."

Rachel redirected her gaze to Kat. "I forgot. Kat, I bought you a buddy cap. A reminder of the good old college days. I'll get it to you when I remember to pack it. Ever since the accident my memory is weak. Every day my recollections grow stronger and something pops up in my brain, like our old times together. On a good day, I've got so many balls in the air I can hardly think straight. Imagine how a bump on the head has added to the clutter in here." Rachel tapped her temple. "Basil's made me Mick's unofficial personal assistant, which I don't mind, but I'm having a devil of a time doing my own job properly."

Kat's gaze shifted from Garrett to Sherry and back to Rachel. Kat's mouth was in a tight line. "Thank you. Please, don't make a special trip to get it. You didn't have to get me a gift."

"Fate brought us back together. I feel like you're my good luck charm. I'll tell you why when I get back. I wanted to make sure we could dress for the occasion if we got a minute to celebrate the olden days," Rachel said with a broad smile. "Be right back." She resumed an urgent pace.

"The olden days are long gone," Kat said. "She's beating a dead horse if she thinks we have anything to celebrate together." Kat's tone stung Sherry's ears. Rachel and Kat were not on the same page concerning their friendship.

Sherry turned to leave Kat's office. She peered back when Kat addressed her.

"See you tomorrow at the courts. What's on tap for the rest of the day?"

"Business as usual. A full day at the Ruggery," Sherry said. She paused, curious if Kat would bring up the subject of the workplace harassment. She was met with silence. Kat would bring the matter up if she thought Sherry could help, she assumed. Maybe tomorrow after the match.

Chapter 5

Juicy Bites

Prepare for more than cooking games. The blame game is fun, until someone gets hurt.

Sherry and Chutney were stationed below Pep's service window deciding on what to order when Pep reached down from his perch and handed his sister a napkin. She read the words with a furrowed brow.

"Where is this message coming from? How does the author know what the show content is? What's the blame game refer to? Why would someone get hurt? It doesn't add up."

"The napkins may have gone off the rails," Pep said. "If I get too many complaints, I won't put them out anymore. That is, if I receive any more."

"Strange. I don't even know more than the bare minimum and I'm a . . ." Sherry caught herself. She studied Pep for any sign he sensed what she almost revealed. She wondered if her dislike of keeping her exciting secret was written all over her face.

"Pep, order up," Angel called out from the kitchen area.

"One sec, Angel," Pep replied. "Sorry, Sher, can you repeat what you said? I didn't catch it all."

"I'm so curious about who's supplying the information for the napkins."

"Me, too," Pep said. "Today's pile of napkins was on the windshield again this morning when I picked up the truck," Pep said. "Whoever left them even wiped the remaining overnight drizzle off the glass and secured the napkins in a baggie before putting them under the windshield wiper. I saw one smeared footprint on the truck's bump-step, and it wasn't made by me."

"How about the garage's security camera? Have they caught anyone?" Sherry asked.

"Yesterday the video filmed one person. Not helpful. He or she is completely hooded and cloaked. That figure dashes out of the frame as fast as he or she came in. They didn't stop to wave at the camera."

"So strange," Sherry said.

Pep boxed a toast for a waiting customer. "Thanks, Angel. You think the writer has inside access to the production process and is sharing something that shouldn't be shared?"

"The writer's got to have good inside access, yes," Sherry said. "What's being shared today seems like a warning."

"Are you involved in the cooking competition, by any chance? Angel and I have a bet going. He says no and I say yes."

"I'm sworn to secrecy. You know how that goes in cook-offs. I can't confirm, although I could deny if that applied." Sherry winked. "Based on those terms, I can't declare a winner between you two."

Pep pinched his index finger and thumb together and swiped them across his mouth. "It's no secret you're the pride of Augustin when it comes to cooking competitions. All clues lead to you being in it. My lips are zipped."

"Thank you," Sherry said. "Word's getting out, but not from me. I know cook-off rules and when the organizers ask for participants to sit on details, they mean it."

"What does the suggestion to be prepared for more than cooking mean?"

"Now we're getting into the shady area where I have to watch what I say." Sherry gave her reply some thought. "I'm sure the cook-off will have other challenges and skill drills besides actual meal prep. You've seen those on other cooking shows. They're par for the course. I'm not giving anything away. That's my best guess."

"I've seen that on shows. The skill drills can be all over the place in terms of testing the cook."

"That's right. Why the message mentions a blame game and suggests someone might get hurt, I can't fathom. That's just silly," Sherry said. "Yes, I might have been witness to a few murders in the cook-off realm. That isn't the norm. I'm not too worried. The *Juicy Bites* author is toying with the readers."

"I hope you're right, especially now that I know you're a participant," Pep whispered.

"Me, too," Sherry whispered back.

"How far is this *Juicy Bites* mystery going to be taken?" Pep asked. "Basil Sturges can't be happy about the leaks. He's an intense guy. Success in his work isn't an option."

"He may not be happy but I don't think you're too broken up over the fact people are coming back to the truck to read the next installment and, at the same time, buying a toast."

"You've got me there," Pep said. "No tennis this morning? It's becoming a regularly scheduled event between you and Kat. Taking today off?"

Sherry shrugged. "Not sure who messed up, but yes, I thought we had a game this morning. The plan was to play, eat here with her, then get over to the store. She never showed up and she didn't answer my call when I checked in with her. So, I went home, changed, and thought I'd eat here anyway."

"Should you be worried?" Pep said.

"She's incredibly responsible and organized from what I've seen of her. Double booking is usually the culprit."

"Been there, done that," Pep said with a laugh.

"Me, too. I've made that mistake before. Could be she had too much on her mind." Sherry considered the words Kat whispered to her in her office yesterday, followed up by the opinion she had of Rachel. Sherry had every intention of talking about the subject of Kat's alleged harassment over breakfast. She also considered delving deeper into Kat's relationship with Rachel if she was open to that. With Kat a no-show, all that was on hold. "I don't want her to feel bad. I left her a message to call me when she got a chance."

• • •

Thirty minutes later, Sherry and Chutney were on their way to the Ruggery for the morning shift. In the summer Sherry parked her car in the distant free lot to stretch her legs and enjoy the stroll along Main Street. She absorbed the colonial flavor of the building housing her family's business as she neared the Oliveris' hooked rug store. She admired the architecture every time she saw it. Depending on the weather and season, the details both varied and astounded. During late August mornings the summer sun nestled in the façade's angular nooks, teasing the onlookers' depth perception. Her favorite dressing on the building was a fresh coat of snow. She would have to wait months for that look and didn't mind one bit. Her gait picked up as she neared the entrance.

The tall windows with the tight pane grids across the glass were dark, indicating the interior lights were off and Amber had yet to arrive. Sherry unlocked the store's side door, switched on all the lights, unlocked the front door, and flipped the *Closed* sign over to read *Open*. She wasn't alone for long.

"Good morning, Sher," her strawberry-haired coworker said as she approached from the kitchen. "Another lovely August morning." She bent down and ruffled the scruff of Chutney's neck. "I brought your best friend." On cue, Bean, Amber's Jack Russell terrier, bounded toward Chutney and initiated playtime.

"You're a golden ray of sunshine," Sherry said. "Your yellow dress is so cheerful. I need to up my fashion game." She looked down at her navy blue capri pants and white polo shirt.

"Thanks. I'm celebrating the last gasp of summer."

Bean and Chutney came to rest in front of Sherry's tennis bag. She had tucked the bag under the sales desk to keep it out of sight. Even then, the bag wasn't hidden well enough to dissuade inquiring canine noses. The dogs poked around her tennis clothes and sneakers, paying extra attention to a used can of tennis balls.

"Bean has sniffed out a tennis ball in your bag. His new trick is to fetch the ball and bring it back to yours truly. World's smartest dog, besides Chutney, wouldn't you say?"

"No argument here," Sherry said. "Chutney has no interest. Can I donate the used balls to your training supplies?" She reached in the bag and rolled the ball away from Bean, who waited patiently for the command to track the ball.

"Thanks. Go get," Amber said. Bean's short legs carried him across the wood floor on command. He returned the ball to Amber's feet.

"Simply amazing," Sherry said. "Maybe you can show me how to teach that trick to Chutney."

"I'd love to," Amber said. "He's a natural, just needs some motivation."

After Bean's demonstration, a man entered the Ruggery.

"Good morning, Sherry," Basil said. He leaned down and picked up the ball at Amber's feet. "Drop this?"

"Thank you," Amber said.

"What a nice surprise," Sherry said. She hoped he hadn't noticed the blatant double-take she performed when he walked in. "Are you looking for a rug? Do you live close by? We ship anywhere."

"I live in Manhattan. But, I apologize. I'm not here to shop for one of your family's fabulous rugs I've heard so much about. Ask anyone you come across in town about the must-sees and must-visits and the Ruggery consistently makes the top five destinations. And I asked a lot of people. As much as I'd love to shop, I'm steering through a mini crisis and wanted to speak to you about it."

"That doesn't sound good." Sherry arched her back to allow Amber to be seen behind her. "Amber, this is Basil Sturges. He's working on a television production here. His crew eats at Pep's food truck sometimes."

"That's exciting. Nice to meet you," Amber said.

Basil nodded in return.

"I'll leave you two to chat." Amber threw up her hand in a casual wave.

Sherry softened her voice even though Amber was out of sight. "I hope there isn't a problem with the contest."

"Don't worry, everything is still slated to begin production Monday. We've selected the other amateur cooks for the cooking competition and nearly every aspect of the schedule is on point."

Sherry blew out an exhale of relief. Maybe Basil was exaggerating when he used the word *crisis*.

"The problem is one of my production team has gone AWOL. Cut off all contact. She hasn't answered calls or checked in since yesterday afternoon. She missed three crucial and mandatory production meetings."

"I'm sorry. That's tough," Sherry said.

"I wanted to assure you in person, the show will go on, and on schedule. But, you'll soon hear we're replacing Rachel Yaro. My hope is she isn't the person who's been leaking production secrets to *Juicy Bites*. The timing of her disappearance raises red flags. That would be a double slap in the face amid an already time-sensitive situation that needs a speedy resolution. Not to mention, she'd have committed a fireable offense."

"Strange," Sherry said. Her thoughts drifted to Kat, who could also fall into the AWOL category.

"It *is* strange. Rachel has been on my team for about a year. I've come to rely on her. She knows the television production industry inside and out. She also knows the strict timeline we run under. I cannot grant exceptions for unexplained absences. She's seen others replaced for this behavior so it shouldn't come as a surprise to her I had to do what I had to do. I'll be happy to hear her reasons for her absence, but she must understand the show goes on, and in this case, without her. Business aside, I sincerely hope she's alright."

Sherry nodded in agreement. She also hoped Kat was alright.

"The reason I'm here is to let you know we've made an immediate replacement for Rachel. I'm letting all the contestants know. I feel like we all must trust each other and be transparent about production changes. Her name is Stacy Trainer. She's been in our organization long enough to understand the process very well. She'll be contacting you soon with more details as need be."

"Okay. Stacy Trainer." Sherry repeated the name to exercise her memory. "Can I ask a few questions while you're here?"

Basil checked his phone. "I only have a few minutes. I need to contact everyone else with this personnel change. Email, phone, messaging. My communication method depends on who, what, where and when."

"I'll be quick." She condensed all her questions into one. "When will I get further details about the entire competition process?"

Basil smiled. "The way these things work, to keep the integrity of a surprise ending, is to cloak the content in secrecy. We want genuine reactions from the cooks, whether it be surprise, confusion, frustration, competitive angst, whatever. All I can tell you is you'll need a clear schedule next Monday through Wednesday. Monday you'll meet the other contestants. Don't worry, we'll feed you lunch and you'll be home by six o'clock each day." He held his gaze on Sherry as she absorbed his words.

"Okay," Sherry said when her mental schedule was somewhat organized.

"I trust your years of experience in cook-offs have given you great insight into what you'll be up against. You understand this isn't cookie-cutter cook-off programming. There will be twists, turns, and surprises that will treat the audience to a cooking competition unlike any other. All this info, and more, will arrive spelled out in an email you'll receive by the end of the day. Stacy is hitting the ground running by putting the details together as we speak. Are you feeling good about everything?"

"I think so. I love the challenge of a new spin on cooking contests," Sherry said. "One last question. Since word about the show seems to be trickling out, when can I tell my family and my fiancé I'm on the show?"

"I fully understand what you're up against. Your fiancé, Don Johnstone, ferried us around on his wonderful boat as part of the production setup and it took all my might not to have an investigative conversation with him about the life of Sherry Oliveri."

"I stuck to my agreement, and he knows almost nothing. What he does know he's deduced on his own."

"I appreciate that. One of the shortfalls of filming in such a tight-knit community as Augustin is the difficulty of keeping the details of the shoot under wraps. I get the feeling everyone in town has everyone else's back. That's a wonderful characteristic of a hometown. You're very lucky."

"I agree," Sherry said.

"It would be alright if you told them you've been selected to compete in a television cooking challenge program. I can't imagine any more details than that will emerge before filming, despite the *Juicy Bites* blurbs your brother is showcasing at his truck." Basil's face screwed up into a frown. "You're not feeding information to him, are you?"

"Absolutely not," Sherry insisted. "I take my pledge of discretion very seriously. I've been in lots of contests where the contestants must stay mum so as not to spoil the timing of the publicity. No worries there. Pep has nothing to do with the information other than enjoying the repeat customers the napkins bring in. He's in the dark about their source like the rest of us."

"Just checking. To tell you the truth, my gut reaction is Rachel may be behind the leaks," Basil said. "I can't fathom her reasoning, but she's now missing and that doesn't bode well for her. Maybe the jig was up. That's another reason it's important to locate Rachel. She needs to be reminded one aspect of a career in the television industry is safeguarding secrets."

"I can only speak for myself, and I'll only tell a few what I'm allowed to tell," Sherry said.

"Appreciated. Keep an eye out for the email from Feral Creations for the finalized schedule details."

"Is there a prize for the winners?" Sherry asked. She didn't want to assume a large prize, but the thought was there.

"Wouldn't be much of a competition if there weren't a whopper of a prize. Right?" Basil said. "One thing about dangling an attractive lure in front of hungry fish: you're sure to see a knock-down, drag-out battle for the fat, juicy worm. What viewer wouldn't want to see the same between motivated cooks? And I'm planning on having a record number of viewers with my show's concept. Be prepared to cook your heart out for America."

The conversation had taken a turn that made Sherry shudder. She was in deep and there was no turning back. Had her years of cooking competitions prepared her to be watched by tens of thousands, possibly millions, of viewers?

"See you Monday at the library," Basil said with a casual tone. He let himself out, accompanied by the piercing chime of the antique brass bell hanging over the doorframe.

Chapter 6

Amber emerged from the storage closet cradling two skeins of cloud-soft lambswool. One bundle was lavender, the other sage. "Hazel Riordan is coming in for these two. I'll ball them up while you tell me all about Mr. Sturges." Amber pulled a stool up to the lengthy wooden sales counter and began her task. "He's the man behind Augustin going Hollywood?"

"That's right. Only he's more Manhattan than Hollywood. His production company is filming a cooking competition in and around town. For three days. Filming starts Monday."

"Three days. That's a long competition. Are you part of the action?" Amber asked.

"I am," Sherry said. "I would have told you sooner, but I've had a gag order placed on me until he gave me the go-ahead, which he did. I've been through the interview process and things are moving in the right direction. Basil said more details are on the way very soon. For now, all I know is the fun begins Monday morning and I've been told to clear my schedule for three days. I'd imagine if I'm knocked out early all that goes out the window."

"How exciting," Amber said. "Remember when we met at my first and only cook-off? I naively thought I could cook against you and do well. Look at me now and look at you now. Goes to show, stick with your talents. Mine isn't competitive cooking."

"You've got more talent for selling, customer service, and retail productivity in your pinkie than I've got cooking talent in my whole body." Sherry helped herself to the lavender skein of wool. "If I ball this up, would you be able to spot me here on Tuesday and Wednesday, if need be?"

"Of course. I still owe you swap time from my bout with the flu last spring," Amber said.

Sherry untied the yarn skein, which fell into a large oval of loose yarn string. She looped one end of the oval around the left post of the nearest chair. She looped the opposing side on the right chair post. The job of rewinding the yarn into a ball was as easy as beginning with the snipped end of the yarn and following the oval round while winding the yarn over itself to form a ball. Thanks to the chair post method, an extra pair of hands wasn't needed. Customers were appreciative of the Oliveri staff saving them the step of winding the fresh wool yarn into a more user-friendly shape to hook with, one that didn't knot or tangle as the loose oval shape was prone to do.

"I appreciate you so much. Thanks," Sherry said. "Hazel Riordan has been hooking rugs for decades. She's one of Dad's oldest customers. I remember coming in the store with Dad when I was about eleven. She came in with one of her three miniature schnauzers for a portrait of the dog to be drawn up on canvas. I thought, 'this lady will have a piece of art with her dog's portrait hooked in gorgeous wool. How amazing is that?'"

"She's so lucky," Amber said. "All our customers are lucky."

"I couldn't agree more."

"Are you looking forward to the competition? How are you practicing? Sounds like it's not your standard cook-off."

"I haven't had time, or even enough information, to give the whole matter much thought," Sherry said. "There's already a hitch."

"What's that?" Amber asked.

"One of the production crew has gone missing. Her job was as assistant producer, and she hasn't checked in with Basil since yesterday. He said he's forced to replace her. I met Rachel on a video call, and she knew her stuff. She was enthusiastic and fully engaged in the project. Too bad."

"I wonder if that'll delay the schedule?" Amber asked.

"He has her replacement lined up. Only a small bump in the road, it seems."

"Maybe *Juicy Bites* will fill us in tomorrow," Amber said. "That's my current local news blotter."

"You've been reading *Juicy Bites*? At Toasts of the Town?" Sherry asked.

"I sure have. I look forward to getting a breakfast toast before work so I can see the latest installment. The content's beginning to make sense from what you've just told me. I'm kind of addicted to the napkin news. And the food is great, obviously."

"There's lots of speculation on the news' source. Basil asked me if I had anything to do with it all because the napkins show up at Pep's food truck. Of course, I don't. I know just as much, or as little, as anyone."

"The logical person to suspect is Pep. What do you think? Does he have anything to do with *Juicy Bites*?" Amber asked.

"He says he doesn't."

"It would be a genius marketing scheme to attract repeat customers," Amber said. While she was speaking, Amber was displaying her mastery at winding yarn into balls. "I'd say Basil Sturges and company are also likely candidates. Think about it. By putting out tidbits of news on the production they're drumming up interest in future viewers." She collected the lavender ball of yarn from Sherry's hands.

"Makes sense."

"Do you have any idea what today's message meant? I hadn't had my first sip of coffee when I read it. I wasn't fully mentally functional. What about someone getting hurt? That was an interesting twist. Any idea what that meant?"

Sherry threw her hands up in the air. "The whole package is a mystery. Who writes it, why they write it, and where's it leading the reader."

The bell over the door tinkled and a woman entered. A high-end purse patterned with designer initials was displayed prominently on her forearm. Her gold-barred ballet flats shuffled across the wide-planked wood floor with as much orchestration as a performing dancer. "Good morning, ladies. Two of my favorite people. I've come for my yarn."

"Good morning, Hazel. We have your yarn right here. Would you like an extra skein of each color? Matching the exact dye lot is always tricky if you run out."

"Oh." Hazel sighed. "Such gorgeous colors. Oliveris never disappoint. No, I think this should be enough." She fished in her purse and pulled out her rhinestone-bedazzled wallet. "Did you see the gigantic car parked outside your store? Honestly, some people flaunt their wealth like a peacock flaunts his feathers. People are collecting around the vehicle as if they expect the president to be getting out soon. It would be great for business if word got out he was shopping in your store."

Sherry laughed. "Is it a long black limousine?"

"Perfect description," Hazel said. "Monstrosity is another word for it."

"I believe the car belongs to a television producer who's in town working on a project. He was in the store a while ago. I'm sure Kat has told you about the production team that's been visiting town hall for permits and such."

Hazel shook her head and not a strand of her silver bun moved out of place. "I've never been a helicopter parent. I don't hover around my daughter as much as I'd like, if only to hear more about her job. Kat's a twenty-seven-year-old independent woman. Ever since she moved out of our house, I hear from her on average of about once a week. I didn't even know you two had made a tennis connection until recently." After Hazel vented, she added, "Yes, she may have mentioned producers were in town. I've also seen the *Juicy Bites* newsy napkins. They've told me more than Kat's willing to share."

Choosing not to incite Hazel's testiness, Sherry changed the subject. "I don't suppose you know where Kat is right now, do you?" Sherry wanted to coax the answer out of the woman without causing her any undo alarm about her daughter's disappearance.

"At work, of course." Hazel's answer was clipped. "Why wouldn't she be? The whole administration is dependent on her good work."

"Okay, thanks. I owe her a call."

"Speaking of the napkins, is Pep writing them as an advertising gimmick?" Hazel asked. "If he is he should speak up and claim responsibility because Kat may lose her job if the suspicion lands on her." She lowered her voice to a near whisper. "Kat has better sense than to be writing them, I do hope."

Sherry chose to keep the conversation as noncombative as possible by not addressing Hazel's comment, even though the point was a valid one. "Pep's not writing them. He's gotten a delivery the last couple of mornings on his truck's windshield. He put the stack out for customers, and they're welcomed. The author's identity is a mystery," Sherry said.

"How thrilling. Except, of course, if Kat's involved. I do need to ask Kat about what's going on. Not in a helicopter parent sort of way. More as one curious adult to another. Here's my card," Hazel said as she handed Sherry her credit card.

"I'm sure she'll happily tell you everything she can," Sherry said, although she herself had many questions for Kat.

"I hope Augustin doesn't let fame go to her head." Hazel giggled so hard she snorted. She dabbed at her nose with a tissue she retrieved from her purse. "Oh, my. I haven't had a belly laugh in forever."

Sherry completed the transaction and Hazel left the store. "This store makes even fussy folks happy."

"Sure does," Amber agreed.

Sherry fidgeted with the temperamental credit card reader before pushing it aside. "I hope Hazel's daughter isn't in any trouble."

"What do you mean? Why would she be?" Amber asked.

"She and I had a tennis game scheduled this morning. We planned the game yesterday. She never showed. I didn't want to alarm Hazel, but how do you forget a plan we made half a day ago? I left her a message this morning and have yet to hear a word from her."

"Hazel said Kat was at work."

"I hope that's the case," Sherry said.

"She'll check in soon, I'm sure. By the way, why do they have different last names?" Amber asked. "Kat and Hazel. Coleman and Riordan."

"Hazel's been married three times. Once before Kat was born, Kat's father was number two, and Mr. Riordan was number three, until he passed away. Hazel was over forty when she had Kat. Kat thinks that explains Hazel's parenting style. She claims her mother was beyond her nurturing years. Those are Kat's words."

"Parenting is way out of my talent zone. I'll stick to sales," Amber said as she headed to the back of the store.

Hours later, Sherry took advantage of a lull in customers. She plunked herself down on a stool and texted Don a message. She knew he'd be out on his commuter boat, picking up or delivering passengers on his daily route between Augustin and Long Island. She needed to ask him about their dinner plans. She typed one word when her phone vibrated. Kat must have played her message and was replying. She read the screen. "Oh, no." A chill rippled down her spine.

Chapter 7

"Hello." Sherry's throat tightened. She choked out a name. "Ray?"

"Yes, it's me. I hope you're doing well. Do you have time to speak? It won't take long. Are you sick? You don't sound like yourself."

Sherry hesitated before replying. "Yes, no, I'm fine. Just surprised to hear from you. The timing of your call is, well, startling. Are you just checking in?" Sherry sensed her question wasn't going to prompt the answer she desired.

"I wish this was a social check-in with only a recipe question, but it's not."

She was correct. "Oh, no," Sherry repeated. His directness reminded her, Detective Ray Bease served dual roles in her life. One was as a friend with similar interests in cooking, recipe innovation, and perfecting baked chicken thighs; the second role was as Homicide Detective for Hillsboro County. He was the man she collaborated with on several occasions during murder investigations. "I dread asking what this call may be about, if not recipes."

"I'll get right to the point. Do you know a woman by the name of Kat Coleman? She's the Augustin mayor's office manager and special assistant."

"Yes, I do. Is she okay? What happened to her, Ray?" Sherry's voice grew frantic.

"Why do you assume something happened to her?"

"The first clue is you're a homicide detective and you said this isn't a social call. The second clue is she missed our tennis game this morning with no word and I'm worried."

"As far as I know, she's fine. Unless there's something else you'd like to tell me."

Sherry mulled over whether to share recent occurrences with Ray. It was only a day ago Kat questioned Sherry about harassment. The conversation was cut short before Sherry could get to the reason for the question. If Sherry brought the matter up to Ray, he'd say there wasn't enough information to go on. Another consideration was the chilly vibe she witnessed between Kat and Rachel at town hall. What was that all about?

Sherry had been a part of multiple murder investigations while clinging to the coattails of the detective. The process taught her inconclusive facts are just that and throwing them in the mix can muddy the waters. Rather than hear Ray's lecture on suppositions versus solid evidence, she remained silent.

"I'd like to speak to her and I'm having trouble locating her. When I called her work number the mayor answered her phone. He was as interested in her whereabouts as I am. The mayor mentioned she often has breakfast with you before work. At your brother's food truck. The mayor claims the young lady's always at her desk at nine on the nose. Today she didn't show up to work per usual and didn't call in a reason. She won't answer or return his calls. At the mayor's suggestion, I stopped by Pep's truck. Both you and your brother said this morning you ate solo because you were stood up for tennis and breakfast."

"That's all right. Call me a worrywart, but I'm concerned. She's one of the most responsible people under thirty I've ever met. And you're not doing much to settle my concerns. Why are you involved? Is this even a police matter? She's probably lost her phone and is in line at the phone store for a newer, more expensive model, as we speak. That's how they get you." She held her breath until Ray responded. Historically, he was patient with her rambling.

"All I asked is if you know her whereabouts," Ray said. "I feel like I've pushed a button."

"If the mayor hopes to locate her, isn't he asking the wrong department? Why not missing persons? Calling the big dogs in, like you, seems like putting the cart before the horse."

"He didn't call me. I called him, or rather her, and he answered. Yes, he was concerned but wanted to give her time to show up and explain herself. I only wanted to question her," Ray said. "You seem quite concerned."

"I admit to overreacting, but you're homicide. You're questioning her?"

"She's a person of interest in a case I'm working on. That brings me to my next question."

The series of unexpected events suddenly lightened Sherry's head. Ray's words became fuzzy. She heard him speaking but the meaning behind his words was gibberish. What was making her so uneasy? Sherry blinked back to clarity.

". . . Rachel Yaro," Ray said.

"I'm sorry. I missed your point. Can you repeat that, Ray?"

"A woman named Rachel Yaro has been murdered. Your friend Kat Coleman was one of the last to see her alive. In the mayor's office. Late yesterday. Now Ms. Coleman's missing, although we have evidence she's fine, just missing."

"Murder? I thought she was only missing. Poor Rachel," Sherry said.

"You know the victim? You knew she was missing?" Ray asked. "She's not from these parts. She's from New Jersey by way of Manhattan. How do you know her?"

"I met Rachel Yaro recently. She's a member of a television production team about to begin a cooking competition project here in town. I'm sure you already know that. She interviewed me to potentially be a part of the show."

On the other end of the phone, Ray hummed a note of contemplation. "Right. Cooking competition."

"Rachel's team from Feral Creations Productions had meetings with the mayor at town hall. They're filming in Augustin, and they need permits, police presence, and that sort of stuff. I think the mayor likes the excitement of national television featuring his town and wants his fingers in the pie as much as possible. He's fashioned himself as the liaison between the project producers and the location management. Kat saw them often over the months of preparation, she said. The whole shebang has been a closely guarded secret until very recently."

"Uh-huh. I see," Ray said. "And Kat works for the mayor. She saw Rachel Yaro and her team frequently in the office."

"Kat's desk is stationed right outside the mayor's office. Visitors must get past her before seeing the mayor."

"She wasn't at her desk this morning, as I said. You two were supposed to play a tennis game and have breakfast together."

"That's right. We play and eat at Pep's truck. The schedule is very convenient for Kat as the truck's parked in the town hall lot most mornings."

"Uh-huh."

Sherry could hear the scratching of pencil on paper. She could even make out Ray flipping the paper over before scratching began again.

"And Kat couldn't make your tennis game because . . ."

"I'm not sure of the reason," Sherry said. Her attempt at maintaining a casual tone didn't ring true to her ears. "I haven't been able to reach her to find out if something came up. There's a good chance she forgot. I've done it myself and I'm sure you have, too. She's a wonderful girl, Ray."

"I would like to speak to her. She may not be picking up my phone call if she doesn't recognize the phone number. If she contacts you, would you please notify me?" Ray asked. "Better yet, pass on my number to her."

"You're a hard sell, Ray, but I'll try to convince her to call a homicide detective because she was late for work this morning."

"I appreciate your cooperation," Ray said.

"What happened to Rachel exactly?" Sherry heard a soft growl on Ray's end of the phone. She recognized the guttural rumble as a signal she asked for details he felt conflicted to share. She understood. Credit to Ray. As often as Sherry collaborated with him, he felt it was his obligation to shield her from any gory details.

"The woman's body was found this morning at Feral Creations' storage sight. The company was given permission to park their container trucks housing production supplies on the side lot of the Augustin Garage, Gas, and Mini Mart. The owner, a man named Juan Garcia, discovered her body."

"That's where Pep parks his food truck overnight," Sherry said. "I'm glad he wasn't the one to find her. The shock would have really rattled him. Poor Juan must be beside himself."

"Hmmm."

"No hmmms. Pep has nothing to do with Rachel Yaro's murder. Don't even 'hmmm' me," Sherry said.

"Hmmm is an expression of thought organization. Nothing more."

Sherry tugged at her short sleeve. The material was clinging to the sudden presence of sweat. "What about Mayor Drew? I mean, you did say he and Kat were two of the last to see Rachel."

"Along with two of her workmates."

"Mick Snider and Basil Sturges."

"That's right," Ray said. "You're familiar with them?"

"Long story, but I've known them for a few days. I was interviewed by all three to see if I qualified for the cooking competition."

"That time frame doesn't constitute a long story," Ray said. "Their production sounds like it's right up your alley of expertise. Good luck."

"Thanks. And Mayor Drew? You questioned him?"

"Mayor Drew has a solid alibi of back-to-back meetings into yesterday evening, followed by a trip to New York to speak at the annual Northeast Political Conference. Sounds as dull as dishwater. He spent the night in the city. He has receipts. Rachel's time of death is estimated to be around six to eight this morning. He's back in his office and concerned for Kat. He said her office phone was chock-full of phone messages."

"Hmmm." Sherry calculated. The murder occurred around the time the napkins are dropped off at Pep's truck.

"Now you're 'hmmm-ing.'"

"Organizing my thoughts," Sherry said.

"Care to share any of those thoughts?" Ray asked.

"Since Monday morning, Pep's found a stack of napkins daily, printed with short blurbs, nestled under his food truck's windshield."

"And napkins pertain to my case how?" Ray asked.

"They may or may not. I'm mentioning their existence in case they do. The stack of napkins was left by an anonymous provider. So far, each day, there has been a two- or three-line news update about that very same cooking competition Rachel was working on."

"Ah, I see. Newsy in a straightforward factual way, or does the news have a certain slant to it?" Ray asked.

"Monday and Tuesday's news was straightforward. They presented a blurb like a coming attraction advertisement. It piqued the interest of everyone I talked to who'd read them," Sherry said.

"Any today?"

"Yes. Very different. The napkins have a menacing tone. They emphasized intrigue involving the shoot. They suggested someone might get hurt."

"And someone did," Ray said. "Someone involved in the shoot. The project Rachel Yaro's working on. I see. Yes. The connection. Now segments of the garage's security footage makes more sense."

"What do you mean?" Sherry asked.

"Mr. Garcia showed me the security footage from the time of the murder," Ray said. "Unfortunately, the camera covers only one angle and couldn't capture any activity between the trucks. It's a Stone Age system, to say the least. One that overwrites itself at the most inopportune intervals."

"Nothing concerning the murder was caught on camera?" Sherry asked.

"Nothing. There's security footage of the person placing something on Pep's truck. Now I know what that activity is all about, thanks to you. That person never approached the big rig containers. A hooded figure dashes in and dashes out. And in a direction opposite the murder scene. That person never approached the Feral Creations' truck area. That's a significant detail. On the other hand, it's not an impossibility the person took a circuitous route to the murder scene. The footage is grainy and the quality too poor to make out any certain identification. Mr. Garcia thought maybe Pep had come in early to work on the truck. He dismissed the activity as not out of the ordinary. Mr. Garcia may have not known he was seeing someone delivering napkins for the past three days. It wouldn't be the first thing I thought of either."

"Pep got that same story from Juan Garcia the first time the napkins were delivered. I wonder what time the napkins delivery was?" Sherry asked.

"The video footage is time-stamped around six ten. Rachel's murder at the Augustin Garage was in that time window. The murder wasn't caught on camera. It occurred between two trucks. No way to see what went on."

"Why is her death categorized as a murder rather than an accident?" Sherry asked.

"Very good question," Ray said, as if Sherry were his star student, which she might be.

Sherry grinned widely.

"Investigators at the scene deduced Rachel Yaro was struck from behind and fell forward, facedown. Yes, that could have indicated an accident except for one more detail. There was one of those iconic slate clapboards resting on her head. Handwritten on the slate was 'finale.'"

"That's awful. Poor Rachel."

"She had the key to the truck in her hand. Basil Sturges said she has a copy because her responsibility is to organize the shoot's clapboards and they are stored in one of the trucks. Her purse was slung across her shoulder. None of the contents disturbed. Preliminary indication suggests she was blindsided by her attacker. He or she came from a direction she wasn't expecting. If she were involved in a struggle with a companion who turned on her, there might have been more disturbance to the surroundings as the situation escalated. Whether she knew her attacker or not, he acted quickly and took off."

"Do you think she knew her attacker?" Sherry asked.

"Could go either way. Nothing around her was out of place, damaged, or disturbed. There was no sign of a struggle. Except the clapboard, which had her hair and blood on it. She was hit with such force her injury was fatal. There was bruising on her legs, evidence they were taken out from under her with a blow from the offender, causing her to go down before she was finished off."

"You're describing a surprise attack. Robbery wasn't the motive. What was? Certainly not that she happened upon the *Juicy Bites* delivery being made and that person was so startled she was murdered. That would be insane." Sherry shut her eyes. The image of the murder scene burned in her mind, and she wanted it gone. "Awful." She paused while another set of circumstances crossed her thoughts. "Is it possible the murder occurred, and the napkin delivery occurred, and everyone involved was none the wiser that so much else was going on feet away?"

"Theory, but yes."

"What would Kat know that would help your case?" Sherry asked.

"As a working detective I'm going to remind you, I do not speculate on the ongoing case beyond what I need to ask you about. As a friend I can say, Ms. Coleman may have overheard something, seen something, been asked something, while Ms. Yaro was in her office."

"Makes sense," Sherry said.

"One last question," Ray said. "Did Ms. Coleman ever refer to the deceased beyond the fact she was in the office waiting to see the mayor? For example, did Kat Coleman share any insight into whether Ms. Yaro was content with her job, her teammates, her social life? Sometimes you gals seek each other out to share concerns."

"If Rachel spoke to Kat about her life, I wasn't aware. Sorry," Sherry said. "I haven't known Kat for all that long. I'm not sure to what extent she would confide in me." Sherry sucked in a breath as she considered how much to tell Ray about Kat. Was it her place to share Kat's statement about harassment? "Do you think Kat's safe?"

"The mayor hasn't heard from her since her workday ended yesterday. She stayed at the office until five. The mayor left town hall in the early evening before boarding a train. As far as I know, she hasn't been to work today. She didn't show at tennis or the food truck."

"But you said there was evidence she's alive and breathing. How can you be sure?"

"I'm going to stop short of naming names, but a family member told me Kat had answered her call this morning. Their conversation was cut very short when Kat abruptly said she had to go."

"Hazel. I'm glad," Sherry whispered. "At least Kat knew enough not to ignore a call from her mother. Ray, did you give Hazel all the details? I hope she's not terrified for her daughter."

"Terrified? No. That woman's a bit testy. She wasn't in a mood to provide much assistance. I identified myself and asked to speak to Kat Coleman. She told me her daughter had a new residence and if I left my number, she'd pass it on. I kept the details vague. She was more put out than concerned."

"I don't want Hazel to panic. I'm glad you didn't alarm her."

"Despite my reputation, I have compassion. I have a good feel for when to pump the brakes. I didn't mention a murder."

Sherry smiled at her friend's empathy.

"You know how to reach me if you hear from your friend. She's a person of interest, that's it. She was with the deceased within hours of her death.

Anything she might have overheard, seen, or witnessed in her office or elsewhere is crucial at this early stage in the investigation. Evidence is freshest in the first twenty-four hours. That's right now." Ray's words tumbled out with muscle.

"I understand," Sherry said.

"Let's speak soon," Ray said. The phone went silent.

Chapter 8

"You look like you've seen a ghost," Amber said when she returned to Sherry's side.

"I may have. One of the cook-off production team has been murdered. Rachel Yaro."

"The person you said was missing? She's been murdered? How awful."

"That's what Ray just said," Sherry said.

"That's hard to understand," Amber said. "Here one minute, gone forever the next at the hands of another."

Sherry lowered her head. "I don't understand it one bit. Poor girl. I suppose that puts an end to the cooking competition. That's not important. Finding Kat is."

"What does finding Kat have to do with the price of milk? You switched subjects so quickly. And why did Ray call you to tell you about the murder? Does he know you're in the cooking contest?"

"Same subject," Sherry said. "Ray called to see if I knew where Kat was because she's a person of interest in Rachel's murder investigation. He knows now that I was slated to be in the cook-off."

"Kat? A person of interest?" Amber asked. "How could that be at all possible? She's such a sweet girl. Her mother's a little all over the place with her moods, but Kat seems as steady as they come. I would venture to say in their family the apple fell far from the tree."

"Kat was one of the last to see Rachel. At town hall. Before a meeting with Mayor Drew."

"Makes sense. She may be of help. Are you worried something bad happened to Kat, too?"

"Ray said he has evidence Kat is fine. She's making herself hard to contact, which is adding to the drama. He said when he contacted Hazel, she assured him she had spoken to her daughter today."

Amber lifted her eyebrows. "Mothers may tell white lies to protect their young. Do you believe Hazel spoke to Kat? I mean, you haven't been able to reach her."

"I want to believe Hazel. On the other hand, Hazel's told me how little Kat's in contact with her. Ray seems to believe her, so that's half the battle. All I know is Kat's not answering my calls or Ray's. In my case, she's probably embarrassed she stood me up. She has nothing to worry about there. I'd never scold her for a simple mistake. I'm sympathetic because I've done it myself."

"She's young and resilient. Who knows what embarrasses a twenty-something these days?" Amber said. "You mentioned Mayor Drew saw Rachel, too. He couldn't be involved, could he?"

"Nope. He has an alibi for the time of death. He was in the city overnight. He left work and immediately caught a train. Rachel's time of death was early this morning. He wasn't in Augustin at that time. And this morning he went straight from the train station to work. He has receipts as proof. Not to mention Ray was able to speak to Mayor Drew and he was fully cooperative. Unlike Kat."

"Rachel Yaro had an enemy. Who was it?" Amber asked.

Sherry shook her head. "There's one detail I haven't mentioned," Sherry said.

"There always is with you," Amber teased. "That's why you're such a good sleuth. You keep your cards close to the vest until needed."

"I don't know if it's even related to Rachel's murder. Kat confided in me that someone is being harassed at work. She couldn't finish her thought because she was interrupted. I don't know if she was referring to herself, but maybe she was talking about Rachel, who is often in the mayor's office. That's a long shot but worth considering. In any case, both women disappeared, and one turned up dead."

"If there's one thing you've taught me about murder investigations, it's that there are no coincidences."

Sherry peered across the Ruggery showroom. The time was coming to pack away the rugs showcasing summer designs and break out the fall foliage, holiday cornucopia, and root vegetable–themed rugs. Staying one step ahead of the impending season is what the customers demanded.

"I guess with this development I'll have more time next week to swap out the seasonal inventory."

"The cook-off isn't continuing? Have you heard from Basil Sturges?" Amber asked.

"No, I haven't heard from anyone regarding the fate of the cook-off. They're probably mulling over the options. I'm putting my money on the whole production being put on hold."

"I have no idea how this should be handled," Amber said.

"I'm not optimistic the cook-off will continue. Too bad. I was warming up to the idea of competing on television. The sheer terror of it all was beginning to subside."

"Television doesn't leave much to chance. I have a cousin who's married to an actor and he once told me the saying the show must go on is real. It won't be long before you know whether the cook-off will happen, I'm sure."

As the last word left Amber's mouth, Sherry's phone buzzed. One glance at the illuminated screen and she couldn't answer the call fast enough.

"Speak of the devil," Sherry said before striking the speaker button. She mouthed the caller's name in Amber's direction.

"Hi, Sherry?"

"Yes, this is Sherry. I just heard the terrible news about Rachel. What a shock."

"Shocked is the best description of everyone's reaction. She was a wonderful assistant. I'll miss her greatly." Basil heaved a sigh.

Sherry let out a contemplative hum. His sentiments seemed to have softened since his last visit to the store. "I'm sorry for everyone who knew her."

"Thank you. That's appreciated. I'm calling because I knew you'd hear the news sooner rather than later."

"I heard a few minutes ago."

"I'm sure you're wondering if Rachel's mur . . . I mean passing, will affect production," Basil said.

"I figured the cooking competition was off."

"Not at all," Basil said with conviction. "Television is an impersonal industry. Some would say heartless. Not much halts production once the wheels have been set in motion. If you've ever seen a photo portrait posted at the end of a program memorializing someone who passed during production, that's how deaths are handled. The same will happen in our case."

"I see," Sherry said. Before Basil's phone call she was prepared to tell Amber she no longer needed her to substitute on the cook-off days. She had to return her mentality back to competition mode.

"There's too much at stake not to continue the process once it's begun," Basil said.

"I'm a little surprised," Sherry said.

"Nature of the beast. I can't say I always agree with the industry's culture, but I'm getting desensitized quickly. You're still willing to compete, aren't you?"

"Yes, yes. Of course, I'm so sorry for Rachel's passing, but if the show's continuing, I'd like to be a part of it."

"Okay, good. She would have wanted that, too. She agreed how talented you are. A great ambassador for all home cooks. The cook-off itself will be wonderful for the contestants and the viewing audience."

Sherry was taken aback how easily Basil slipped back into business mode after expressing mourning. "That's so nice of her. I was looking forward to competing."

"Great. As you can understand, the delivery of the shoot schedule is running a bit behind. The schedule will be on its way after I've reached out to all the contestants by phone to ease their minds. In the next hour, in all probability. I finished touching base with everyone about the shift in personnel and suddenly I must regroup, reconnect, and relay the awful news about Rachel. I never can predict all my job entails. I certainly never saw this coming."

"Absolutely not," Sherry said.

"Watch your email. Thank you for your patience during this trying time."

"Of course. I'll see you Monday as planned?" Sherry asked.

"No change there. Absolutely."

She took a chance posing one more question. "Is there any recipe I should practice or prepare for?"

Basil laughed. "Being the seasoned veteran you are, I was wondering when you'd ask me that. The answer is no. You don't need any practice whatsoever. Cook your most successful meals for the next couple days if you feel the need to warm up your cooking chops. I know you'll be more than ready. See you soon."

After Basil's call went silent Sherry turned to Amber. "The cook-off's on. Beyond that information, Basil's phone call wasn't instructive at all. I sure hope the contestant email gives me more of an idea what I'm in for."

"I see your wheels turning," Amber said. She tapped her temple. "The minute he said don't bother practicing, you were mentally running through your winning recipes to choose which to get to work on. Admit it."

"How well you know me, my friend. I might even dust off my biggest winner, Ranch Steak Bruschetta, to make sure I still have what it takes. That recipe has a lot of steps that require good technique to get the best results. The bread must be sliced a certain way, toasted to perfection; the steak sliced thin, against the grain, with consistency; and the bruschetta topping cut in uniform dice. The seasoning of each layer affects the overall taste. A light hand doesn't do anyone any good. The steps to preparing that recipe can translate into so many other recipes."

"Practice makes perfect. Go with what you do best."

"You're right. I have a few days. I'll do it."

"And if you have any leftovers, remember your hungry coworker," Amber said with a pronounced grin. "You should've asked him if he had any idea who had a problem with Rachel."

"Would you have asked that question if you were in my shoes?" Sherry knew the answer.

"No way. But I'm not known for my amateur sleuthing like you are."

Chapter 9

Thursday brought an early-bird text request for tennis. Sherry was awake after seeing Don off but was nowhere near ready to run out the door and face stiff competition on the courts. She accepted the last-minute, unexpected invitation nonetheless. She had other reasons to make the effort, beyond getting exercise. Kat had some explaining to do. When Sherry arrived at the court, she approached with caution. First things first, Sherry offered Kat her condolences.

"I'm so sorry for the loss of your friend Rachel," Sherry said as they filled the court's player bench with their equipment. "You were college friends who reconnected in Augustin?"

"Thanks. It's been crazy. Yes. You heard us talking the day you were in my office. She went into television work after college. Once someone relocates to the city, you're bound to lose touch. And we did, until her team showed up in Augustin. She put in fourteen-hour days, so even here I hadn't seen her except when she met with the mayor. We made tentative plans for dinner once the filming was complete."

"That's tough," Sherry said. "I'm so sorry."

"I appreciate that, thanks."

"On a lighter note, pardon my appearance. I didn't do my laundry yesterday because I didn't think I needed clean workout gear today. It was quite a surprise when you texted this morning." Sherry was sporting a T-shirt she found at the bottom of her dresser drawer.

"You look as good as always. It's me who could use a wardrobe refresher," Kat said with a chuckle.

Sherry made the decision to leave the conversation uncomplicated until after the match. No sense drumming up controversy until there was time to hash it out. When the two finished their match and made their way to Toasts of the Town, they were greeted by Pep and Angel. The women ordered both daily specials. Sherry lost the match and, per the terms of their standing wager, pulled out her credit card in preparation for the payment.

While Kat waited for Sherry's order to be filled, she pinched off a morsel of her Tex Mex Brex Toast and placed it on her tongue. "This is so good. Angel and Pep's combination of eggs, salsa, spinach, thick-cut bacon and cheddar on a massive whole-grain toast slice hits the spot."

"You made the right choice," Angel said from his service window vantage point. *"Muy delicioso."* He slipped back into the kitchen to retrieve Sherry's order.

"No napkin delivery today," Pep said as he wiped the counter with a dishcloth. "I guess the magic is over."

"Will we ever find out who the author was?" Sherry asked.

"I could hire a private investigator," Pep said. "Interested in footing the bill?"

"No, thank you. Let the mystery live on," Sherry said. "Right, Kat?"

"I'm sorry. I'm so excited to eat my toast I wasn't listening."

Angel delivered Sherry's Greener Goddess Frittata Crunch Toast.

"Thanks a lot, guys. Have a great day," Sherry said. "Okay, Kat. It's finally time to eat. If you have any left."

Kat turned tail and was halfway to the picnic tables when Sherry finished her sentence. The two nestled in opposite each other and began to admire their breakfast toasts. Kat's gaze drifted from her meal to her hands as she unfolded a napkin.

"If you're looking for some news on the napkins there aren't any today. Maybe you didn't hear Pep say he didn't receive any under the truck's windshield wiper this morning."

"I did. Just checking," Kat mumbled.

"Just checking?" Sherry asked. She saw her opening. "Do you know any more about the *Juicy Bites* author than you've said?"

Kat tipped her head toward her shoulder. "Not really."

Sherry put a bit of toast in her mouth and concentrated on Kat's twisted lips. "Do you think that's the end of *Juicy Bites*? Maybe whoever the author was played out their hand and will find another way to entertain the town?"

"May not be a bad thing the end has come," Kat said with a sigh. "I'm sure people think the mayor's office leaked production news. Honestly, we didn't. Mayor Drew wouldn't be well-served at all by leaking inside information. He considers filming in Augustin his baby. Keeping the project cloaked in secrecy has been the norm. The meetings in his office are about procedural steps taken to ensure all logistical aspects of the shoot are covered. Feral Creations' lawyers' guidelines dictate the way. No wiggle room there. The production team follows them with the strictest adherence. No secrets are spilled. To us, most of the show content itself is as much a mystery as those silly napkins. All we ask is the final product reflect Augustin in a positive light, and Feral Creations hears us." The level of distress in Kat's voice rose as she made her point.

After both women had nearly devoured their toasts, Sherry seized on a moment of quiet to continue the tough conversation. To her surprise, Kat made the first move.

"Let's address the elephant in the room. Detective Bease must not be very happy with me," Kat said as she polished off the last bite. "I'm not willing to cooperate with the investigation right now."

"I can't speak for him, but I'm glad you're safe and sound after giving us all a scare. The fact you disappeared without a word the same day as Rachel's murder gave me quite a fright."

"Getting back to Detective Bease. I did return his call, eventually. Problem was, he asked more questions than I was willing to answer. I have no other choice."

"Why don't you have a choice?" Sherry asked.

"I can't go into it. Not yet," Kat said.

"I'm sure you're not the first uncooperative witness."

"Hah, witness. I think I'm a suspect, not a witness."

"Don't be silly. No one thinks you're a suspect. Don't let Detective Bease intimidate you. He's doing his job, step by step. If you have nothing to add to the investigation, he'll move forward to another source."

"I may have been one of the last to see Rachel alive, yes, that's the truth. Remember, she had two teammates that always came with her to the meetings at town hall. What about them? Basil and Mick."

"Do you suspect either of them of killing her?" Sherry asked.

"Mick, no. He was very close to Rachel. She went above and beyond to help him in and out of his wheelchair and attend to so many of his needs. She took up a lot of the slack on tasks he couldn't physically manage. He must miss her tons. Their boss, Basil, on the other hand, is a tough cookie and hard to read. He and Rachel had words on occasion but those appeared to be nothing more than your run-of-the-mill spats. Heck, Mayor Drew and I have them all the time. Do you know how often I've nagged him to send you that newsletter article so you can finish your editing and I can distribute the darn thing?"

"Cheers to your efforts," Sherry said. "I know you're loyal to your boss. You need to think outside the box now that the detective has you on his radar for one reason or another. You need to stand up for yourself and tell him what you're telling me."

"That's a nice way of saying I'm a suspect in Rachel's murder and I'm in charge of clearing my own name," Kat said. "This is not a good day. Not only have I become a murder suspect, I'm considered a secret leaker. What else can go wrong?"

"Who killed Rachel and why is one mystery. Who the author of *Juicy Bites* is, and the purpose behind the effort of providing the newsy napkins, is another. Unless the two are somehow connected."

"Sherry, you're a sleuth extraordinaire, but this is getting too complicated." Kat closed her eyes and raised her head toward the sky. When her attention came back around, she exhaled. "I need your help. I'm in a bad spot and I can't say what that is. Can you trust me when I say I'm not guilty of murdering my old friend Rachel? And I'm not the author of *Juicy Bites*?"

"Of course I can. That's what I've been trying to get through your head," Sherry said. "When you disappeared yesterday without a trace, it raised red flags since you were one of the last people to see Rachel and you have a relationship with her."

"I agree I had unlucky timing taking the day off at the last minute."

"Yeah, I suppose. Unlucky is one way to frame it. Deliberate is another."

"I had my reasons for my sudden decision to get away, and now's not the right time to go into it."

Sherry knew better than to push her friend any further. The task of delving into her motives seemed an impossible one anyway. If Kat felt pressured by too many questions she'd remain shut down, or worse, disappear again. Sherry needed to be patient and let Kat share on her own terms. Sherry had a cook-off to prepare for, *Juicy Bites* no longer existed, and Rachel's murder investigation was in the capable hands of Ray Bease. Kat would be fine. The cook-off was the priority.

Chapter 10

The end of the week brought a preview of autumn weather. Two days of cool, wind-driven rain kept Sherry indoors. She found time to outline goals for next year's growing season at the Augustin Community Garden and put the finishing touches on her concept for a rug-hooking class aimed at budding rug artisans. Her hope of putting the town newsletter to bed was still on hold while the mayor withheld his article. He must have a good reason, so Sherry set the deadline aside until further notice.

She spent whatever free time she could salvage working on the various steps of her tried-and-true winning recipe, Ranch Steak Bruschetta. She practiced more than she had ever worked on a cook-off recipe. From blending the horseradish ranch dressing to creamy tangy perfection, to achieving crispy edges on the thinly sliced steak, she jotted down notes on how to improve her technique with each result. Successfully shingling the steak on grilled baguette slices resting on a bed of peppery arugula wasn't a given until the eye was treated to a glimpse of each savory layer that made up the recipe. The tomato-scallion bruschetta topping was drizzled, not drowned, in the dressing to enhance the fresh flavors and tie the whole dish together. If every one of her recipes was as simultaneously complex in flavor yet as simple in concept, she'd be sitting on the amateur home cook champion throne for a lifetime.

At the same time, Sherry kept an ear to the ground in hopes of any updates on Rachel's murder investigation. None came. Wet courts canceled Friday's tennis game with Kat and, as a result, she hadn't spoken to her concerning the situation. When the sun and the warmth returned, the game remained postponed, as Kat preferred not to play on the weekends because the courts were notoriously overbooked and the wait time was unbearable.

When Monday morning rolled around, a rush of adrenaline woke Sherry up at the crack of dawn. By the time she made it downstairs, Don was nearly out the door to start his day.

"Happy cook-off day," he sang. "Are you excited, nervous, raring to go, or all of the above?"

"I thought hearing I was in a cook-off and then finding out it would begin in only a few days would be too much for my little brain to handle. I was wrong. This day couldn't come fast enough. I hope all cook-offs in the future have an equally fast turn-around time from entry phase to cook-off.

That way there's no chance to overthink the event."

"That's good news. I like your attitude. Will I see you by dinnertime?" Don asked. He sipped the last of his coffee and brought his mug over to the kitchen sink.

"I hope so." Sherry masked a yawn with the palm of her hand. "I wish I'd gotten more sleep last night. I stayed awake mulling over details for hours before conking out."

"You didn't have to get up so early with me, sweetie," Don said. "I do appreciate the Monday morning send-off."

"You're my good luck charm. I had to get one more kiss from you," Sherry said. She met up with him at the sink for her good luck kiss. "And there's something I've been meaning to ask you about."

"Shoot."

"When you motored the Feral Creations crew around in your boat, you said their driver went along too?"

"He did. He was very helpful. The man named Mick has trouble with balance and leg strength. The result of a car accident. Yonny, the driver, said he's been working for the crew since Mick returned to work after some time away. They decided they needed a driver when they got this big project, assuring they'd all arrive and depart together. Not a bad idea for a time-sensitive group dependent on each other."

"Makes sense."

"Does that answer your question?" Don asked.

"One hundred percent."

"Why do you ask?"

"I was on my way downtown to go to the bank, and I took a small detour by the marina. I saw the group heading toward your boat, and the man I assume was Yonny was with the team."

"A small detour?" Don asked. "Were you on a reconnaissance mission?"

"You could call it that. I wanted to get a better visual of my interviewers. I was curious whether he tagged along on the boat ride."

"Sure did, and I was glad for his help," Don said. "Gotta go. Text me during the day to let me know what's going on."

"No phones allowed," Sherry said. "They don't want anyone filming for personal use or, heaven forbid, having someone's phone ring during the competition."

"Okay, then I'll see you when I see you," Don said with a laugh. "Good luck and kill the competition."

• • •

Sherry arrived at the Augustin Library two hours later. She was escorted to a cordoned-off holding area for those on the production call sheet. There, Sherry was assigned an aid who led her to a gathering of checked-in contestants. She took time to acclimate herself to the hubbub of people and equipment bustling around her. A tent was assembled over the library's courtyard adjacent to the outdoor amphitheater, which was a preemptive move because there was a threat of rain. Sherry and the other cooks complied with the order to take a seat on the tiered steps facing the tent as soon as the announcement was made to do so.

Sherry was able to see much of what was housed inside from her vantage point. Cameras were strategically located in the upper corners of the tent. There was a distressed wood cupboard wedged against a faux backdrop. She could see an impressive collection of spices, canned goods, broth containers, and dry goods. And that was only the first row of each shelf. In front of the cupboard was a row of tables aligned next to one another. At first, she couldn't locate any cooking appliances, which baffled her. On closer inspection, there was an area blocked off with material draped from the tent ceiling, large enough to contain stoves or cooktops. The best clue the drapes concealed appliances was the proximity to a spiderweb of power lines and cables running across the floor.

As was often the case at cook-offs, there was an air of anticipatory anxiety hovering over the scene. Conversation was held to a minimum with only an occasional utterance of amazement concerning the transformation of the library's grounds into a cook-off extravaganza.

A woman sat down next to Sherry and extended her hand. "Hi, I'm Silvia."

"Hi, Silvia. Nice to meet you. I'm Sherry. Are you a competing cook?"

"Yes, I am." She waved the credentials hanging from a lanyard around her neck.

Sherry pegged Silvia's age as being in the ballpark of her own. Cook-offs had no steadfast age demographic. Over the years, Sherry collided with cooks of all ages, genders, sizes, and cultural backgrounds in the kitchen arena—another reason she loved cooking competitions. More importantly, the woman next to her exuded a calm Sherry was grateful for.

Silvia lowered her voice to a whisper. "Here comes the head honcho."

"Everyone, may I have your attention. Good morning," a familiar voice announced. A hush swept over the crowd. Basil strolled into view and waved in several stragglers. "Contestants, welcome. Please have a seat and we will get the show on the road."

Mick was wheeled in by a young woman Sherry didn't recognize. She parked him next to Basil. Each member of the crew wore a headset. Four large-screen monitors were anchored on tripod stands across the grassy arena in front of the seating. The screens powered on when Basil cued someone on the side of the tent entrance. The cameras picked up various angles of the tent interior, a close-up of one of the worktables, and a posterior shot of Basil, Mick, and the woman Sherry assumed was Rachel's replacement, Stacy.

"All the cook-off contestants are here and seated in front of me. I will walk you through today's competition. The concept is simple. We have scoured the country in search of twelve of the country's best amateur cooks and we'll narrow that number down over the next three days. The cooks will be given challenges to perform. Ingredients will be transformed into recipe masterpieces. Techniques will be scrutinized. Judges will judge, prizes will be awarded. Above all, I stress, have fun and enjoy yourselves.

"Mick, Stacy, and I are your contacts for any troubles, questions, concerns you may have." Basil pointed to each of his assistants as he named them. "I'd like that fully understood. I don't want miscommunications, rumors, and whispers floating around. If there is anything out of order, please, see one of the three of us and we will address it. We're here for you all. Thank you."

Mick and Stacy nodded.

"Let's get right down to business. You cooks have been chosen because you are all veterans of the cooking competition circuit."

Sherry craned her neck to get a look at the other cooks. She hadn't had a chance to assess her opponents. In her years of cook-offs and recipe contests, countless other cooks had become more of a community of friends enjoying a common hobby rather than feared competitors. The anticipation of seeing some of her old friends was dashed when she didn't recognize one face among those in sight. She'd have to settle on a mindset of making new friends.

"Today we will have the twelve contestants partake in an elimination cooking challenge," Basil continued.

"Right off the bat," Silvia said. "This got serious really fast."

"You will be paired up with another contestant, and as the show gets underway you will hear the challenge rules. Stay alert to your name being called. When it is, you will be minutes away from your ninety-minute cooking challenge."

Sherry's heart rate ticked up as she listened. "Am I the only one with a million questions?"

Silvia tipped her head. "Just go with the flow. And have fun."

"We are lucky to have had a huge response to a social media call last night for extras to show up extremely early this morning to be our audience. Their responses will be your inspiration to give the challenge your all. Remember to light up the crowd with your personalities."

Sherry peered behind her. She came across two sunny faces donning warm smiles and waving. Eileen and Hazel gave Sherry the thumbs-up.

"We are going to begin calling up the pairs in a few minutes. If your name is not called, you will follow Stacy to a holding trailer behind the amphitheater to pass the time until your turn comes around. It is also where you will wait to be called for your turn to compete. From now on, the overall competition journey you are embarking on will be referred to by its production name, *Relish*. So, on behalf of all who are working to make this a successful and popular television series, welcome to the first round of *Relish*. Would Sherry Oliveri and Jada Jackson please follow Stacy and Mick to their cook stations inside the tent for further instructions.

"Audience, please only clap when the cue card is raised." Basil pointed out a young man holding an "applause" cue card over his head. The audience gently clapped until the sign was lowered. "Perfect. Except, more exuberance next time, clappers. This is television, remember."

"Good luck," Silvia said as Sherry glanced in her direction.

"I'll need it." Sherry rose to her feet. She tried to locate the other cook, Jada, preparing to step forward. She couldn't spot anyone definitively. She left her seat and made her way to the tent entrance. At the entrance she was joined by a petite woman who introduced herself as Jada. Both women entered the tent, where they found themselves in a well-lit cooking arena stocked with an abundance of supplies and ample workspace on each of two tables. Dodging the cameras and cables to get to their marks required cautious footwork.

"This is impressive," Sherry said to Jada. Jada gave a weak nod.

"Ladies, I would like you to meet Jason Kilmartin. You may recognize him as the host of the long-running game show *Flashback*. Jason is the *Relish* host."

Jason stepped forward and shook each cook's hand with vigor.

"Jason will give you the rules of the elimination challenge," Basil said. "Don't be concerned with any gaps in the intro monologue. We will be applying effects later and need to allow blank air space for those. We are under time restrictions to get all the contestants' shoots done today. Please listen closely and, above all, be yourselves."

Stacy handed each cook a bright green apron, not the color Sherry felt most comfortable wearing, but she imagined it was eye-catching on television. She unfurled the rolled apron and admired the *Relish* logo embroidered on the front. A crossed whisk and a wooden spoon bordered the show's title. Sherry tied the apron on and the urge to compete kicked in.

"Contestants, welcome to the newest and most exciting cooking competition on television, *Relish*," Jason said in a polished address. His enunciation was as charismatic as his features. "The elimination challenge you are about to compete in is called Worldwide Local."

The name of the challenge did little to narrow down the theme. Worldwide Local was a great example of an oxymoron. But which word carried more weight, worldwide or local? Was practicing on her primarily American cuisine–inspired Ranch Steak Bruschetta a good idea after all? Sherry blinked away the colliding questions.

"You must use all the provided ingredients in your recipe. The cupboard items are additional, as is any ingredient you find on the butcher block table." Jason pointed out a gorgeous New England–style block of thick grainy wood, about four feet long and four inches thick, resting on carved wooden legs.

Sherry envisioned the table as a centerpiece in her colonial home and the corners of her mouth turned up. There were several herb bunches, fruit baskets, and vegetable collections on the table waiting to be considered for use by the cooks.

"Your time limit is thirty minutes from start to plating finish. You must adhere to the theme, which is local in a worldwide sense. That will become clearer as we proceed. You are both very experienced cooks and shouldn't have any problem with the challenge. There are three judges who will taste your prepared recipes. You will be judged on presentation, taste, adherence to theme, and taste. Yes, I said taste twice. Taste is of utmost importance." Jason smiled. His teeth were perfect, if not too bright. "Please secure your aprons and we will begin. Remember, there are no retakes. The scheduled breaks Basil alluded to will come in the following intervals: after the ingredients have been revealed, when the recipes are complete, and when the judging is complete. Go with the flow if any others materialize. You will be filming confessional recaps after the contest is complete. Good luck, ladies. Most of all, have fun."

"Thank you, Jason." Basil walked over to the back of the tent. He whisked away the material hanging from the ceiling and unveiled the ovens.

Behind the gleaming stainless-steel ovens, the tent flaps were open to the library's garden. Sherry's racing heart was settled by the sight of a last gasp of late summer hydrangeas and dozens of wildflowers turning to seed.

"When I give you the signal, you will receive the ingredients for a local recipe of your choice. It may not be the definition of local you are conjuring up in your culinary brains. That's the challenge. Local is all relative."

Sherry and Jada exchanged glances.

"Thirty seconds," Basil announced when he returned. "Mick, thirty seconds."

Sherry followed Basil's line of sight to his assistant. Mick was out of his wheelchair and into a walker. He was shuffling several clapboard slates balanced on the walker's railing.

"Contestants, stay on your marks behind the tables, please. We will be presenting your mandatory ingredients after a brief introduction."

Mick lifted one clapboard over his head after placing multiple clapboards on the floor. The juggling act was not an easy task while steadying himself on compromised legs. Stacy was at his side overseeing his attempt.

"Can everyone see the clapboard?" Basil called out. Sherry spotted a distant cameraman raising his hand.

"Want me to hold it?" Stacy asked.

Mick threw his shoulders back and straightened his arms and legs with a moan before reaching full height. "Better?"

The cameraman flipped a thumbs-up. Basil marched over to Mick.

"Good job, Mick. Thank you, Stacy," Basil said. "Rachel did a good job organizing these slates. Even though she was new to the task, Rachel had a good system in place before she . . ." He sighed.

"I double-checked them this morning. They are in perfect order," Stacy said. "Her system needed no translation. Only the finale board is missing, as it's in police custody. Kudos to Rachel for making our jobs easier."

"Agreed. Folks, silence, please," Basil called out.

"Even though Basil said he wanted authentic cook reactions, they might have some regrets," Sherry whispered as she adjusted herself over her mark behind her assigned table. "The pace is shockingly fast."

Mick clapped the board. The cameras began to roll.

Jason rehashed the explanation of the Worldwide Local challenge. A second time around was a welcome refresher because Sherry missed a sentence or two as she mentally sorted out the steps required to take her recipe concept from inception to completion. She made sure she was fully attuned to Jason when the camera lit up.

"Sherry and Jada, here are your local ingredients," Jason said. He had what looked like Easter baskets on each arm. "Local is a relative term. You may be thinking, 'local to where?' If you are, you are on the right track. Not local to the lovely state of Connecticut." Jason held a lengthy pause. "That would be too easy. We want you to relish the challenge and show us your cooking chops."

Sherry and Jada groaned.

"Here comes the twist," Jada whispered.

"I thought worldwide local was twist enough," Sherry replied.

"You both must cook a dish local to the Middle Eastern style of cuisine. Being the knowledgeable cooks you two are, there shouldn't be any problem. Let's look at your ingredients."

Sherry and Jada reached in their baskets as Jason listed the contents.

"You will find pistachios, cilantro, pita bread, ground lamb, yogurt and cucumber. Oh, and bamboo kebab sticks."

Sherry was pleased with the ingredients, but not the time allotted. She was going to have to dumb down a full recipe to a micro recipe. Kebabs were out of the question due to the obvious choice to make them. A lack of creativity would equal a deduction in points. She paged through the recipe archive in her brain. In a moment of clarity, she made her selection. No turning back. She glanced over at Jada. Her opponent's cheeks were puffed out as she glared at her basket.

Chapter 11

Sherry laid out her ingredients on the table and willed them to speak to her. Time management was of the utmost importance. Her decision to transform her ingredients into Middle Eastern–inspired lamb pistachio meatball lollipops with tangy raita dip in a limited window of time was a tall task. Toasting the pita bread would take five to six minutes, not including a trip to the food processor to turn the flat rounds into breadcrumbs. That was the best place to begin.

The next step required a dairy ingredient to transform the toasted crumbs into a binder that would marry the meatball ingredients while achieving a moist consistency. In case she was asked about the purpose of toasting the crumbs, only to then soak them in a dairy product, she had her technical answer at the ready. On cue, Jason and a cameraman stopped by her table to check on her progress.

"Sherry, did I hear you're preparing meatball lollipops? Genuis."

"That's the plan. Kick on a stick with a dipping sauce to boot," Sherry said.

"What's in the small bowl here?" Jason asked. He lifted the small glass bowl up to the camera.

"Pita crumbs. The beginnings of a panade," Sherry explained.

"Can you explain what a panade is?" Jason asked.

"It's a combination of a starch and a liquid. It helps prevent the protein fibers in the meat from stiffening and becoming a gummy burger consistency. The word literally means bread mash. Meatballs are a technique dish. One that my grandma taught my father, and he taught me. I tweaked the recipe and put the Sherry spin on my meatballs, but the foundation's been there for a few generations."

"I love the family tradition of handing down recipes."

"As fun as cooking is, it's also a lesson in chemistry. If I skipped the panade step and served the judges mini hamburgers instead of tender meatballs, I'd be dinged for poor technique, and tough meatballs."

"But using pitas as breadcrumbs? That takes imagination," Jason said.

"I like to think I'm resourceful. Thanks," Sherry said. "The best use of the pitas was to incorporate them into the meatballs to showcase their importance in the recipe. Toasting them contributes one more layer of flavor."

Jason nodded in agreement. "Amazing. You go the extra mile. The devil's in the details."

Sherry left her station, trailed closely by a camera operator, equipment slung over his shoulder, and an associate monitoring the dragging cables. She went in search of milk to add to the bowl of crumbs. She lost valuable time eyeballing the butcher block table selection before resigning herself to the fact there was no milk. Instead, she picked up one of her favorites, spreadable herb and garlic cheese. She'd add a splash of water to the cheese to liquify it before stirring the blend into her pita bits. She mentally patted herself on the back for thinking on the fly without getting rattled.

With her meatball binder blend in hand, she passed Jada's workstation. She snuck a peak at her progress. Even a subtle check on her opponent was caught on camera. The camera operator, following her every move, panned from Sherry to Jada and back again.

Sherry returned to her workstation, where she incorporated the panade into her ground lamb. Her choice of utensil was a fork, so as not to over-mash the meat and toughen the final product. All was going as planned when an alarm went off in her head.

Oh! I forgot the chutney for the raita. My secret ingredient. I hope the pantry has a jar. Don't get your steps out of sequence. Finish the meatballs first.

Competitors could lose focus deep into the process when thoughts grew clouded by what-ifs and maybe-I-should-haves. Sherry recognized the symptoms coming on. An overlooked ingredient here, a forgotten heating pan there. She needed to get back on track.

What was once an orderly plan became an exercise in recovery. She glanced at her watch. The minutes ticked by as if they were seconds. She sucked in a deep breath and settled her thoughts. She formed and cooked the meatballs before feeding them onto the bamboo sticks. She constructed a foil tent to trap the heat before she moved on. One component of the dish was done. She found the chutney in the pantry and with it concocted her version of elevated raita using yogurt, lime, and cucumber. She hit a speed bump when she saw her cilantro resting on the table, untouched. Big mistake.

She couldn't use the herb as a garnish as she would have liked, because she'd be penalized by the judges for using a provided ingredient as an afterthought. Instead, she minced the herb and stirred it into the dipping sauce, which morphed into Green Goddess Raita Dipping Sauce. Thank you, Pep, for inspiring the new sauce's concept and name. The breakfast she had enjoyed at Toasts of the Town, Greener Goddess Toast, popped into her head at just the right moment. Without the new definitive name, the dip may have been seen as having no real direction. She laid the meatball lollipops in a circle on the stark white platter supplied by the organizers. She filled the vacant center with the bowl of dip.

Her recipe was complete with minutes to spare. Sherry checked on her opponent's progress. When she glanced over, Jada was wringing her hands. Her face was blanched and there was a teardrop rolling down her cheek. Sherry surveyed the scene for any sign help may be on the way but only saw the camera operator aiming the lens in Jada's direction.

"Are you okay?" Sherry whispered.

"I burned my finger, and I can't finish plating," Jada said with a whimper.

"Let me help you," Sherry said. If she were reprimanded by the contest officials, so be it. She didn't want to win by Jada's default. She wanted to win in a talent-versus-talent showdown. Under Jada's direction, Sherry hoisted a bubbling saucepan off the stovetop behind the prep tables. She brought it over to the soup bowls Jada had laid across the identical platter Sherry had used. Jada used her battered hand to sprinkle pistachio croutons across the surface of the soup and shower on a remainder of cilantro to add a pop of color to each bowl.

"Smells wonderful," Sherry said.

"Thank you," Jada said. "I owe you big-time."

"You do not. Happy to help." Sherry returned to her table as time was called.

Jason stepped into the camera frame. "Sherry. Jada. These platters are fantastic. Looks as if you've both crushed the Worldwide Local challenge. The judges will be out soon to taste them."

"I can't wait to meet the judges," Sherry said in a whisper.

"Me, too," Jada said.

Basil motioned to the camera operator and the red light dimmed.

"In the meantime, would you two follow me to the confessional tent, where we'd like your play-by-play of the morning's artistry," Stacy said as she stepped toward the cooks. "Jada will be first."

"Are we going to meet the judges?" Sherry asked. She wasn't sure who to direct her question to.

The point was moot when Stacy shook her head.

Basil replied, "Not today. That's part of the journey." Basil didn't wait around for Sherry's reaction. He turned and was quickly lost in a group huddled in conversation.

"It would be more fun if we met them," Sherry said to Stacy, whose shrug left Sherry slightly deflated.

"This isn't your typical cook-off. It's important to remember that," Jada said.

"I see what you mean," Sherry said. "I haven't figured out what we're in for and I think that's the point."

Sherry spotted Ray in the distance on her way back to the contestant trailer. He was standing alongside Basil and Mick. She couldn't recall Ray ever coming to more than one of her cook-offs. The detective had a love of cooking and, while off duty, picked Sherry's brain to build his cooking skills. On duty was another story. He was single-minded and not tolerant of deviations from the task at hand. Still, as a friend, she wanted to fill him in on her exciting morning. He was on Sherry's turf, and he'd have to adhere to her rules. Hah! If only.

Basil waved Sherry over. "Sherry, the detective would like a word with you. We're taking Jada's interview first, so you two can talk. Stacy, give them ten minutes, please, and then escort Sherry to her interview. Excuse me." Basil scurried off to his next task.

"I'll be back soon," Stacy said. She guided Jada away.

"Ray, I haven't heard from you since last week. Was Rachel's killer caught?"

"On the contrary. We've hit an impasse. The investigation has stalled." Ray studied his lace-up leather shoes, an unusual footwear choice for a warm late summer day. "We're circling back to your friend Kat Coleman."

"Why is that?" Sherry asked.

"Kat must know more than she's willing to say, which is not much so far. Mr. Nice Guy Ray is getting stonewalled, and Mr. Hardcore Detective Bease is about to show up at her door."

"I'm not sure why she's not speaking up," Sherry said.

"I have a theory. The news leaks printed on the napkins are coming from town hall. No one else is privy to the information except the production team. After questioning, everyone from Feral Creations checks out as following the strict nondisclosure protocol," Ray said. "Kat doesn't want to be exposed as the author. Now her friend's been murdered, and she can't offer any help or she'll be cornered. She's stuck."

"You think Kat thought she was doing the mayor's office a good deed by spilling tiny amounts of production tea to tantalize the viewers? Then the timing turned horrible?" Sherry asked.

"That's where I'm at. Mayor Drew's been forthcoming about his aggravation someone is putting news out there. He doesn't realize he may be facing the source of his aggravation every day at work."

"Oh, Kat. You are in a pickle," Sherry said.

"And I haven't been able to clear her name from the murder suspect list thanks to her uncooperative attitude. She won't speak to me. I'll have to go to the next level."

"There's no more *Juicy Bites*, so your theory needs some tweaking," Sherry said. "*Juicy Bites* ended with Rachel's death. Wednesday was the last day."

"Not the case," Ray said. "The napkins ended for only one day, Thursday. You must not have eaten out Friday? And I'd imagine you wouldn't have gotten over to the truck before coming here this morning. You haven't talked to Pep?"

"My tennis game was rained out Friday. Pep was away on the weekend. The only way he can take a day off is if he takes the family out of town, he says. And no, I ate at home this morning. *Juicy Bites* is back?"

"To bring you up to speed, no *Juicy Bites* Thursday, but the napkins were back with attitude Friday," Ray said.

Sherry spotted Hazel and Eileen over Ray's shoulder, standing at the amphitheater steps. They appeared to be involved in an animated conversation. "Even if the napkins are back, why would they have anything to do with Rachel's murder? The napkins were teasing the television production."

"They may or may not have anything to do with the murder," Ray said. "Finding the author will narrow down the options. Rachel Yaro could have been in the running because she's in the inner circle. But, obviously, we must rule her out. There are a few more suspects to consider that fit the bill. After that, the pool of suspects gets murky."

"And what do you expect to achieve here today?" Sherry asked.

"The reason I'm here today is to get more out of Basil Sturges. Here on set, in his element, he's vulnerable to rushing his answers. A slip of the uncensored tongue could yield valuable information."

"And did anything slip out?" Sherry asked.

"He was more than willing to share that Rachel Yaro had a beef with him. His words. When I questioned him about his team's working relationships, he was eager to tell me Rachel never felt adequately compensated for her efforts. He said she asked for a raise almost every pay period and he couldn't oblige. His bottom line couldn't support a higher wage at her level. She was a team player, but she was growing resentful toward her boss for freezing her pay at a certain scale she considered low. Her title was Associate Producer. She was still green, he said."

Sherry was reminded of Eileen's comment she'd seen the production teammates having an argument.

"Rachel's beef was with Basil. Where does Kat fit in? Why are you circling back to her?" Sherry asked, while keeping an eye out for Basil and Stacy.

"Her incomplete alibi. It really gnaws at me."

"Two egos locking horns?" Sherry asked. "She's a strong character and so are you."

"She's testing my resolve. She's your friend. You can't get through either. We're not sure if her mother can get any word out of her daughter. What's her motivation to be so stubborn? In this case, her attitude's not doing anyone any good." The exasperation in Ray's tone fascinated Sherry. She'd never seen him thrown for such a loop.

"I can't tell you how to conduct your investigation but, have you checked out a man named Garrett Stein? He's an entertainment reporter. His current assignment is covering the cook-off production. My gut tells me he's the one spilling production secrets under the guise of *Juicy Bites*."

"How would he benefit from writing *Juicy Bites*?" Ray asked. "You're not covering for Kat, are you? Throwing me off her scent won't work until I've sniffed thoroughly."

"Keep sniffing. You have my blessing. Don't let your frustration with the stalled investigation get personal. I'm in your corner."

"Sorry," Ray said. "And I don't use that word often. Now, what about this Stein fellow?"

"I accept your apology," Sherry said with a smile. "Garrett Stein may be writing *Juicy Bites* to be relevant. Or to impress someone. Or to get back at someone. Think about it. When the author is disclosed, he or she may be celebrated," Sherry said. "And yes, those are speculations."

"Okay. Noted. No one's out of the running right now," Ray said.

"I'd like to run the theory of Garrett Stein being the *Juicy Bites* author by Kat. She sees him often," Sherry said. "Him writing the napkins makes a lot of sense for the promotion of his career. Plus, he's been spending tons of time at the mayor's office, where the Feral Creations crew hangs out quite often."

"Is this relevant to Rachel's murder investigation? Aren't we getting too far off track?"

"Hear me out, Ray."

"I always end up hearing you out. And I admit, it's almost always worth the extra time it takes to get to the point."

"Glad you think so. When I was in Kat's office, the day before Rachel's murder, Garrett Stein was there. Kat called me in close to ask me if I'd ever been harassed at work. She was seeking advice on the matter and the timing was noteworthy. Rachel was murdered the next day and Kat went missing."

"Is her boss bothering her?"

"I truly don't believe Mayor Drew would behave badly. Was she talking about Garrett Stein? He was sitting right beside her desk. Kat turned down the volume when she told me. I'm assuming she did that so he wouldn't hear her."

"*Was* she talking about him?" Ray asked.

"She couldn't finish her thought because we were interrupted."

"And?" Ray prompted. He rolled his hands around one another to speed up Sherry's point.

"And, I'm not sure how that might play into Rachel's murder. I wanted to mention it because the timing was so close to Kat disappearing and Rachel passing." Sherry rewound the memory of Rachel's offer to get Garrett a glass of water as she passed through Kat's office. The suggestive glance Rachel gave him was enough of an invitation to give the impression of a heightened interest in more than hydration.

Ray was an expert at wearing a poker face. Sherry couldn't decipher whether he agreed with the noteworthiness or not.

"I'll speak with Garrett Stein."

"Two minutes until your interview," Stacy said as she approached.

"Okay, thanks," Sherry said. Stacy turned her back and busied herself with her phone.

"I didn't get a chance to ask. How did your cook-off go?" Ray asked.

"Hard to say. The judging criteria is based on using the provided ingredients, sticking to the theme, taste and presentation. I have no idea who the judges are. The whole process feels like on-the-job training with an air of mystery hovering over the contest. The cooks aren't given more guidance than the basic rules. I have no idea how I did in the first round. There are many more pairings to go before I know anything concrete. But I'm having a good time."

"Before you go, I'd like to show you Friday's *Juicy Bites*."

"I haven't seen today's, either," Sherry said.

"Let me show you. I've got both days in the vault."

"Where is the vault?"

"Right here at my fingertips." He dipped his hand in the pocket of his khaki pants. He removed a scrunched napkin covered in smears of a white saucy residue. He wiped his hand on an accompanying handkerchief. "Here we go. I had a Smoked Salmon Schmear Toast this morning and I wasn't disappointed. It was a little oozy but worth it. Salmon, capers, chive cream cheese, pickled onions. The best. Anyway." He unfolded two wrinkled papers and read the printed messages to Sherry. Friday's first."

Chapter 12

Juicy Bites

Who cooked up a murder? Feral Creations wouldn't write this script.
Note: Two-faced stories need two endings.

Juicy Bites

How is a good mystery like a cook-off?
Beat the clock, stick to the theme, nothing is as it appears.

"Don't you ever empty out your pockets?" Sherry asked while sporting a grimace.

"I'm on a case. I've taught myself to never throw anything away without showing someone else what I found. A second opinion could break a case." Ray handed Sherry what was left of the used napkins. "One for Friday. One for Monday."

Sherry inspected her hands. She frowned when she discovered her finger was spotted with cream cheese. "What's your take on the messages?"

"To be determined. I'm going to talk to this Garrett Stein fellow. If I need you tomorrow, you'll be here?"

"I'm certain we'll be changing venues tomorrow. And I'll only continue in the cook-off if I win this first round," Sherry said.

"Knock 'em dead." Ray tapped Sherry on her back with the tips of his fingers.

"You're not wiping your hands on my back, are you?"

Ray threw up his arms in surrender. "Not guilty."

"Here's my ride," Sherry said.

"This way, please. Time for your follow-up interview," Stacy said with a briskness that matched her gait. She didn't give Sherry time to bid Ray more than a fleeting farewell.

Stacy's pace showed no mercy to a cook who'd competed hard for the last two hours. Sherry's fatigued legs stumbled over a tuft of grass before Stacy slowed down. Sherry was relieved when they reached the tent, which was not much larger than a walk-in closet. Sherry lowered herself down in a seat facing a camera. Stacy was positioned behind the cameraman's shoulder.

"I'm going to ask you some questions about your experience this morning. Talk straight into the camera, not to me," Stacy said. "Are you comfortable?"

"Pretty good, thanks," Sherry fibbed. She wriggled to find an ounce of comfort on her unpadded folding chair.

During the interview, Sherry was asked about how she utilized the supplied ingredients, her inspiration in choosing her recipe, and any roadblocks she may have encountered along the way. She did her best to recount the steps she took to reach the final product. Stacy's last request was for Sherry's to elaborate on her relaxed demeanor in comparison to her opponent's during the competition.

"I felt like everything went as well as I could hope. I felt confident."

"We witnessed Jada burn her hand," Stacy said. "You never hesitated to assist her."

"I was more than happy to lend a hand to an injured cook. I never thought twice about it."

Sherry's brows pinched together when panic set in. Had she broken a rule by assisting Jada? More explanation was needed.

"I've been in plenty of cook-offs where another cook needs more pepper or a paring knife or a piece of plastic wrap you may have on your table. I always share. I can't ignore someone in distress. I just can't." She gave her statement some thought before continuing. "I never want to see anyone get hurt." If the officials wanted to disqualify her for being a fair competitor, then so be it.

Stacy nodded and tapped the cameraman on the shoulder. He cut the camera shoot and Sherry hoisted herself off her chair.

"The winner announcement doesn't come until all the others have competed," Stacy said as they left the tent. "We're aiming for midafternoon to wrap for the day. Another pair of cooks is already underway. If you wouldn't mind stepping into the trailer until then, we'll call you when the time comes. Lunch follows." Stacy pointed Sherry in the direction of the contestant trailer.

Mick was reviewing notes resting on the crossbar of his walker when Sherry passed by.

"Hi, Mick."

She stopped when he lifted his attention off the papers.

"How'd it go, Sherry? You must be relieved you're done," Mick said.

"Done? Did I lose?" Sherry asked.

"No, no, no. That announcement hasn't been made yet. Not until all the pairs have competed. Take a seat inside. The other competitors will join you as they complete their challenge."

Inside the trailer, Sherry watched a full morning news program with partial attention until the remaining competitors began to filter into the trailer. She made a fast friend in Silvia, who was more than willing to share her life story with Sherry. They made a date to eat lunch together when the catering truck opened. By the time two p.m. rolled around Sherry's stomach was rumbling. She'd only eaten a snack bag of popcorn and downed an iced tea since breakfast.

"Cooks, lunch is ready," Stacy called out from the front of the trailer. "We've dismissed the audience and it's you and the crew, our treat. Today's shoot is a wrap, but please stay through lunch and enjoy yourselves. Take off your aprons and return them to me as you leave, please. We will wash them and return them to those competing tomorrow. The announcement of those moving on to day two will be made at lunch."

Silvia clutched Sherry's arm. "Good luck to both of us."

Lunch was standard catered fare: pasta salads, turkey finger sandwiches and fruit bowls. It was pleasant to eat outside on the library common and served to both reenergize Sherry and stoke her excitement for the cook-off's round one results. When Basil, Mick, and Stacy huddled together at a corner table, the time had come. Sherry listened as the volume of their conversation increased to the point Basil used his hands to signal the others to take the level down a notch.

"What's that all about?" Sherry asked Silvia.

"Maybe they're not agreeing on the outcome?" Silvia said.

• • •

"I live to cook another day. I go back tomorrow for round two," Sherry said. "I'm expected at the Augustin Inn tomorrow at nine a.m. sharp. Can you hear me over all that engine noise?"

"Yes," Don said. "Congratulations, although I'm not exactly surprised. You're the best cook around."

"Thank you," Sherry shouted. She wondered how Don heard her over the rumbling engines, blaring horns and screeching gulls. "I'm here at the Ruggery for a few hours."

"I'll see you at your house after seven tonight," Don yelled out over another blast of a boat's horn. "Bye."

Sherry set her phone down.

"Erno picked a heck of a time to take a week off. He's missing all the action. He didn't want to come home early when you told him you were going to be on television?" Amber asked.

"First of all, the show won't air immediately. They said it will air on Labor Day weekend. Dad has plenty of time to get home to watch it. And second, miss his first trip away from Augustin in five years? I don't think so. Plus, Ruth Gadabee made all these elaborate plans for them on Nantucket. It would be such a shame for the happy couple to cut their trip short. He's going to be a new man when he returns. Mark my words."

"All he's missing here is a murder, Augustin starring in a TV cook-off program, and an anonymous mystery writer teasing news on napkins," Amber said.

"When it rains, it pours," Sherry said with a laugh.

"No more newsy napkins at Toasts of the Town, right?" Amber asked. "You said they stopped after last Wednesday. I don't eat out as much as I'd like, but the napkins had me hooked while they lasted."

"I thought so. Ray told me otherwise. The delivery started up again Friday with an edgier bent to them."

"Edgier? How so?"

"Murder was referenced, and a vague warning was issued. What does it all mean? How and when does the escalating mystery end?" Sherry asked.

"Is there no more talk about the cook-off?" Amber asked.

"More than ever. The napkins make a comparison between a murder and a cook-off. They mention Feral Creations, saying the company wouldn't write a script that included a murder. I certainly wouldn't think so. The real puzzle is what's the two-faced story that needs a second ending? And Monday's napkins say at the cook-off, nothing is as it seems."

"I'm sorry I asked. Now I'll be thinking about all those odd terms and phrases all day," Amber said. "Two-faced story? A second ending? That's a riddle."

Sherry and Amber exchanged head shakes as the Ruggery's front doorbell tinkled.

Mrs. Raymond, eighty years young, shuffled through the doorway. "Good afternoon, Sherry and Amber. I'm on my way back from the beach. I was unceremoniously evicted from my favorite observation point by some highfalutin television crew who proclaimed the beach theirs."

"Good morning, Mrs. Raymond. I'm so sorry that happened," Sherry said. Mrs. Raymond had been a Ruggery customer for longer than Sherry was alive, and then some. Her citizen résumé was what impressed Sherry the most. She was a staple of the Augustin community, assisting in the community garden upkeep, and she was known to have a near perfect attendance record at any public forum debate held at town hall. Back in the day she'd been the school board president and headed up the town's annual half-marathon committee. "You, of all people, should be allowed to claim your piece of beach for as long as you'd like, any day of the week."

"Thank you, darling girl," the woman said. "I didn't come to complain. Life's too short for that. Everything evens out on Judgment Day."

Sherry cringed at the thought, which was one hundred percent accurate. "Is there something we can help you with?"

"Yes, please. My friend Hazel told me her daughter has moved into her very own townhouse. That's always a huge milestone for the youth of today. She also mentioned Kat, that's her name, I don't know if you know her, is incapable of wrapping a present correctly, let alone decorate her new home."

Sherry summoned her will to not side-eye Amber with a knowing glance. "I do know her. Kat Coleman, yes. She's a wonderful girl. Works at the mayor's office. She works so hard she may not have the time to learn correct wrapping techniques."

Mrs. Raymond's penciled eyebrows arched. "Of course you know her. I should have remembered. You edit the town newsletter. That handsome young mayor always writes the most seductive articles. He was born to be a politician."

"I never considered his articles seductive, but I see what you mean."

"You should play tennis with the girl. Hazel says her daughter can beat anyone at tennis and hasn't found a worthy opponent yet."

Amber couldn't suppress a cough. "Excuse me, I need some water." She left Sherry's side.

"I'll be sure to ask her to play. I have some wonderful rugs to show you," Sherry said. "Take a seat and I'll bring some over." Sherry slid an armchair over to the front window, where Mrs. Raymond would have natural light to view the rugs' color schemes.

"Honey, since you said you knew Kat, I'd like to ask you something about her," Mrs. Raymond said as she lowered herself carefully down into the chair.

"Of course. I don't know her very well, but I'm sure I can help you pick out a wonderful rug she'll adore," Sherry said as she walked across the showroom to the mountain of oval rugs.

"Which rug to choose wasn't my question. I'll do the choosing, but thank you for your offer."

Sherry absorbed Mrs. Raymond's self-assured comment. With age comes the wisdom to recognize your strengths, and Mrs. Raymond's noble strength was belief in herself.

"Do you think she's a lesbian? I mean, her mother mentioned she has no interest in finding a husband. Hazel says she's nudged her daughter toward some eligible bachelors and Kat's turned up her nose at all of them. Hazel may be barking up the wrong tree. Putting her eggs in the wrong basket, so to speak. Hazel swears she's spent her life staying out of Kat's social life, but maybe she should have known this much about her own daughter. And if she is, my lovely granddaughter may be a perfect match for her."

"I can't speak with any authority on Kat's love life. I'm sorry, Mrs. Raymond," Sherry said, eager to change the subject. She presented four oval rugs draped across her forearms.

"No matter. Hazel also mentioned Kat was bothered by a workplace conundrum. An issue pressing her to do something against her better judgment. Oh my, life can get so complicated." Mrs. Raymond shook her head. Her gray curls flipped in all directions.

"Kat mentioned something about that to me, too. Do you have any details?"

"I don't. Kat can speak in riddles sometimes. Most youngsters speak in riddles these days, in my opinion. Poor Kat. No love life, and her career's turning messy. There's so much pressure on today's youth."

Sherry didn't steer the conversation back to Kat but made a mental note of what Mrs. Raymond had to say. Instead, she paraded a selection of rugs before Mrs. Raymond, after the first four were refused.

"Those look beautiful. You have made some wonderful selections, dear. Thank you for narrowing down the choices."

Mrs. Raymond chose a beige rug with a border of ivy and pink geraniums. Sherry helped her to her car when the transaction was complete, where, thankfully, a driver was waiting behind the wheel. Mrs. Raymond was a bundle of octogenarian energy whose reactions had slowed markedly since the last time Sherry spent time with her. Sherry used the opportunity of helping her to the car to ensure she had a safe ride home. Relieved Mrs. Raymond was taken care of, Sherry stored away her pending offer to taxi her.

"Dear, one last word about Kat Coleman," Mrs. Raymond said as Sherry held the car door open. "I shouldn't tell tales out of school but I will this one time. Her mother says her daughter's holding on to a big secret. One that could cost her the job she has worked so hard to get."

"People need support at times. I'm glad Kat's confiding in her mother," Sherry said.

"That's the problem. I don't think she is. Hazel found this out from a man named Garrett Stein who has befriended Kat. He has something to do with the television production that kicked me off the beach. He's a looker, too."

"I think he's a reporter or journalist in the entertainment field. He's probably covering the television shoot."

"Oh, dear, you seem to know so much about the filming. Are you in the show?" Mrs. Raymond asked.

Borrowing an expression from Ray, Sherry considered her "vault" of unused, evasive replies concerning the cook-off nearly empty. She was tired of white lies and flimsy explanations. Rather than bend the truth one more time, Sherry decided on a different tactic.

"I am, but it's hush-hush. Please promise me you won't tell a soul. I'm counting on you keeping this quiet."

"I promise." Mrs. Raymond's pale complexion bloomed with color. She positioned herself to face Sherry as best she could while confined to her cramped backseat space. "I'm thrilled you consider me a confidante."

Sherry hoped Mrs. Raymond would return the favor by sharing some information. "Do you know how Hazel knows Garrett Stein?" Sherry asked. "I've only met him briefly. He seemed like a nice guy."

"Hazel met Garrett Stein in the lobby of town hall, on one of her many trips to check something out over there. My goodness, you'd think the woman was running for office with how much time she spends *not* checking up on her daughter but finding a reason to be at town hall. She said he bumped into her, but I wouldn't be surprised if Hazel launched herself at the unsuspecting fellow."

Mrs. Raymond scooted back in her seat. Sherry buckled the shoulder strap across the woman's tiny frame.

Sherry could see the driver's eyes darting from the car's side mirror to his rearview mirror. He cleared his throat, as if reminding Mrs. Raymond the day was moving forward, and they hadn't left the parking spot yet.

"Hazel managed to interest Garrett Stein in taking her daughter out,"

Mrs. Raymond said. "Hazel's a smart lady. Been married three times, so maybe not so smart in the love department. If I were Kat, I wouldn't want Hazel anywhere near my potential love connections."

"For someone who claims she doesn't meddle in her daughter's affairs, she does seem to have her finger in a lot of Kat's pies," Sherry said.

Mrs. Raymond paused and adjusted the belt strap. "This thing isn't made for someone under five feet tall. It always strangles me." Mrs. Raymond went silent.

Sherry studied the woman as she closed her eyes. Sherry understood if she needed a nap. Sherry put her hand on the door handle to close it when Mrs. Raymond's eyelids popped open with a jerk of her head. Sherry's back was beginning to ache from her unwieldy crouch to catch all of Mrs. Raymond's words.

"Hazel was sidetracked by the fact that he had no wedding ring on, had a sweet face, and was obviously sent from a higher power to marry Kat. One thing led to another, and Hazel convinced him to ask Kat out. That's as far as her efforts got, from what I gather. He's still trying to get a date with her. That's why I asked if she dates men. Better to know sooner rather than later."

"As long as she's happy," Sherry said.

"For Hazel's sake, I hope Kat doesn't end up headlining in *Juicy Bites*. That's a worry of Hazel's. She's concerned Kat's the author tattling the information. So much so, she made it her mission to discover and announce the name of the author. Kind of nipping the napkins in the bud before Kat gets nipped."

"I'd like to know as well," Sherry said. "I wish Hazel good luck."

"Hazel has a nose for news. She loves solving a good mystery. I think she has too much time on her hands. Hazel did some sleuthing to find out who was writing the *Juicy Bites* napkin news. In the process, she got Garrett Stein to tell her Kat wouldn't accept his date invitation because a work situation was souring her mood." Mrs. Raymond dabbed her lips with a tissue after snickering at her own comment.

"That's a concern," Sherry said. "Did Hazel mention whether she had a lead on the identity of the *Juicy Bites* author?"

Mrs. Raymond shook her head slowly. "She would have mentioned if she cracked the case. And she didn't."

"My worst fear is Kat may be in danger and isn't able to ask for help. From who, or what, I can't be sure. If her mother told you she's concerned, that's a worry."

Mrs. Raymond's hand swept across her forehead. "Oh, my. I don't like the sound of that. Tony, would you please take me home. I need to rest from all this excitement."

"Yes, ma'am," the driver said.

"Goodbye, Sherry. Let me know if you hear anything. Unless it's horrible."

"Bye, Mrs. Raymond. Thank you for your business." Sherry gently shut the car door and waved as the car rolled away.

"Where have you been?" Amber asked. "I thought you were seeing Mrs. Raymond to her car."

"I was. She was telling me some interesting tidbits about Kat Coleman. She mentioned Kat was holding on to a secret that could cost her dearly. I hope it has nothing to do with Rachel's murder. Rachel and Kat were friends. At least they used to be friends. I'm confident Kat can take care of herself, except if there's a murderer roaming around."

"You've got a cook-off to concentrate on. Maybe let the authorities, namely Ray, do their job, so you can do yours."

"Wow, Amber. Strong words."

"It's just that you can get sucked into a murder investigation and I don't want to see *you* hurt. I know you. If you think you can lend a hand to someone in need, you will. Without regard to your own well-being." Amber walked over to her friend and gave her a hug. "You're a national treasure. We need you to stay safe."

"Message lovingly received," Sherry said. "Now, let's get back to work. I'm out tomorrow and I doubt if the day will run as smoothly as today."

Chapter 13

Juicy Bites

Food and suspects will be grilled at the Augustin Inn.
Whoever's sitting on an explosive secret—
someone at the cook-off has the match.

Sherry handed the printed napkin back to Eileen. She pulled her cardigan closed as an early morning chill brought on a shiver. She had only planned on being outside for as long as it took Chutney to relieve himself, not for a lengthy inquiry from her neighbor and Kat's mother.

"Are you at all concerned? I wanted to show you before you left for the Augustin Inn. Hazel and I can't go today. No audience allowed. Who will look after you?" Eileen said. The concern in her voice didn't do much to warm Sherry up.

"I'm not worried in the least. Only about the rain and humidity in the forecast. I assume we'll be cooking indoors and not grilling. So, *Juicy Bites* isn't completely on point. Don't worry about me. I don't need looking after," Sherry said. "But I appreciate your concern."

"The weather wasn't our greatest concern," Hazel said. "I don't like the new tone of the napkins. I was hoping they'd be more upbeat today, like they used to be. But no, they're getting so dramatic. I wish the poor girl's murderer would be found so these shenanigans will stop."

"You could stop reading the napkins," Sherry suggested.

"And miss something? Not on your life. That's why I rushed over to Pep's truck and bought us breakfast so I could see what news the napkins put forth today."

"And then you rushed here to make me nervous by delivering the news?" Sherry asked.

"We came over to wish you well. I do enjoy my beauty sleep, but this was so important I set my alarm. *Juicy Bites* has taken such a turn," Eileen said. "It's as if one pleasant author has been replaced by another who enjoys spreading fear."

"So far, nothing untoward has happened at the cook-off. This publicity stunt may have worn thin and is grasping at straws predicting doom and gloom," Sherry said. She thought about Eileen's comment. She made a valid point. It's as if the author had changed along with the messages. She had yet to pinpoint the first author and there was a possibility of a second? "Thank you both for walking Chutney today. I'm told I'll be back before dinner."

"My pleasure," Eileen said. "Good luck. Hazel and I would be there if we were allowed."

"I'd like to say I'll let you both know how the day goes when I see you, but as you know, I signed a confidentiality agreement," Sherry said as her body leaned toward home. "At least you got to see some of yesterday's event."

"As long as you share with me as much as you share with Effie Raymond," Hazel said. "She called yesterday to tell me you were in the television cook-off. I said, 'tell me something I don't know.'"

Sherry cringed. "You know the same as her. I'd be more forthcoming if I could." How was she getting in so much trouble partaking in the hobby she loved so much? "By the way, yesterday, did you two watch the judging portion of the competition? I'm so curious about who the judges are. Are they celebrity chefs, sponsors, town folk?" Sherry asked. "The cooks are in the dark about their identity."

"No. Sorry," Eileen said. "They closed the tent flaps and left us guessing what was happening. The audience left when it was clear we weren't needed anymore." We did get to see the other cooks perform and they are nowhere near as proficient as you. You should clean up, no problem."

"Interesting," Sherry said.

"Before you go, dear, I wanted you to hear what Hazel's telling me," Eileen said. "You see her daughter more often than she does, and I thought you could ease her motherly worries."

Sherry checked her phone for the time. "If I can, I will."

"The problem is, Hazel received a second call from your friend Detective Bease," Eileen said. "Right, Hazel?"

"That's right, dear," Hazel said.

Sherry took a deep breath. "Kat was one of the last to see Rachel Yaro before she turned up deceased the next morning. If she knows anything useful, it would be helpful for him to learn."

"He's a homicide detective," Hazel said. "He didn't say that the first time we spoke. He didn't even mention the murder. I had to do my own investigating, which I'm good at, starting with who the heck Detective Ray Bease is."

"It sounds like you've done your homework," Sherry said.

"Except her research uncovered one overriding fact," Eileen said. "He doesn't speak to anyone unless they're directly involved in the act. I know because I watch reruns of *Hawaii Five-O*."

"*Hawaii Five-O* is your idea of a factual resource?" Hazel side-eyed Eileen.

"Well, why not?" Eileen asked.

"Does he think my daughter is capable of murder?" Hazel asked. Her cheeks reddened.

"Don't worry. I spoke to the detective. At no time did I get that impression. What exactly did he say to you?" Sherry asked Hazel.

"He called once last week in hopes of locating Kat. Now a second time to give me an earful about how Kat won't speak up for herself."

"That's outrageous," Eileen added. "Kat's being coy. No harm in that."

"There might be," Sherry suggested.

"Again, the detective wanted to know if Kat had issues with Rachel," Hazel said. "He wanted to know where Kat was the morning Rachel was, oh, I can't say those sorts of words."

"That's okay, dear," Eileen said. "We know what you mean. I'll say the word. Murder."

"I had to remember what I told him the first time we spoke. I hope my story was consistent. I told him she and I had just spoken. And I use the word *just* loosely, give or take a day or two." Hazel waved her hand back and forth, demonstrating the nonspecific time frame she shared with Ray. "He said Kat wasn't willing to speak on her own behalf. He said it was his duty to pursue a red flag."

"It is," Sherry said.

"Well, he needs to know I was told years ago to not speak on her behalf. They were harsh words for any mother, but I honor them to this day," Hazel said.

Eileen's eyes drifted skyward before her gaze settled back down to Sherry. "Hazel and I have been friends through four marriages. One of mine and three of hers. Three, right?" Eileen glanced at Hazel for confirmation. A nod confirmed their friendship and a trio of nuptials for Hazel. "She didn't raise a killer."

"Of course she didn't," Sherry said. "I wonder why Kat doesn't offer up the information he's asking for. He wants to pinpoint where she was when she took off for a day without any advance notice. That way he can put the issue to bed." Sherry peered at Hazel, whose head was lowered. "If we knew, her unapproved day off can be labeled coincidence and nothing more."

Hazel put her hands up to her head. "I knew I should be more of an overbearing parent. What's the point of staying out of your child's business when something like this occurs? I can't help her." She sucked in a breath. "Can you, Sherry? Please?"

It was difficult to downplay the urgency in Hazel's plea. "Does Kat have any guy friends at town hall she's dated and it didn't work out? I can't imagine she doesn't get lots of date invitations; she's such a cute girl," Sherry asked.

Hazel thought long and hard, pacing a small circle as she did. When she came to a stop, she patted her hair into place. "Not dated, as far as I know. Maybe a dabble here and a dabble there. Recently she stated she's on hiatus from men. I'm a modern woman. I can accept her decision. Why do you ask?"

"Think hard, dear," Eileen said. "All your visits to town hall must have turned up some young eligible man Kat had a fancy for in the past. One that she might have dismissed the advances of, and he didn't take it well. You said Kat has a workplace problem that she can't get a grip on. Maybe it's a jilted lover?"

"There is one recently. He's not jilted, but he is being rebuffed, as far as I can gather. He's interested in her and biding his time until she appears receptive."

"You make it sound like a breeding program out in the wild," Sherry said with a snicker. Hazel wasn't amused. "Would this be Garrett Stein?"

"Yes, dear. Garrett Stein. He has my blessing to pursue Kat should he be inclined. He's quite a dashing fellow."

"But you're not pushing him, are you?" Eileen asked. "Honestly, Hazel. Pick a lane. Either you're all in as a matchmaker or you're not."

"Me? Huh! I do have to say, I could speed up the process if Kat would let me. I met the young man. He checks all the boxes. Don't blame me for lighting a small fire under him to act fast before she's taken. I know Kat would never listen to a suggestion from me, so I attacked from the other side. When her mind is made up in a certain direction, only the most strategic of negotiations can change it."

"Couldn't it be she's playing you right into her hands?" Eileen said.

Hazel tipped her head.

"Maybe she's telling you one thing about Garrett Stein but doing the opposite. That way she maintains control while keeping you at arm's length while you wait for the outcome you've chosen for her," Eileen said.

"You raised a strong adult," Sherry said.

"And a clever one. Maybe you're right. But the right man is hard to find, and I have some experience in that department. She should listen to me sometimes. When I was young, I had many polite admirers who used to follow me around town assessing my eligibility. When the time was right, they'd court me properly. I know today's social world is rather aggressive and behavior has grown so crass. Young men have no idea how to capture a girl's fancy. Showing up at her office and staring at her like a forlorn puppy isn't going to get him anywhere. Why are you asking about Kat's dates at work? Do you think there's a situation I should worry about?" Hazel asked.

"What I'm looking for is a reason she didn't show up for work Wednesday. Maybe a date ran long?" Sherry asked.

"I'm going to ignore that insinuation. My Kat is a busy girl who wouldn't choose extended playtime over her responsibilities. On the other hand, do you think Garrett Stein is a bad seed and Kat is having trouble with him? Should I be regretting having pushed him in her direction?"

"I have no idea," Sherry said. "Something's amiss with Kat, though."

"You're not easing my worry. For heaven's sake, I look like a fool because I told the detective she was at work that morning. She wasn't. Now I'm an accomplice in hiding the truth," Hazel said.

"I don't think Detective Bease thinks that," Sherry said. "Not at all. You told him what you thought was the truth at the time."

"I told the detective she would eventually tell him what he wants to know. She sets her own timetables. No one can rush her. That's the truth. Whatever else I told him was more fluff than substance. I may have left out a fact or two."

"Detective Bease can rush her if he feels inclined," Sherry said. "Time-tables are important in an investigation."

Hazel held her gaze on Sherry and groaned. "Sherry, can you help find the murderer? I only have one child and she needs help."

"I know as much as you do about Rachel's murder," Sherry said. "If Kat knows something, she could break the case wide open. Unless she's in a tough spot and is protecting herself or someone else."

"Sherry? Please?" Eileen pleaded.

"Will you?" Hazel asked. "Please? I do think she's in some manner of trouble. What if he's the problem?"

"I'll try," Sherry said.

A glance at her phone confirmed Sherry would make it to the inn as early as she liked if she left the conversation where it was.

"When time permits," Sherry said. "I have an issue with the town newsletter, and I need to pay a visit to the mayor's office. It's a good excuse to speak to Kat."

Chapter 14

The Augustin Inn had been renovated within the last two years. The construction maintained the delicate balance between updating the structure for full function in modern times and preserving the history the walls witnessed since the Revolutionary War. One of the rooms on the lower level originated as a storage facility for ammunition, while another stored dry goods for visiting colonial troops. Much of the inn was refurbished after the mid-1800s, and blending multiple eras seamlessly was another hurdle the contractors had to grapple with. In the end, the inn remained the simplistic, symmetrical building with six chimneys, but the real magic was the warm, welcoming New England style of the interior.

As she neared, Sherry drank in the inn's visual history she'd read about in a newsletter article written by the mayor while the renovation was underway. Modern-day reality hit when she was required to clear strict cook-off security protocol before entering. After checking in she followed directions to the contestant gathering. The muted blue and gold carpeted hallway was cluttered with cameras, cables, and personnel trading instructions on the day's schedule. The calm she woke up to earlier dissolved as the tornado of commotion swept her up. Her nerves settled a bit when she spotted a familiar face.

"Welcome to *Relish*, day two, Sherry," Stacy said. "And welcome to the orderly chaos. Basil and Mick are meeting with Jason now. They'll address the remaining cooks afterward."

"Thanks," Sherry said. She had a hard time making sense out of all the activity in the tight hallway space. "Where are we cooking?"

"Don't worry. You'll have plenty of elbow room in the inn's kitchen. We won't have an audience today. It's all about the cooks and their creations. You must generate the excitement without any clapping, ews, or ahs. Follow me. I'll try not to lose you in the crowd. It's time to put on an apron."

On her speed walk to the kitchen Sherry weaved in and around equipment waiting to be positioned and crew members hustling to and fro. She only lost sight of Stacy once before finding her huddled with Mick. He was struggling to place his walker over a thick bundle of wire.

"You're doing a good job under the circumstances," Stacy told Mick.

"I count to ten when I feel like giving up," Mick said. "Re-centers me." He straightened up and rotated his shoulders. "Thanks for the help."

"I'll continue on? I don't want Sherry to be late," Stacy said.

"Carry on," Mick said. "I'll be there soon." He resumed navigating the cables.

"Got to give him credit," Sherry said. "A for effort."

"He'll be better soon," Stacy said. "No rush. I enjoy the extra responsibility."

"You're doing a great job, too," Sherry said in hopes of countering what she sensed could be a touch of resentment on Stacy's behalf.

Sherry reached the inn's spacious commercial-grade kitchen and gathered with the other cooks. Stacy informed the six competitors they'd be cooking in two teams of three. One team was made up of Sherry, Silvia, and a stout man named Orlando. Orlando greeted his teammates with a smothering bear hug that took Sherry's breath away. He proceeded to pump his fists and proclaim the team's name Triofante, Italian for triumphant, Trio for short. They were cooking against Summer Sizzle, also made up of two women and a man.

At first sight, the kitchen looked to be one of the most accommodating facilities Sherry had the pleasure of competing in. The four huge stainless-steel ovens were a sight to behold. She was transported back to the time she cooked outdoors under adverse conditions of blazing sun and high humidity, on a tiny two-burner portable cooktop. The heat was slow to come up and impossible to control as she'd like. She was certain the other cooks were having the same issues but that didn't help her chances. She came in dead last, serving the judges a broken sauce over pink chicken thighs. They refused to eat the meat after a knife cut revealed the degree of uncooked meat. Sherry's stomach flipped at the thought of making the judges sick had they tried a bite. The memory lingered and served to motivate her to expect the unexpected during cook-offs.

"Stacy," Mick said, "Orlando would like to use the men's room before we begin. Anyone else?"

Four more cooks raised their hands.

"Glad I asked. Follow me." Mick shuffled forward on his walker, leading four cooks in his wake.

"I'll take them," Stacy said abruptly.

"Must be the nerves," Sherry said as the procession left the kitchen. "I don't drink a lot before a cook-off, only during. I learned the hard way."

"A veteran move," Silvia said.

Mick nodded in agreement. "Let's wait out in the hall for them to return.

I don't want anyone to have an unfair advantage familiarizing themselves with the layout in here before the others."

"Can I ask you a question?" Sherry didn't wait for permission from Mick to proceed. "I admire how well your team works together."

"We try," Mick said.

"How is Basil as a boss? I hope he's a breeze to work with. I mean, the circumstances must be difficult with someone new stepping in for Rachel at the eleventh hour."

"I understand your curiosity," Mick said. "Stacy's not all that new. She's been an intern, come through the Feral Creations page program, and she's very driven to succeed. As a matter of fact, I'm reminded constantly to watch my back, or I'll lose my position as Basil's number-one production assistant to her. Basil's not taking it easy on me, despite my injury, that's for sure." His gaze drifted over her shoulder. "In the end, Basil is Basil, Stacy is Stacy, and I take who they are with a grain of salt." He waved his hand to flag down two cooks returning from the bathroom.

"Did I hear my name?" Basil cocked his head as he approached.

Mick made an audible gulp. "Only good things said."

"Mick, would you mind taking Silvia to supplies and swap out her apron for a stain-free one, please?" Basil asked. "Sam pointed out a visible stain under the logo. The stain will show up on camera."

"Who's Sam?" Silvia asked as she inspected the front of her apron.

"Camera two operator. He has a great eye for variations," Basil said.

"Of course. Silvia, this way." Mick and Silvia moved slowly down the hall, quickly swallowed up among those milling about the hotel's corridor.

Sherry opened her mouth to begin small talk about the weather but was interrupted.

"While I have a moment with you," Basil began. "Detective Bease asked me several questions about my working relationship with Rachel Yaro. We had a productive team, and we got the job done." He paused. "What was he getting at? I may have given him the wrong impression of the dynamic between Rachel and me."

Sherry willed the others to return, unsure of the direction Basil was going in. She had cooking on her mind and needed to focus.

"I'm sure that information was helpful," Sherry said.

"You know the man. Do you believe he has me on his list of suspects?" Basil asked.

"I would never presume to speak for him," Sherry said. "He's doing his fact gathering. I wouldn't worry." Sherry had no idea whether Basil should worry or not. The words came out without much regard to where the investigation was headed.

"One more item. My driver, Yonny, found a gift bag in the limo with an envelope inscribed *To Kat Coleman, Cheers, Rachel.*

"That's nice and sad at the same time," Sherry said.

"Would you mind delivering the gift to Kat? I know you play early morning tennis with her."

Sherry winced at the thought of such a personal errand for Basil. "You probably see her more than I do."

Basil's face twisted into a scowl. "I don't want to be seen giving her a gift after going through the detective's questioning, as benign as it was. The impression any witness might get could be detrimental on many levels. If I get it to you by the end of today, would you deliver it to Kat next time you see her? And would you mind full discretion on the matter, please?"

"It's a shame Rachel isn't here to deliver it herself. It might have mended some fences." Sherry's voice drifted off as the other cooks approached. When she returned her gaze to where Basil stood, he was gone.

"Okay, folks, back to work," Stacy said. "Follow me."

"Can I help?" Sherry asked as she skirted Mick's walker. By the time the words were out of her mouth, Stacy was yards ahead. Mick had a nifty sling hanging from the side bar of his walker sporting several items overflowing from within. As slings will do, it swung from side to side as he lifted and lowered the hardware. He was forced to adjust his grip with every step forward.

"I don't want to be rude, but why didn't you get the walker that has four wheels?"

"The doc said I was a better fit for the two wheels in the rear model. He wanted me to have to lift and lower the front as a strength exercise."

"I get it," Sherry said. "Let me help you."

"Thanks for the offer but I'm okay," he said. "Stacy forgot a few things and now she's on to something else, so I'm left to pick up the pieces."

Sherry jutted her hand toward Mick as one leg of his walker wedged itself between the carpet edge and the floor. With a yank she freed the walker's front leg.

"Thanks. You know, I'm really seeing the other side of things, being in this situation," Mick said. "Some people are dependent on getting around this way for life. I'm lucky. I'm coming close to the other side."

"That's a good attitude," Sherry said. "My first instinct is to lend a hand. I hope people don't take it the wrong way."

"Better to err on the side of compassion," Mick said. "You obviously do. Thank you."

"Do you mind if I ask about your accident, Mick?"

"I don't mind at all. I had a bad one, but I'm making progress. The team were all in the car. We were on a drive to scout out possible locations for background footage of Connecticut in winter. At the time Feral Creations was in the running for one of those house makeover shows. I was hoping we didn't get the project. Those shows are overdone to death. The pressure is always on to get behind a unique show. One that would turn the industry on its ear and win us the praise we deserve. You're only as good as your latest award winner. Anyway, the roads were nearly impassable. We hit a patch of ice that put the car into a spin. The driver died and I broke some major bones. Always wear your seat belt. And avoid icy January roads. Thanks to Augustin's finest, we were all well cared for," he said.

"You have a good outlook. That makes a big difference in recovery time," Sherry said.

"It's been a long haul. Slow and steady's winning the race. Not much longer on this thing."

"Teams, can I have everyone over here, please," Stacy called out.

"Time to go," Sherry said. She joined the other cooks. Her nerves were once again heightened.

"Does everyone have on your aprons? No stains?" Stacy asked. She inspected each cook, taking care to smooth down some apron wrinkles. "Great. Basil will begin by reading you the rules today. When Mick gives the go-ahead by lowering the arm on the clapboard, Jason will make his introductions. The cameras are rolling at this point, so smile and face Jason. The cameras will not stop rolling. Ignore them. They're part of the scenery. Any questions?"

Once again, Sherry had a dozen questions on the tip of her tongue but chose to reserve them when no one else chimed in. She had no time to dwell on what she didn't know about the cook-off because Basil stepped in front of Stacy.

"Good morning, folks. Time to get started. Six cooks remain in the *Relish* cook-off," Basil said. "All of you are vying for the forty-thousand-dollar prize, half of which will be going to the charity or nonprofit of your choice. If that isn't inspiration enough to cook your hearts out, I don't know what is."

Spontaneous applause broke out. *Forty thousand dollars* was repeated throughout the group.

Basil continued when the murmur died down. His gaze drifted beyond the cooks. "Jason? Are you ready to welcome the two teams and present them with their challenge?"

The kitchen space grew tight when the cooks joined the cameras and production personnel. The space shrank further as everyone soldiered together to give Jason a wide berth to perform his introductions. Jason flowed into view with his hair styled to be stationary under all conditions. His white polo shirt was crisply ironed, and his makeup was applied flawlessly, lending him an orangey summer glow that screamed commitment to the day's theme.

Sherry raised her hand.

"Yes, Sherry," Basil said.

"When will we get full instructions on how the cook-off works?"

"The cameras start rolling. Jason makes his intro and addresses the cooks. The element of surprise is priceless. Catching real-time reactions on camera, that's what the viewers tune in for."

"When will the explosive secret be revealed?" Orlando asked. "*Juicy Bites* predicted a bombshell."

Basil sighed. "Hah. I wouldn't count on that happening. If you're worried, I advise staying vigilant. Security is on scene. Okay, Mick. Ready when you are."

Mick gave the go-ahead with a slam of his clapboard's arm.

Jason's smile was timed perfectly with Mick's signal. He radiated enthusiasm. The red recording light on top of the camera lit up. The operator raised a hand with his thumb pointed skyward. Jason gave a subtle nod.

"Welcome back to day two of the *Relish* challenge. Half the cooks have been eliminated. The remaining six cooks are relishing success. Stay hungry if you're aiming for the big prize." Jason swept his arm toward the camera.

"Behind me, the cooks have been divided into two teams: team Trio, short for Triofante, and team Summer Sizzle. Survivors from yesterday's *Relish* challenge face a daunting test today. Teams will be presented with mystery ingredients to be grilled, indoors, and assembled into a meal for the judges. Teamwork, creativity, and decision-making will all come into play. The challenge today is titled"—Jason lowered his mike and made eye contact with every one of the six cooks, then he lifted the mike to his lips—"*Not Burgers Again This Labor Day, Please*." He paused again. "Cooks, please take your marks next to your team's prep area." He pointed out stars stenciled on the linoleum floor in front of each of two ovens.

Sherry glanced at the massive steel oven on her way to her mark. The traditional burner grates had been replaced with ridged grill inserts. Sherry wondered if the forecast for hot, humid weather with a good chance of thunderstorms shifted the grill competition indoors and the theme shifted along with the contest's location.

Team Trio and Team Summer Sizzle settled in front of their ovens, alongside which was a large preparation area. A young man and woman entered the area carrying large wicker baskets.

"Thank you, Pauline and Trey," Jason said. The baskets were set down on tables beside the ovens. "The ingredients you must incorporate into your recipes are in these Labor Day picnic baskets."

Sherry looked to her Trio teammates for reassurance they were up for the challenge. The blank looks on their faces didn't offer much in the way of confidence.

"You will find portobello mushroom caps, pesto, goat cheese, corn on the cob, cherry tomatoes, and your choice of *either* quinoa or walnut halves. To your left you will find a minimal amount of pantry items such as oils, vinegars, dry seasoning, fresh herbs, fresh fruits and some canned goods, such as beans. In your allotted cook prep time, we have factored in some time for you all to acclimate to this unfamiliar kitchen. You may also ask our runners, Pauline and Trey, if a certain ingredient you desire is available, and where it may be located. You may need to substitute, so keep an open mind."

Sherry held her gaze on Jason in anticipation of his command to begin.

"Okay, teams. When I give the go-ahead, you will have two hours to prepare a dish to wow the judges. Be a team player and you will have the advantage." Jason froze in place, as did the cooks.

Sherry held her breath.

Chapter 15

"Cooks, it's time to create recipes the judges will relish," Jason announced. "You have one hundred and twenty minutes. Good luck. The clock begins now."

"Okay, Sherry. What's the plan?" Silvia said in a pronounced whisper.

Orlando leaned in. "Huddle," he said. When the Trio huddle broke, they had a plan to make Southwestern Charred Portobello Bowl with Tangy Pesto Cheese Drizzle.

"Bowls are in this year, we need to jump on the trend bandwagon," said Silvia. "That's a good idea, Sherry."

"Teamwork makes the dream work," Orlando said.

"Who wants to marinate the mushrooms in Southwestern flavors?" Sherry asked.

"You're speaking my language," Orlando said. "I'll need the mushrooms, tomatoes, and corn from the bucket of ingredients. They can all take a bath in marinade before we char them on the grill."

"Silvia, would you like to cook the quinoa in a saucepan over the grill flame? It's a great bed for the bowl contents to sit on because it doesn't get mushy. We'll slightly undercook it. By the time it's plated and sits a few minutes it'll absorb all the drippings and yummy drizzle. The texture will be perfect." Sherry pointed out a saucepan in the pantry rack. "Can you grab the appropriate pot, too?"

"Yes, of course. My mouth is watering already," Silvia said.

"I'll grab the goat cheese and pesto and search for sour cream, vinegar, lime, and a touch of whatever chili they have in the pantry. When I get back, I'll concoct the tangy pesto cheese drizzle," Sherry said. "Wish me luck."

"Maybe grab some canned black beans while you're over there?" Silvia suggested.

"Will do," Sherry said.

Sherry left her team and met Carla from the Summer Sizzle team browsing the pantry selection. Despite sporting a slim athletic build, she was huffing and puffing to an alarming degree.

"This is terrible," she complained. "Our team is making a big mistake. We can't agree on our menu choice. I came over here for some inspiration, and, frankly, to clear my head."

Carla had yet to make room for Sherry to scan the pantry. The camera

95

operator, with his camera's lens aimed squarely on the two women, was blocking the alternate opening.

"Can I help? It's not worth getting all worked up about. Just breathe. I don't think it's against the rules if you tell me which part of the team's plan doesn't appeal to you."

Carla glanced at the camera lens, then back to Sherry. "They want to make a salad and I think that's so boring, not to mention an easy cop-out. We can't win with a salad."

"Did you have another idea?" Sherry glanced back at her teammates, who were buzzing around the preparation table. She caught a glimpse of Garrett Stein in the wings taking notes. No audience was allowed into the day's cook-off. He must be on duty.

"My idea is portobella pizzas," Carla said.

"How about a compromise? Grilled portobella pizza salad. The pizza can be cut in slices and sit on top of a yummy salad with a pesto vinaigrette."

Carla hugged Sherry, pulled away, and shook her by the shoulders. "Perfect. Thank you so much."

"You have to get your team's approval, but it was mostly your idea, not mine," Sherry said. She put the blonde locks that sprang forward during Carla's energetic hug back in place behind her ears. A drip of sweat trickled down her forehead. "You're welcome. Good luck."

Sherry got back to the task of collecting ingredients for the Southwestern-inspired drizzle. She found jarred chipotle in adobo sauce, garlic and onion powders, vinegar, a lime, honey and sour cream. She also picked up a can of black beans and toted the load back to the Trio station.

"The sauce fixin's have arrived," Sherry announced upon her return. "They should give a smokey bite."

Orlando and Silvia were well on their way to completing their elements of the recipe.

"The mushroom is rubbed down with spices and ready to grill," Orlando said.

"The quinoa is almost cooked, then I'll keep it warm until presentation time," Silvia said.

"It's all coming together. Orlando, do you think you can scout out a good-size bowl? A glass one would really showcase all the layers," Sherry said.

"I'm on it. When I get back, I'll get to grilling." Orlando repeated a fist pump and stumbled forward. "Phew, it's getting hot out here." He regained his balance when he grabbed the corner of the prep table.

"It is getting hot in here. You okay?" Silvia asked. "There's some water back there. Trey or Pauline can help you find a sports drink."

"I might need to sit for a minute," Orlando said. He made his way to a corner of the kitchen and went down hard onto a folded chair.

"Take your time," Silvia said. "Get back here as soon as you're able."

"Hope he's alright," Sherry said. "Luckily, we have plenty of time if it's only down to the two of us." Sherry separated a medium-size mixing bowl from a stack on the table. She whisked together the drizzle ingredients. She dipped a spoon into the bowl and tasted for balance of flavors.

"How is it?" Silvia asked. She wiped her brow with a hand towel provided by Pauline.

Sherry's puckered lips answered the question. "Needs more honey. Too much acid. The lime is strong." She spooned in more of the sticky honey and retasted with a new spoon. If the judges, whoever they may be, saw her double dip with a used spoon that could spell trouble, or elimination. "Perfect now."

"How much time is left?" Silvia asked.

Sherry checked the watch she put on before she left her house. She seldom wore a watch, as her phone served as her go-to timepiece. The problem was, no phones were allowed on the contest floor. Monday she noted a countdown clock, prevalent at all the cook-offs she'd been a part of, was nowhere in sight. She was at the mercy of Jason calling out various intervals of time and that was something she wanted more control over.

"By my calculation, we have close to forty minutes left," Sherry said. "That's not much time to grill, slice, arrange and assemble. There's always a fine line between waiting until the very last minute to assemble so the dish doesn't sit around getting sloppy and cutting it so close you miss a detail."

"Okay, now I'm nervous," Silvia said.

Orlando stepped up to the prep table. "Hey, guys. I'm not feeling very well. This heat is kicking my butt."

"I've got a bad feeling they've turned off the air-conditioning to recreate the great outdoors," Sherry said. "Or test our resolve."

"Ugh, my resolve has dissolved." Orlando's reply seemed to sap the last of his energy. He lowered his head and hung on to the edge of the table for dear life.

"Go back and rest. You'll get a second wind. If not, don't worry. Nothing's worth getting sick over." Sherry watched Orlando lumber back to his chair. She handed Silvia three ears of corn. "When you get a chance, can you please shuck these. We need to grill the corn until the kernels smell sweet and char the tomatoes until they're about to burst. Once we take them off the flame, they'll burst as they cool. We can capture the oozing goodness."

"You really romanticize cooking, don't you?" Silvia wasn't posing a question as much as she was framing Sherry's passion.

Sherry blushed, either from the increasing heat or Silvia's accurate assessment of her emotions. "I'll brush the tomatoes with oil. Let's bring the corn and tomatoes over to the grill tops and get them going. Be careful, the grill tops are flaming hot. The tomatoes will need to be turned often so they don't overdo."

Silvia stood vigil over the vegetables as they achieved perfect, on the verge of charred, grill marks. She and Sherry downed two bottles of water while they debated the presentation arrangement. They agreed to wait and see how the mushrooms looked when removed from the heat. They were hoping Orlando would rejoin the brainstorming and put in his two cents since he was the mastermind behind the mushroom's flavor profile. Their wish was granted when he emerged.

"My second wind has blown in. You'll be needing these." On cue, Orlando labored up to the table carrying a white oval bowl containing the portobellos swimming in marinade. "A brush of oil and these beauties hit the flame. Four to five minutes a side should do the trick. Give or take a few minutes."

Twelve minutes and three flips later, the mushrooms were grilled to perfection. The edges were charred, and the centers were moist and meaty. Orlando sliced them into half-inch-wide strips.

Silvia set down a layer of peppery arugula to nest at the bottom of the bowl before the quinoa was spooned in. The corn, tomatoes, mushrooms and black beans were each given their bowl space allowance to occupy. The mushrooms claimed the center spot because they were the stars. Sherry dabbed some errant juices from the rim of the bowl. The sauce was drizzled artistically over the ingredients and all that was left was to wait for the closing word from Jason.

"How does team Summer Sizzle's recipe stand up against our masterpiece? Anyone catch a glimpse of theirs?" Silvia asked.

"Sherry, I saw you talking to Carla earlier. She had distress written all over her face. I can fully sympathize if she succumbed to the heat," Orlando said. He patted his forehead with a dish towel. "Except no one from the other team offered me any help."

"The stress got to her for a second. She was fine after a good word. I can't get a proper look at their dish, but she said they're making a pizza or a salad or some combination of the two," Sherry said. Her lack of certainty wasn't an evasion of the facts; she made a friendly suggestion and had no idea whether Carla followed through.

"Time's up, folks," Jason said. "Team Trio and team Summer Sizzle, would you both please place your completed recipes on the table behind me and they will be brought to the judges. You can then enjoy some much-needed rest while the judges relish your cooking."

Silvia volunteered to carry the bowl over to the table. Sherry kept her sights on her teammate, noticing Silvia's shaking hands clutching the bowl as she took cautious steps. She returned and blew out a triumphant exhale. "Phew. Glad that's done."

Team Trio traded high fives all around.

"Cooks, may I have your aprons, please?" Stacy asked as she approached. "Great work today. Would you all mind attending recap confessionals as I call your name?" She checked the clipboard in her hand. "Sherry Oliveri. A reporter would like a word with you. Afterward, you're wanted in the confessional room, please."

"Thank you," Sherry said to her teammates. "Hmmm. A reporter? I thought the set was closed today."

"Maybe a good sign," Orlando said.

"Hope so," Sherry said.

"Follow me, Sherry," Stacy said.

The inn's air-conditioning was localized in rooms and the front lobby and everywhere else in the building was uncomfortably warm. Sherry's energy level was draining as the heat of the day was becoming oppressive. Stacy's breakneck pace wasn't helping her recover. When they reached a small room down the hall from the kitchen entrance, Stacy pointed inside the room.

"Sherry, I think you know Garrett Stein. He's an entertainment reporter and we're relying on him to cover the making of *Relish*. He'd like to ask you some questions. I'll be back in a few minutes to take you to the next interview."

Before Sherry could open her mouth in response, Stacy had stepped away. She turned her attention to Garrett, who stood when she entered the room.

"Nice to see you, Sherry. Please, have a seat." Garrett was dressed in shorts and a collared shirt. He had a computer tablet in his hand. He sat across from her and positioned his fingers over the keyboard to capture her responses.

"Gladly. The day started out cool and the humidity is now rearing its ugly head. Typical New England August day."

"It would be nice if they'd turn on the AC," Garrett said. "I'm writing articles about the various stages of the *Relish* production. I have a few questions for all the contestants."

"I hope my answers make sense, my brain's a bit fried," Sherry said with a laugh.

"I have no doubt you'll do fine. Ready?"

"Sure," Sherry said with a sigh.

"This televised cooking competition runs for three days of elimination challenges. Have you ever been in a cook-off of this variety?" Garrett asked.

"Never. I've cooked on television before but only for an hour. And it was more of a demonstration than a competition. I had already won the contest and the sponsor wanted some television exposure for publicity's sake. I really enjoyed it. No pressure whatsoever."

"In your opinion, is this cook-off pressure-packed, so far?"

"This is intense to say the least. I've been in three-hour single-day cook-offs and those are also exhausting. This is different. Extreme. I never know what I'm in for from one day to the next. The uncertainty of even being around the next day is disconcerting. Not knowing the theme, the ingredients, the venue—now that I'm saying it all out loud it's a wonder I haven't been more anxious about the process." Sherry laughed at her confession.

"Proves you're a veteran," Garrett said. "You give everything a lot of thought and consideration. One more question: since you mentioned all the uncertainties of the next day's theme, ingredients, and venue, how would you have prepared if you did know any or all of these factors?"

"In a cook-off it's unusual not to know the theme and venue beforehand. Very. My main criterion for entering a cook-off is the attraction to the theme."

"Begs the question, why did you enter this cook-off then?" Garrett asked.

"I didn't. They called me. That's not unusual for a television cooking competition. They know what they want out of the participants, and they seek you out."

"Interesting," Garrett said. "Almost as if they were creating the cook-off around the cooks instead of the other way around."

"I never looked at it that way," Sherry said. "You're right."

"Back to my question. If you knew the theme, venue and other variables, how would you have prepared?"

"Easy. When I do know the theme and so on, I research what's been a winner in that contest over the last years. That way I don't duplicate a recipe by mistake, and I can head in a fresh new direction the judges will hopefully appreciate. I also research trends in food, cooking, and kitchen products. All those elements are important to the twist in the recipe's concept. Always keeping recipes on trend is a good way to garner the judges' favor. I've also been practicing my signature recipe, Ranch Steak Bruschetta. Kind of like an athlete lifting light weights to warm up their muscles. That recipe exercises a lot of my cooking skills and flexes my culinary muscles."

"Good answer. Thank you, Sherry. I think we have enough content for today. You look a little worn out." Garrett set his tablet aside. "Would you mind if we have a chat off the record?"

Sherry huffed out a breath. "That sounds like what I have just enough energy for."

"Did you see *Juicy Bites* this morning?" Garrett fished in his back pocket and pulled out a neatly folded square of paper.

"I did."

"What do you think the full scope of the message refers to? *Food and suspects will be grilled at the Augustin Inn. Whoever's sitting on an explosive secret—someone at the cook-off has the match.*"

"Well, we grilled our recipes today. The author knew that much before the cooks did. I wasn't sure we'd be grilling because of the forecasted storms, and the author still knew," Sherry said.

"And the suspects getting grilled? What piece of the puzzle is that?"

"Has to refer to Rachel Yaro's murder investigation. It must be a continuation of yesterday's note." Sherry furrowed her brow. "I was grilled by Basil before the cook-off began. He had some questions about how Detective Bease is leading the investigation. He wanted to know if he was a suspect."

"Interesting." Garrett dipped his hand in his other back pocket and retrieved a second fold of paper.

"Is that your vault?" Sherry couldn't resist asking.

Garrett had no trouble interpreting Sherry's meaning. "I guess a pocket could be considered a vault. Guys use their pockets for all sorts of collections." When the napkin was unfolded, he spread it across his lap. *"How is a good mystery like a cook-off? Beat the clock, stick to the theme, nothing is as it seems."*

"Beating the clock in both situations is critical," Sherry said. "The theme of this cook-off is Labor Day in the broad sense. Each day, so far, has been about summer food, but with a mystery element involved. We don't know the ingredients, the venue, the cooking method or the specific daily theme until the cameras roll." She eyed Garrett with a challenge to respond.

"A good mystery certainly has a theme. In the case of a murder, the theme is the motive. The story behind the actions of the murderer. After the murder occurs, if the guilty party can keep the theme under wraps, he's done his job. From the outside looking in, solving a murder can be daunting. If you're on the inside, though, maybe what others overlooked is obvious."

"Maybe the notion *nothing is as it seems* is overstating the fact that the obvious theme is right before our very eyes, we just don't see it," Sherry said. She rubbed her temple.

"Do you think you're the target audience for these napkins? You have a reputation for solving murders involving cook-offs."

The thought had crossed Sherry's mind. "You tell me. Anyone here today may know something. People here worked with Rachel. Including you. Including me for a short time. The question is who would put in such an effort to promote solving the murder?"

"Someone who has more to lose while the investigation is continuing than when it's complete."

"Makes sense," Sherry said.

"Or someone who is guilty and is desperate to throw out diversions to buy time," Garrett said.

Sherry scowled. "You've been working in TV entertainment too long. That sounds like the script of a bad movie. We all know how those movies end."

Garrett's expression broke into a scowl, followed by a smile. "Don't discount the possibility."

"Maybe. I don't know of any suspects being grilled. Detective Bease isn't even here as far as I know. I'd think he'd be the one doing the suspect grilling. It's his job."

"Do you know who the suspects are?" Garrett asked.

Sherry took a long hard look at the man sitting across from her. "Are we playing a game here?"

"If we are, the ball is in your court. The cook-off clock is ticking. Solving the murder might be on the same timetable. The napkins do say 'beat the clock,' for both activities."

"I have nothing to add. Except, maybe someone knew you'd be asking questions off the record." Sherry motioned a tennis forehand. "Here. Now the ball's in your court."

"What about the explosive secret someone's holding on to that could be ignited by someone involved in the cook-off?" Garrett asked.

"Again, you tell me," Sherry said. She'd served up the million-dollar question, and it was up to Garrett to remain in the game or default. "If you put these ideas out in the universe, they might come to fruition. Do you have an explosive secret?"

"Maybe." He leaned toward Sherry. "Rachel wrote *Juicy Bites*, not me."

"You do see the hole in that theory, right?" Sherry asked. She tried hard to not let cynicism creep into her voice. She was failing. "Rachel's been gone since Wednesday. *Juicy Bites* lives on. Despite what you say, you're a good candidate for the position of author."

"Someone has picked up where she tragically left off. Someone with a different agenda."

"And you have proof Rachel was the first author?" Sherry asked.

Garrett's cheeks bloomed a rosy red. He remained quiet.

"If you want my opinion, I maintain the author might be you," Sherry said. "Digging up dirt is part of your job description. And uncovering who murdered a Feral Creations employee would be a nice feather in your cap. A good move on your part, unless you're outed."

"Do *you* have proof I'm the author?" Garrett asked.

"Besides the fact you are getting me to grill a suspect, namely you, just as *Juicy Bites* stated would happen? Okay. What about the obvious? You work with the Feral Creations crew. You have prior knowledge of every word that's been written."

"Why do you have a vendetta against me, Sherry? What have I done to you? Talk about making a fast judgment about someone. You don't even know me."

The hair on Sherry's forearms pricked up. "I'm team Kat. I'm worried you're not. I'm interested in finding out who writes *Juicy Bites* to see what that connection is to Rachel's death. I'm not convinced it was Rachel, as you suggest. You check a lot of boxes when it comes to who is in the know enough to put out production news before it happens. You could easily have written the napkins before and after her death."

"Me and many others," Garrett said.

"When we were introduced in Kat's office you were reading a book, the title of which showed up today in *Juicy Bites*."

"I'm reading *Script for Murder*. No crime in that, pun intended."

"*Script, murder*, both words were in *Juicy Bites*."

"Ask Kat, she'll vouch for me," Garrett said.

"Kat isn't even willing to vouch for herself. I think someone is harassing her and I'm afraid it's you. She told me as much."

"Kat said I was bothering her?" Garrett's expression dropped to a pout.

"The same day I met you in her office she began to confide in me about an office harassment situation that was going on. I saw her eyes shift in your direction. The story was incomplete, so I'm only left to put the pieces together myself. And I want to if she feels threatened."

Garrett put his hands up to his face and rubbed the stubble on his square jawline. "What she said is true. But, it isn't her story. Kat's protecting Mick. He's been told to keep a secret or face terrible consequences. Rachel told Kat before she was murdered. Kat thinks the circumstances may be destroying Mick. That's all Kat told me."

"Oh, Kat. I'm beginning to understand. She's the one with the match to ignite the explosion?"

"You must believe me. I don't write *Juicy Bites* now and I never have. I don't know who killed Rachel. I would never hurt Kat. But I do know Kat's in danger if she knows what Mick knows. We need to find the murderer before she's punished, too."

Sherry's mouth dropped open. "Was Rachel punished for the same secret?"

"Sherry? Time for your debriefing interview," Stacy said as she tapped on the door.

"Thanks for the chat," Garrett said. "We'll be in touch."

Chapter 16

Sherry employed every trick she knew to compartmentalize her chat with Garrett as she walked down the hallway. The effort was worth it. At the debriefing interview, She spent twenty minutes recounting various stages of her team's participation in the cook-off without interference from wild thoughts of murder and intrigue. All went well until Stacy, who was again positioned behind the camera operator, clipboard in hand, posed a question that shifted the mood.

"Sherry, can you explain why you gave a member of the opposing team a solid, and probably game-changing, tip during the height of the recipe brainstorming? Wouldn't that compromise your team's chances?"

Sherry was suddenly aware of the uncomfortable chair she was seated in. She shifted her weight to find a more pleasing position. She crossed and uncrossed her legs. Her mind raced with questions. Was there a right answer? Had she again come close to breaking a rule only to face a penalty, taking her teammates down with her? How close were the microphones to the conversation with Carla? At the time, she wasn't tuned into being recorded, only helping a fellow cook in need. She pictured the camera closing in on the two cooks while ideas were exchanged. What was the saying—no good deed goes unpunished?

Stacy rolled her index finger, prompting Sherry to respond.

"Carla was in some distress."

"Yesterday you helped another cook, Jada, who burned her finger," Stacy said. "What if those actions came back to penalize your team?"

"I have no apologies. I have a ten-year mental archive of cook-off experience to reach into, so I did, to help an opponent. I didn't see any harm in giving her a leg up when she was stuck in the mud. This is supposed to be a fun competition and I'm not having fun if someone is miserable and I can help."

"Thanks, Sherry. That's all for now," Stacy said. She tapped the camera operator on the shoulder and the red light dimmed.

"Were my responses okay?" Sherry asked. "I meant what I said."

"All good," Stacy said. Her muted tone did little to ease Sherry's concern.

After the interview, Sherry was relegated to the stark contestant lounge, where she snacked on bite-size sandwiches and fruit. Her mood lifted when, one by one, five contestants joined her after they'd been debriefed. The next step was unclear until Basil made an appearance. He squared up in front of the cooks, who rose to greet him.

"Hello again, everyone. It's been a wonderful morning of grilling magic. Team Trio presented the judges with a Southwestern-influenced portobella bowl. The use of one of the biggest trends in the food world right now, bowls, was brilliant. Team Summer Sizzle matched the effort with a creative portobella pizza salad—a combination of two of my personal favorites. The team that prevailed exhibited elevated technique, presentation and flavor. Not to mention teamwork on many levels." Basil instigated a round of applause.

The cooks exchanged smiles and looks of encouragement.

"Everyone did a wonderful job today despite the heat. Orlando, how are you feeling?" Basil asked.

Orlando was reclined on a two-seat couch with his head resting on a pillow. "Better, thank you. My team was amazing. I hope I didn't squash their chances of moving on."

"On the contrary, Team Trio will indeed be moving on to the final round of *Relish*. Congratulations."

Sherry and Silvia squealed with delight and gave each other a hug before enveloping Orlando. Team Summer Sizzle congratulated Trio.

"I wish we could meet the judges," Sherry said. Her suggestion was shrugged off by Basil.

"Part of the game," Basil said. "Their anonymity. Team Summer Sizzle, you did a wonderful job today. We're sorry to see you go."

The cooks were given another round of applause.

"Sherry, Silvia and Orlando. We will see you tomorrow at Bluefish Run Beach. The episode will air on Labor Day, so dress appropriately. You've all done a wonderful job as a team and tomorrow it's time to prove yourself solo. Check your texts for the start time. It's a logistically tricky venue and will take a while to set up, so the start time may be later than today. I, for one, can't wait to crown the *Relish* winner. Have a good evening."

The bulk of the afternoon was nearly over by the time Sherry returned home. Despite being physically tired, she was restless and decided to see if Kat would hit some tennis balls with her to loosen the tight muscles in her legs. She prepared for Kat to claim she couldn't play on such short notice and was elated when the invite was happily accepted. Kat said the mayor cleared the final hour of the day's schedule to finish his newsletter article and she was free to leave the office early. Sherry celebrated a double win with her version of Orlando's fist pump.

• • •

Sherry was rejuvenated after an hour of exercise. "Getting outside and running around was what the doctor ordered. I needed to move my legs after standing pretty much in one place for the morning." She slid her racket into her tennis bag and took a seat on the players' bench. "I'm not sure I'll be able to get back up, though."

"It's hot today. August is holding on with a vengeance," Kat said. She opened her water bottle and chugged her refreshment.

"I owe you a can of tennis balls," Sherry said. "I must be getting stronger if I wacked that ball over the fence, never to be seen again."

"You don't owe me. Would you like these? They've seen better days," Kat said. She offered Sherry the can containing the remaining two balls. "Maybe for Chutney?"

"Sure. We're working on fetch. He's the only dog in the world who has no idea what all the fuss is about chasing a ball and bringing it back to the thrower."

Kat handed the can over. Sherry tucked it away in her bag along with her racket. Kat was slow and deliberate while packing up her equipment. She hadn't initiated much conversation throughout the practice, other than debating line calls.

"You're very quiet today," Sherry said as she watched Kat zip her bag. "Anything on your mind?"

"There is. I haven't had the courage to ask until now. I'm desperate. The cook-off filming is over tomorrow. I think any chance to find Rachel's killer will disappear with the production team." She held her gaze on Sherry. "Leaving me front and center on the suspect list."

Sherry studied her friend's frown. "Before you go on, why haven't you told Detective Bease what you know?"

Kat's face blanched. She lifted a shaky hand and fumbled the scrunchie out of her ponytail. "So many reasons. I can't go into it." She waved her hand as if brushing away Sherry's question. "Most of all, I want your help. I trust you."

Sherry's concern for Kat was growing with each accelerated breath. "I'd like to help you, but you're making the process so difficult. The detective needs some facts to work with and so would I, if I were to help."

"There something weighing on my mind. I haven't confided in anyone except Garrett because he's been around Rachel and has sensed some issues,"

Kat said. "Mayor Drew is so excited about the filming going on in Augustin I didn't want to shake him from his dream. And you're in the cook-off of a lifetime. I didn't want to shut down the project or cause any undo harm to anyone if I was wrong."

"All this concern is why you disappeared the morning Rachel was killed?"

"Part of the reason."

"Now we're getting someplace," Sherry said. Her tone was laced with all the optimism she could drum up. "Go on."

Kat closed her eyes.

Sherry wasn't going to let the moment go by. "Okay, I'll start. I was interviewed by Garrett today for the cook-off. Afterward we had an off-the-record chat. Your name came up. He said you mentioned workplace harassment the other day and you weren't speaking from personal experience. You were asking for Mick."

"True," Kat said. "I honestly don't know much about why Mick was being threatened beyond that he knows something that someone would go to extremes to keep from leaking."

"How is he being threatened exactly?" Sherry asked.

"Threats to his livelihood. He'd lose everything if he didn't comply. Rachel told me as much."

"Did she tell you the secret he's sitting on?"

"No."

"Why did Rachel tell you about Mick if she wasn't going to share the secret he was keeping? On the other hand, you two didn't seem to be on the best of terms," Sherry said.

Kat sighed. "We aren't. Weren't. Maybe that was the reason she didn't tell me everything. Just a teaser. Like *Juicy Bites*. She was good at teasers. She got lots of people hooked on *Juicy Bites*. Or maybe she didn't know the secret, only that Mick was being put on the spot."

"Do you think Rachel wrote *Juicy Bites*? Garrett does."

"I do," Kat said.

"What makes you think she did?"

"She surprised me Tuesday night with a text that asked me if I would deliver the napkins to Toasts of the Town at the garage early Wednesday morning. We had built up a bit of a rekindled friendship by then. She made some friendly gestures toward me and I was receptive. In her text she explained she wrote the daily blurbs and they had attracted increasing interest in the production."

"*Juicy Bites,*" Sherry said.

"That's right. She thought her idea to go rogue with a publicity stunt was working well."

"It kind of was," Sherry said.

"She tried to recruit me to deliver the napkins because she had an appointment Wednesday morning and couldn't make it to the garage until after six thirty. Her days started extremely early. By the time she was available, the chances of being caught were high. The sun would almost be up, and Pep would be on his way to pick up his truck. She was insistent she didn't want the news drips to be interrupted."

"But you must not have accepted her request because she was murdered there," Sherry said.

"That's right. I didn't. I love my job too much to put it in jeopardy by following her silly plan. She took a risk by going later and it didn't pay off."

"That could have been you who was murdered," Sherry said.

"Don't think that notion didn't haunt me to such a degree I left town for the day. Garrett texted me very early that morning with the news and I got in the car and drove until I finally caught my breath," Kat said. "I had her murder, the knowledge Rachel was the *Juicy Bites* author, and the mystery of what Mick was being harassed for to contend with."

"Rachel was murdered Wednesday morning," Sherry said as she sorted her thoughts. "And she got *Juicy Bites* out before she was gone."

"If you look closely at last Wednesday's *Juicy Bites* you sense the tension. It read, 'it would be a crime if someone got hurt.'"

"Do you think she was predicting her own demise?" Sherry asked.

"At the very least she was admitting there was trouble," Kat said.

"Did she give you any sense she was a target when she texted you?"

"Not at all."

"Garrett passed on the information about her murder to you?" Sherry asked.

Kat turned to face Sherry. "Yes. He and I are getting on well."

"I have my reservations about Garrett. Maybe I'm being overprotective, but he might be playing both sides of the fence. I saw the way Rachel looked at him. It would serve him well to befriend you and Rachel."

"Rachel threw herself at Garrett, but he chose me," Kat said.

"Oh, I'm an idiot," Sherry said. "I'm so focused on believing Garrett writes *Juicy Bites* it never occurred to me you've followed your mother's dating referral."

"Please don't give my mother the credit for Garrett and me spending quality time together. We were together before she had any input."

Sherry held up her hand. "I promise. It's not the worst thing in the world if your mom feels good about helping you out."

Kat shrugged.

"Was it awkward between you and Rachel if she was interested in Garrett?"

"Sure. But I had to get over those feelings. I vowed I would never let personal issues get in the way of my work with Feral Creations. Easier said than done. Plus, I've known her longer than Garrett by a long stretch. She surprised me when she told me she bought me something in hopes of rekindling an old friendship. I was skeptical. I'd believe it if I ever saw it, which I didn't."

"The gift," Sherry said. "I almost forgot the gift." She reached in her tennis bag and retrieved the gift bag Basil had placed in her hand as she left the Augustin Inn earlier. She passed the gift bag to Kat.

"Oh, Rachel. Why'd you have to go and get yourself killed?" Kat moaned. After opening the gift and showing it to Sherry, she zipped it into her tennis bag.

"This whole time I'd have bet the house Garrett was the *Juicy Bites* author," Sherry said.

"No doubt about it," Kat said. "Rachel got the idea to promote the project by supplying the town with slow drips of news. If the plan went as she hoped, Basil would be impressed with her initiative and reward her with more responsibility. With more responsibility would come higher pay. She was having some bumps in the road on her path to success and she knew she had to push the envelope to get ahead."

"I'm not sure going around the boss rather than through him is the best way," Sherry said.

"She told me the plan was nearly dead in the water before the first *Juicy Bites* delivery. She left a napkin in the Feral Creations limo on the first day of printing. She was still having bouts of forgetfulness from her auto accident concussion. She had to run out of a meeting in the mayor's office and recover it because they hadn't visited Pep's truck for breakfast yet and she'd have to concoct a story about where the napkin came from. She passed it to me as she ran back to the meeting. That's how I figured out what she was up to. Garrett saw the exchange and put two and two together. He's such a good journalist." Kat smiled. "I still have the day-one napkin."

"I wonder if anyone else on her team made the same deduction if he saw the napkin in the limo," Sherry wondered aloud. "The concept was her idea of job security, I suppose."

"As it turned out, she didn't have long enough to get a reading on how the public or Feral Creations was receiving her idea."

"I'd imagine she had access to some powerful printers to get the job done," Sherry said.

"She had access to full printing capabilities in one of the trucks. That was one of the reasons she rallied hard for the clapboard prep assignment each morning. She printed the napkins last thing at night and delivered the stack the next morning. Basil gave her the key to the trucks for her clapboard assignment and that made the process of printing the napkins a slam dunk."

"I might owe Garrett an apology. I prejudged him in your defense. At least I got some facts out of him, and you, finally."

"Sherry, I need your help. There's a connection between *Juicy Bites* and Rachel's murder. You must agree. I know you do."

"There's a piece of the puzzle missing," Sherry said. "A crucial one. I agree with that."

"I have an obligation to at least try to find Rachel's murderer. She wasn't a bad person. We had some good college times."

"And Garrett? Can't he help you?" Sherry asked. "Do you think he took over writing *Juicy Bites*?"

"It's not out of the realm of possibility. If he is writing the blurbs, he's playing a dangerous game."

"One where he might lose favor with Feral Creations. And one that could get him killed if he dives too deep into ferreting out the murderer," Sherry said.

"I've only known Garrett since the spring. How can I ask him whether he'd be willing to take part in clearing the name of his new girlfriend?"

"Maybe that gives him more of an incentive. He's very keen on keeping you out of harm's way."

"He said that?" Kat asked with a dreamy lilt to her tone. "He's so sweet."

"Yes, he did, and I can relate. When I discuss this with Don, I'm going to get the same reaction," Sherry said.

"That's a good sign." Kat paused while she squared up to Sherry. "I have a plan and it involves both of us. Before you say anything, hear me out."

Sherry pinched her lips shut tight.

"We go over to the Augustin Garage very early tomorrow morning and stake out the trucks to see who shows up to deliver the stack of napkins."

Sherry sighed. "I was afraid it would come down to this. There's only one problem. Tomorrow is the last day of the cook-off. I'm lucky enough to be in the final round and I don't want to sacrifice my chances by going over to the Augustin Garage beforehand."

"You're so right. We can't mess around with the cook-off proceedings. Would you go Thursday morning?" Kat pleaded. "You're the only one I trust to partner up with me."

"I would, but if you think it's someone connected to the production, won't they all be gone? Shoot's over tomorrow."

"The full production crew, all twenty-three members in total, will be in town until Friday. They don't wrap filming, pick up stakes and roll out in an instant. There's lots of loose ends to tie up before they call it quits."

Sherry closed her eyes and fought the sensible voices in her head. "Okay. Let's do it." Sherry paused. "Only on one condition. If no one shows up with the napkin delivery, you talk to Detective Bease and tell him everything you know."

"You have a deal," Kat said. She hoisted her tennis bag over her shoulder.

"Kat, to quote *Juicy Bites*: *How is a mystery like a cook-off? Beat the clock, stick to the theme, nothing is as it seems.* Time may be running out before someone else gets hurt. The theme seems to be what's the secret that has deadly consequences. What seems to be a cook-off is getting mighty complicated."

"Good luck tomorrow. Hope the weather holds." Kat raised her sights skyward.

A foursome of elderly gentlemen sauntered toward the players' bench. "Hey, are you gals going to get back on the courts or are you going to discuss the weather all day?"

"The court's all yours, Mr. Washburn. Have a good game."

"Thanks. Maybe you two would hit with my grandson one day. Eli will be a star, mark my words. My son's not bad either." Mr. Washburn pointed out the father-son duo playing on the end court.

"Love to," Kat said. "We see them here every day. I love the dedication."

Chapter 17

By the time Sherry warmed up leftovers from the previous night's chicken alfredo, Don was one beer deep into the television news. He kept to a two-beer limit on work nights. He was usually so worn out from the day's activities that the bubbly brew was more of a sleep inducer than a supercharger. A yawn was the first indication he might slip into a pre-dinner siesta. Sherry popped the cork on a bottle of chardonnay with the intention of having only one glass to celebrate her passage into the cook-off finals.

Don carried his beer to the kitchen table. He sat down and shared a smile. Sherry brought two plates to the table. Three sips of her wine gave her the courage to address the elephant in the room only she was aware existed.

"Don, Kat Coleman would like me to help find Rachel Yaro's killer. She's on Detective Bease's radar and she was also Rachel's friend. Oh, and her new boyfriend, and her mother, would also like me to prove Kat had nothing to do with Rachel's murder." Sherry braced in preparation for Don's response.

"You're my fiancée. You're the love of my life. You're also more than that, someone who can't be labeled. You don't need my permission to move ahead in whatever interesting adventure you choose to partake in. You have my blessing, my support, and my concern for your safety. Call me a fool for asking but, what's the plan of action?"

"Kat wants to stake out the Augustin Garage Thursday morning with the idea of catching the *Juicy Bites* napkin author in the act of delivering the goods to Pep's truck."

"And the napkin author has to do with the murder how?" Don asked. He took a swig of his beer and studied Sherry's face. "I can see your wheels spinning."

"I'm not sure. That's why I'm not willing to go tomorrow, as Kat would have liked. I need to concentrate on my last cook-off day. Her plan may be a bust, but she promised to talk to Ray if it is. That makes the time spent worth it."

"You're the world's best multitasker, but even you shouldn't take on much else during a big cook-off." He spun some noodles around his fork before steering them into his mouth.

"I agree. That's what I told her when she wanted to go tomorrow morning," Sherry said. She matched Don's fork twirl and added a chunk of chicken to the prongs. "I have a suspicion the author of *Juicy Bites* knows more about the murder than the two- to three-sentence tidbits of information offered each day. The author might be trying to lure in Rachel's killer by tossing out factoids. An informed napkin reader might be tempted to come forward and offer up valuable info. The overriding factor in the author's identity is how much the person knows about the cook-off details that shouldn't be public."

"There's a connection," Don said.

"I agree, but I need concrete evidence."

"Yum, this is so creamy. One of my favorites," Don said. "Did you use goat cheese?"

"I sure did. And some Romano for the salty bite. The chopped parsley adds the freshness that perks up the chicken. Pretty simple and delicious."

"Who do you think you'll catch at the garage? I know you. You have some suspects in mind already. You never set out on a wild-goose chase without some narrowing of the suspect field."

"Basil Sturges is on my list," Sherry said. "Going against popular sentiment, Kat's mostly, Garrett Stein is, too. He isn't very high up, but something tells me he should be under consideration in some regard."

"You don't think Kat may be behind *Juicy Bites*? I mean, she is invested in a successful cook-off," Don asked. "What about the new team member, Stacy? She could have come on the scene and thought no one would ever consider her. Meanwhile, she could get the credit for finding Rachel's murderer if the *Juicy Bites* puzzles were solved."

"Kat and Garrett are adamant Rachel wrote the napkins before her death. I had every reason to believe one of those two took up the project where Rachel left off. The tone of the blurbs changed from the promotion of Augustin's role in the cook-off to finding Rachel's killer. The one consistency is the prior knowledge of the details of the next day's cook-off. How would either of those two have access to that level of detail? It's not impossible but they aren't as privy to information as others, like Stacy, Basil, or Mick, for example. The Feral Creations team would have full information access. That's why we need to find the author of *Juicy Bites*. Whoever that person is wants the killer found and is putting loads of effort into the cause."

"Go with your gut. But first things first. You have one more day of the *Relish* cook-off. Are you preparing in any way?" Don asked. He scooped a bite of creamy chicken into his mouth. "This is so good. You cooked all day, won the second round and still had the wherewithal to feed me a winner-winner chicken dinner."

"It was leftovers, mind you. The fact you're satisfied is all the prep I need for tomorrow." She used her fork to point to Don's plate of cheesy goodness. "If I do what I do best, and my confidence stays high, I have a fighting chance." Sherry slurped up a spaghetti noodle to punctuate her determination.

"Are you having a good experience at the cook-off?" Don asked.

"The overall cook-off vibe is a mystery to me. One minute we're cooking to stay on the show and the next minute I feel as if my character is being tested when a mishap involving another cook is thrown into the mix. The incidents have happened each day and I'm asked about them in the recap interview afterward, as if it were important to get my answer correct." Sherry threw up her hands. "Maybe I'm reading too much into it."

"If they have you guessing then they're doing something right. Any idea what tomorrow's theme is?" Don asked. He took a sip of his beer and chased it with a bite of pasta.

"Tomorrow we're cooking at Bluefish Run Beach. I don't know if it's grilling again, but I'd bet it is. This is the Labor Day episode. Today was a twist on a Labor Day menu challenge."

"That's a wonderful theme," Don said. "Labor Day menus are getting stale."

"My goal is to rev them up," Sherry said with conviction.

"If anyone can, you can," Don said.

"The venue, Bluefish Run Beach, is an interesting choice. It's very underdeveloped, on the wild side. Tourists hardly ever go there because there's no parking. The effort to keep the beach pristine is working. You hike in through a gorgeous woodland, then a protected meadow, then tall dunes. It's really a treasure, but it's not for everyone. It's too much effort to get to for a lot of beachgoers. I can't imagine we'll have much in the way of equipment and foodstuffs. Let me rephrase that. I have no clue what to expect."

"What time do you have to be there?" Don asked. He twirled a noodle on his fork and popped it in his mouth.

"I got a text saying the start time is two o'clock. I have the morning off. Not sure I like that. Too much time to get nervous. I need to find some way to pass the time in the morning."

"I have a few ideas." His sly smile warmed Sherry's cheeks. "Unfortunately, I'm on duty early tomorrow. After my commuter runs, I'm ferrying some of Feral Creations' supplies to their shoot site. Thanks to you, now I know the location, Bluefin Run Beach. I was kept in the dark so word didn't get out."

"I can strike you off the *Juicy Bites* author list. That person is never in the dark," Sherry said with a smile.

"All I was told was we were taking the boat to a nearby beachhead. That beach is a difficult location to access by truck. Makes sense. That's how I got the assignment. What will you do to pass the time in the morning?"

"I'll think of something," Sherry said. "I always do."

"How about relaxing? Half the population does that when they have bonus free time."

"That concept is too foreign. I'm going with what I know and that's staying busy. What's the saying about old dogs and new tricks?" Sherry broke into a chardonnay-fueled chuckle. She peeked at Chutney curled up next to a ragged tennis ball. "I'm not talking about you, boy. But, on second thought, the term does apply."

• • •

Wednesday morning, Sherry missed Don's departure altogether. He must have left the house unusually early, because she was awakened at dawn by her neighbor's garbage collector and there was no sign of him sleeping next to her. She had a surprisingly restful night's sleep and was a bundle of energy from the get-go. She chose her dog to help release some pent-up adrenaline. Chutney rose to the occasion and accepted the invitation to learn a new skill.

Sherry gathered Chutney's nap accessory, the well-worn tennis ball, and instructed him on what was required. She laid out the two-step process: Keep his eye on the ball when she throws it and bring it back to her. Easy. He'd seen many dogs succeed at the simple task. After twenty attempts on her front lawn, Chutney mastered locating the tossed ball. Each time Sherry threw the ball, he chased it down, only to leave the ball where it lay.

"Honey, can I give you a tip? You know I had a dog way back when, so I do know a few training tricks." Eileen's words were strained as she crossed the road in a moderate jog. She picked the ball up from its grassy nest. She danced around while waving the ball in front of Chutney's snout until he was caught up in her enthusiasm.

"That's progress," Sherry said.

"Get him on board with the game." Eileen tossed the ball a short distance. "Not too far at first, otherwise he won't bother. Get involved." She raced the terrier to the ball and made a huge deal about him picking it up in his mouth. When he showed it to her, he was rewarded with what Sherry guessed was a spare cat treat. The fact Chutney sat at Eileen's side until she repeated the performance was evidence he *was* on board with the game.

"Amazing," Sherry said. "Thanks. You're the best." Sherry raised her arms overhead and gave Eileen a bow. "Kudos to the Chutney whisperer."

"It's nothing. Don't you have to be at the cook-off this morning?" Eileen asked. "Where is it today?"

"Bluefin Run Beach. Not until two."

"What are you going to do until then, besides grow anxious?" Eileen asked.

"Good question. I offered to help in any way at the Ruggery. Amber said I wasn't needed. I thought she'd like a break from all the solo time she's put in this week, but she said no thanks. She has matters well in hand. I would have played tennis, but my wrist is sore from cooking. I'm out of cook-off shape."

"Is Erno coming back soon? He and Ruth must be having a great vacation."

"He's coming home tomorrow."

"Just in time to hear the results of the cook-off."

"By the way, have you spoken to Hazel since I saw you two yesterday morning?" Sherry asked.

"I spoke to her this morning. At breakfast. At Toasts of the Town. We enjoyed Pep's latest superstar toast, Southern Not-Fried Tenders on Waffle Toast with Cajun Maple Butter."

"Wow," Sherry exclaimed. "How did I miss the grand reveal of that masterpiece?"

"I needed three *Juicy Bites* napkins to de-stick the yummy sauce from my lips."

"Glad you liked it. He and Angel are really expanding their repertoire," Sherry said with a grin.

"And I'm happy as a clam to try every last item they offer," Eileen said.

"I'm curious whether Hazel has any new ideas about . . ." Sherry paused while she formulated her wording. "Any new ideas about what Kat might know concerning her friend Rachel's murder. I wish I had more information than that."

"You do love your murder investigations, don't you," Eileen said. "I don't know how much Hazel and Kat have talked recently. Hazel was all out of sorts because Kat told her she was at town hall too often."

"I think Kat is in control of her life. Hazel means well but she should trust Kat. She has a good amount of common sense." After Sherry stated her case for her friend's independence, she realized some of the words rang hollow. The real reason she wanted Hazel to take a step back from her daughter's activities was Kat may be in a heap of hot water. Sherry didn't want Hazel in too deep with a killer on the loose who may have a vendetta against Kat.

"Try telling that to Hazel. She has a renewed sense of mama bear instincts suddenly and it's worrying me. I'm afraid Hazel's going off on her own and will start digging deep to clear Kat's name. We're hoping you'd have some idea who killed Rachel by now. I suppose the cook-off is your priority, as it should be." Her tone wasn't convincing. "*Juicy Bites* isn't helping ease my worries. I'm worried for you too after reading today's news."

Eileen pulled a napkin from the pocket of her velour sweatpants.

Chapter 18

Juicy Bites

Labor Day! Forage for the win. The key is:
Beware of deadly impostors—plants and people.

"Now that's a head scratcher," Eileen said. "Any idea what the words mean?"

"Well, this afternoon's cook-off is airing on Labor Day. I knew that. I'm not sure about the foraging or deadly impostors. The napkins say that's the key. Every word seems to have meaning. If the napkins are a continuation of yesterday, it's alluding somehow to the murder of Rachel Yaro. Whoever wrote this has an investment in solving the case. But what is that investment?"

"That's what Hazel said at breakfast," Eileen said.

"Really?" Sherry asked. "Quite an astute observation of hers. And it's interesting because she has something invested in finding the murderer. Her daughter would be absolved of suspicion."

"Are you suggesting Hazel may be the *Juicy Bites* author? She is an avid napkin user, but cloth napkins are her first choice. I suppose it's quite costly to print up new cloth napkins daily. I just don't see her having a stockpile of paper napkins in her closet. That's not her style."

"She can't be ruled out," Sherry said. "No one can be ruled out so far, except Rachel."

"Where would Hazel be getting the inside information about the cook-off?" Eileen asked. Before Sherry could open her mouth to reply, Eileen continued. "Don't bother. I know. Garrett Stein. At town hall."

"You're right. You said it yourself. Kat told her mother she was at town hall too much. Eileen, do you have any evidence Hazel might be behind *Juicy Bites*?"

"I don't, except that she's worried for Kat's sake and catching the young lady's murderer would ease her mind. But I do know how busy you are," Eileen said. "Where there's a will, there's a way, I always say."

"Sure," Sherry said.

"As much as I'm rooting for Hazel or you to find the murderer without getting hurt, I'd be surprised if she had the initiative to get down to the food truck every morning at the crack of dawn. You should see how long she spends grooming her hairdo to make an appearance at the grocery store. She'd have to get up at four a.m. to make herself presentable on the security camera footage."

"I tend to agree," Sherry said. "If the author knows so much about the cook-off filming, it makes sense the person works for Feral Creations. But maybe not. Remember the napkin that read *Who cooked up a murder? Feral Creations wouldn't write this script. Two-faced stories need two endings.* The suggestion is there's a story that's been told and there will be a new ending. That's a brain teaser if there ever was one."

"My dear, departed husband used to talk in riddles," Eileen said. "Drove me crazy, may he rest in peace. If I had my druthers everyone would get to the point and move on. When he made me guess the meaning of his words, I knew he was camouflaging the fact he'd done something wrong and couldn't break it to me. He didn't realize I always knew *he* was the answer to his riddles."

"Interesting," Sherry said. "The author could be the answer to the riddle. Thank you, Eileen. You've been extremely helpful."

"I have?" Eileen asked. "You mean with Chutney or with the murder investigation?"

"Both."

"I've always wanted to help solve a murder. I'm so excited you said I was useful. Yay, me." Eileen headed back home with a lift in her step.

Sherry collected the tennis ball Chutney had discarded. "I need to speak to Ray while all these scenarios are rattling round in my head." She checked her phone. There was plenty of time to meet up with the detective before heading to the beach. She placed a call to Ray.

Rather than meet in town as she'd have liked, Ray proposed an alternate location. He couldn't pull away from desk duty before Sherry had to head to Bluefish Run Beach. She was more than willing to meet with him at the Augustin police station, on the grounds he give her a tour of the facility. Having passed by the precinct on her way to the Ruggery countless times, she was curious about the interior. She had a mental image of small-town police stations that lay somewhere between the menacing urban lockups portrayed in movies and the modest layout of a television sitcom sheriff's office she watched. When she expressed her desire for a tour Ray didn't understand her curiosity, explaining most people try their hardest not to visit the precinct in their lifetimes, but he relented. He commented that Sherry's fascinations were often on the unconventional side, which she agreed was true.

• • •

The Augustin police station had undergone a facelift over the past year. A third floor was added, the cell tower was shored up, and the entrance was modernized with all manner of security features. The stately façade didn't jibe with her preconceived notion of a gritty police barracks but was impressive nonetheless. When Sherry walked inside the visitor lobby, she immediately grew self-conscious about not hiding her hands behind her back. Cameras were everywhere and she didn't want to be recorded concealing something she wasn't concealing. She raised her palms as she approached the receptionist who was behind a window paneled with extra-thick glass.

"You can put your hands down. I'm not going to search you," the woman said. The name tag on her uniform read *Officer Hastings*. The officer smiled and asked what she could do for Sherry.

"I'm here to see Detective Ray Bease."

Officer Hastings scoured her clipboard. "Sherry Oliveri. It's an honor to meet you. I follow you in every cook-off. Thank you so much for representing Augustin. And may I add, you are a damn good amateur sleuth."

"Thank you. I wasn't expecting that. I don't know what to say except another thank you." Sherry watched her name being added to the visitors' log.

"I'll ring Detective Bease. He should be right out."

Officer Hastings turned away from the window and picked up the intercom receiver.

Sherry couldn't hear what was said until the officer returned her attention to Sherry.

"He's on his way. Say, are you involved in the cook-off being filmed here in town? I was assigned to patrol the library grounds on Monday. I didn't get to watch the actual cooking, but I felt the excitement. Best assignment of the week."

"I'm in it, yes. I'm cooking at Bluefish Run Beach later today. It's the last day."

"I wonder if I can get down there when my shift is up. I hope to see you there."

The door opened and Ray appeared. The metal door was weighty enough to knock him off-kilter as he held it open with his shoulder. "Good morning, Sherry. Thanks for coming down. Come on in. Watch the door, it's taken out more than one criminal."

Ray let it close slightly before Sherry wrestled it wider. She managed to slip through the sliver of an opening. With a bang of metal on metal, the door slammed shut behind her.

"No one's escaping from here," Sherry said.

"More concerning is someone getting in uninvited," Ray countered.

Sherry browsed the area once she was inside the fortress door. Grays and browns dominated the color palette of the walls and floors. The desks were industrial chic—too shiny and the grain too perfectly patterned to be natural material. The space exuded testosterone despite the fact there were at least three uniformed female officers attending to paperwork. They peered at Sherry when she entered the room. Sherry sent them a subdued wave.

"Over there are holding cells," Ray said as he pointed to a corridor. "That's where the action is. Detention, interview, booking all take place in that wing. It's off-limits to visitors." He pointed to the opposite end of the room. "That way are lockers, roll call room, a kennel for Trooper, dispatch, and records. Upstairs is the chief's office, file storage, evidence storage, another interview room, and a few secrets I can't divulge. That's it. I have an office up there when I'm here, but we'll take a seat down here."

Sherry followed Ray to a desk. She was offered a rolling chair, which she gladly accepted. She glanced at the neighboring desk and recognized the seated officer when he raised his head. The Belgium Malinois curled up at his feet pricked up his ears. His canine vest was printed in a large font with K-9 UNIT.

"Troy and Trooper," she said. "I can't wait to tell Amber I saw you today." Immediately after her greeting she regretted sounding so enthusiastic. Amber's boyfriend wasn't an anomaly who was barely ever sighted in his place of work, as she made it sound. He was a police officer filling out paperwork. Par for the course. "I mean, it's nice to see you. Trooper, you are as amazing as ever."

"Sherry, everyone here is rooting for you to win the cook-off. As security for the filming, we know some of what goes on, but not much. I'm assuming you're still in it, right?" Troy asked.

"I feel ridiculous telling a police officer I can't tell you due to a nondisclosure agreement, but I'll just say you're on the right track."

"I knew. Amber told me last night," Troy said.

Sherry chuckled. "Hah! Augustin is a hard place to keep a secret. I work with Amber, she dates a town police officer, Augustin police provide security for the cook-off. We're all in it together."

"Officer Sedgeman and Detective Bease, are you going to introduce us to the infamous Sherry Oliveri or do we have to arrest her for breaking into the precinct?" The three female officers whispered among themselves as they waited for a reply.

Sherry's mouth dropped open.

"My mistake," Ray said. "Everyone, this is Sherry Oliveri. I'm lucky enough to call her my friend. Let's all wish her the best of luck in her competition later today. That is, if we can clear her of all charges."

After the wishes for cook-off success were complete everyone settled back into their tasks.

"I feel like this is my lucky day," Sherry said.

"Every day is your lucky day," Ray said. "What is it you want to speak to me about?"

Chapter 19

"Would you be able to get your hands on an auto accident report that involved a fatality?" Sherry asked. "The accident happened in Hillsboro County within the last twelve months. Let me refine that search. It happened in the winter. Conditions were icy."

Ray's dramatic sigh brought a smile to Troy's face. "Here we go," Troy said.

"Have I said something wrong?" Sherry asked.

"Thank you, Officer Sedgeman. I've got this." Ray returned his attention to Sherry. "I'm a homicide detective. If I can't get access to fatality reports, then I'm handcuffed."

"Forget I asked that silly question," Sherry said. "Let me start over. There was a car accident with a driver fatality months ago, somewhere in Hillsboro County. In the car were Basil Sturges, Rachel Yaro, Mick Snider and another person who was killed."

"I got you covered, Sherry. The accident was the first motor vehicle fatality of the new year, thanks to the administration's tireless efforts to keep the roads safe. It's etched in my mind. I was first on the scene," Troy said from his neighboring desk. "It was last January. Icy road conditions. The driver, Kyle Lemke, was ejected and died instantly. When I arrived the others were standing by the car trying to help Mr. Snider onto the grass in case the car exploded. He was badly hurt and in no shape to help himself. The woman had a head injury. I was told she was knocked out briefly but was sitting outside the car conscious."

"Sherry, do you still need the report?" Ray asked. "What's going on in that head of yours?"

"Thank you. That's very helpful. That might be enough information. I wanted to run my theory by you," Sherry said. She glanced over to Officer Sedgeman. "Troy, you can chime in any time with your firsthand expertise."

"Uh, I think that's my line," Ray said. "What's your theory?"

"As you know, Don, my fiancé, captains a commuter boat for a living. He had a special charter with the Feral Creations team before they began the cook-off. The production team was scouting locations and shooting some footage of the environs. On board were Basil, Mick, Rachel, and their limo driver, Yonny. I asked a few questions about what went on during their time on the water. Don said while Basil and Rachel left the boat to check out Bluefish Run Beach, he had a casual chat with Mick and Yonny. Yonny volunteered that he was hired to drive the team around after the accident, so everyone felt safer. He described the traumatic accident pretty much as Troy did. It sounded so frightening. Apparently, the fatality was another member of the production team who was never replaced."

"Interesting," Ray said. He shifted his chair and woke Trooper up. The Belgium Malinois rose with a graceful lift of his body and proceeded to check Sherry's sneakers with his snout.

"He smells Chutney. Maybe they'll be friends one day," Sherry said as she cautiously ran her fingertips through his shiny neck fur.

"He's not a dog's dog. He's aware he's a working member of the unit," Troy said. "He's deciphering whether you're a perpetrator of any importance."

"Okay, well, I'm not," Sherry said with a deadpan laugh. "Hope my law-abiding scent doesn't bore him." As she said the words, Trooper yawned and curled up alongside Troy's desk.

"A fatal crash. One member of the team was the fatality," Ray said. "His name was Kyle Lemke."

"The driver was the crash fatality," Troy said. "He was ejected from the car. Tough way to go."

"Explains why they hired a driver," Ray said. "Did Don have an opinion on the driver, Yonny, one way or another?"

Sherry searched her memory for any outstanding comments made by Don. "He said he was a nice man. Very helpful. Interested in boats. No red flags."

"So, the team suffered some trauma together. That may have brought them closer," Ray said. "During questioning they seemed close, with a few grievances. Par for the course. You'd imagine most folks who spend countless hours together would have disagreements."

"And they made another hire besides the driver," Sherry said. "Garrett Stein was hired in the following months to rebrand Feral Creations. That way the accident wouldn't define them. He did his job and business picked up. Work began on the new cook-off production not long after. And here we are."

"And?" Ray prompted. "The connection to Rachel Yaro's death?"

"I'm not sure. If part of the rebranding includes the *Juicy Bites* napkins, isn't the logical assumption Garrett Stein is the author? The napkins were originally written by Rachel. I have that on authority from Kat Coleman and Garrett Stein."

"Kat Coleman?" Ray asked. "She told you that?" The annoyance in his tone stung Sherry.

"Yes, she did," Sherry said. "Are you upset she told me or that she didn't tell you?"

"You'd know if I was upset. You're mistaking frustration for upset. I gave Kat the chance to talk to me. I'm doing my job when I question someone. In the initial stages of an investigation, I don't press harder than someone is comfortable with. In her case, I didn't even get off the starting block."

"She doesn't know you like I do," Sherry said. "I told her to talk with you. That you provided a safe space to be in."

"Rachel Yaro definitely wrote *Juicy Bites* until the time of her death," Ray said. "Okay. Thank you for confirming that. Did Kat or Garrett confirm who writes the news now?"

"That's the question on everyone's mind," Sherry said. "I do know there were the makings of a love triangle going on. Rachel had a thing for Garrett and actively pursued him. Garrett has a thing for Kat Coleman and vice versa. The women were friends. Murder is often a crime of passion."

"Sherry, you could be a murder mystery writer," Troy said. "I'd buy your books."

"Thanks, Troy. You do see my point, though, right?" Sherry asked. "Between you and me, as many times as Kat has tried to convince me Garrett is a man with good intentions, something's bugging me about him. I can't help but question his involvement in Rachel's murder. He's around the scene too often."

"I don't see a strong motive for anything but heartache and annoyance with what you're suggesting," Ray said. "As a matter of fact, you're making a stronger point that Kat may be the jealous one, or that Rachel and Kat may have come to blows over Garrett Stein."

"No, no, no," Sherry said with conviction. "That's not the point. There's more."

"Now who's upset?" Ray said.

"Putting the love triangle aside, the fatal crash was a turning point for Feral Creations. In a weird way, the tragedy led to the team flourishing. At least that's how it appears from the outside looking in. But, things aren't always as they appear."

"Go on," Ray said.

"The dynamic between Basil, Rachel, and Mick is fickle. What I mean is, there's an undercurrent of unrest. Like *Juicy Bites* hints at, there's something that could explode at any minute. A tension. I get that vibe from spending time with each of them."

"And you think it stems from the auto accident?" Ray asked.

"Or at the very least the time frame of the accident," Sherry said. "Change, upheaval all came about on that icy day."

"There you go with your mystery writing again," Troy said. "Let me know when the book drops."

Ray sent Troy a glance, the meaning of which was surely to stay on point. "I'll pull the accident report for further review. It would be upstairs. I don't know if it'll tell me anything I don't already know, but following leads isn't always a straight line." Ray wrote down something on a notepad.

"Kat opened up," Sherry said. "That's progress. The problem is she says there's more to the story."

"The story with two endings? The two-faced story riddle from *Juicy Bites*?" Ray asked.

"I wish I knew," Sherry said with a sigh. "Kat is steadfast that the time to speak isn't now. I'm hoping after the cook-off concludes she recognizes the time has come."

Ray tapped his pen on the desk. "One more day. That's all I'll give her."

"She'll have to beat the clock," Sherry said. "She's aware of the time ticking away."

Ray jotted down more notes. "I've got work to do."

Sherry watched the pen busily transcribe Ray's thoughts. When he was done, he set the pen down.

"Anything else? Troy, do you have anything to add?" Ray asked.

"All good here," Troy said.

"Need some recipe advice before the big event?" Ray asked.

"I appreciate any advice you'd have for me," Sherry said. "I don't know what today's theme will be. Beachy cuisine? Labor Day picnic menu prep?"

"I wasn't being serious. I can't role reverse," Ray said. "You share your cooking experience with me, and I gladly soak it in. It doesn't go both ways. All I can offer is a wish for a win. We believe in you, don't we, folks?" He and all the other officers seated at their desks stood and gave Sherry a round of applause.

"Wow. Thanks. I'll do my best." Sherry threw out a wave as she left the room.

• • •

The Bluefish Run Beach entrance was a throwback to the final days of summer every year of her childhood. Her father preferred to take the family to the more remote beach rather than the crowded public beach. Erno invested in all the necessary summer fun equipment, including a pull wagon, umbrella, large cooler, chairs, a football, beach paddleball and plenty of towels. Sherry recalled her mother directed the parade of supplies and children across the hot sand to the perfect spot, one far enough away from the approaching tide to keep the towels dry yet close enough Erno could reach a child in danger in seconds flat. Her mom's untimely passing left Erno with many summers of single-parenting trips to the beach. Sherry said a silent thank-you to the summer tradition kept alive by her father all those years ago as she drove the car through the beach entrance.

She wore a long-sleeved shirt and capri pants to shield herself from the sun's rays despite the heat and humidity of early afternoon. The minute she stepped out of her car she second-guessed her wardrobe choice. The breeze was warm and sticky, providing no relief from the humidity. She followed posted signs directing the cook-off participants to the gathering location.

The beach was a hike and she was perspiring. The footing was tricky and required extra effort to navigate. More energy burned meant more perspiration. She wished she brought a backup set of clothes. She was satisfied she was making headway when she crossed under an overhead banner declaring *Farewell to summer* strung on posts across the sandy walkway. American flags and potted sunflower plants lined the path. She was inspired by the organizer's efforts.

"Isn't this amazing?"

Sherry turned to see Silvia standing behind her donning a red, white, and blue apron. "Hollywood magic," Sherry said. "You already have your apron?" She checked her watch. "I thought I was early."

"I was told to be here at one p.m. I had an interview to catch up on," Silvia said.

"I double-checked, I wasn't expected to show up until two," Sherry said as a ripple of anxiety traveled through her core. "Nothing has begun in the cook-off, has it?"

"Nope. They wouldn't start without you. Pardon me, I'm getting my comb out of my car. The wind is crushing my attempt at a hairdo. I'll also spruce up my makeup since I have a minute. Don't wait for me."

"I'll see you there," Sherry said. "Where do I go?"

"Follow the signs. You need to check in with Stacy and Mick and it's a bit of a walk. Have you been here before? You must have. You're a local," Silvia said.

"We came here every summer of my childhood. My dad's choice. Me and my siblings preferred the crowded public beach because of the easy access, cute lifeguards and a snack bar. At the time we didn't appreciate Dad's need for some quiet after working all week long. At the town's main public beach, people would constantly come up to him and ask for tips on rug hooking and rug repair. Here at Bluefish Run we had the place to ourselves most of the time."

"So, you know it well?"

"They couldn't have chosen a more familiar venue for the cook-off. Although, I've never cooked here. We always brought a cooler of sandwiches."

"That's a lovely memory," Silvia said. "I'll see you in a bit." Silvia took two steps then turned back to face Sherry. "I have a strange question. You mentioned you played tennis."

"Well, I don't remember mentioning that, but yes, I do," Sherry said.

"Maybe I just imagined you did," Silvia said. "Since I made a lucky guess, would you happen to have two tennis balls you could donate to Mick? He's having a devil of a time getting around in these environs. I'm certain if he covered the bottoms of his walker's front legs, he'd have a smoother trip around. I've seen it done a million times. I'm sure you have, too."

"I absolutely do have two tennis balls in my car. My dog is learning how to fetch so I save used balls for his lessons. I'll go retrieve them."

Silvia laughed. "I see what you did there. Mick will appreciate the donation."

As soon as Sherry made the offer, she was reminded of the terrain she had crossed over and how she just volunteered to do it all over again. Sherry trotted back to her car. She found two tennis balls loose on the backseat floor mat. She was tempted to turn on the car's air-conditioning and dry off the glistening sweat soaking through her shirt, but the minutes was ticking. She swiped a comb through her hair, dabbed her forehead with a tissue and made the trek back down the sandy walkway.

When she reached the beachhead entrance, Sherry was met with a sight she wasn't accustomed to. As she passed the dune grasses there was a makeshift veranda where there had only been sand before. The structure's construction material was a form of wood composite that appeared too lightweight for long-term stability. Sherry went so far as to label it flimsy, spruced up by a good paint job. The structure would work for one day of filming, she estimated.

There were grills and tables on the plank flooring. Most thankfully there was a thin roofing cover overhead. Protection from the blazing summer sun was a concern Sherry could strike off her list. The heat would have to be squelched with plenty of drinking water.

The back of the veranda was crowded with four good-sized grills. The beach beyond was littered with red-checked tableclothed tables, reclining chairs and open umbrellas planted in the sand. The scene made for an enticing shoreline backdrop, yet no one was partaking in the summer fun except Stacy, who was smoothing beach towels strewn across the recliners. Sherry felt a tap on her shoulder.

"Good afternoon, Sherry," Orlando said. The outfit he sported upped the festive atmosphere to another level. His short-sleeved orange shirt both clashed with and matched his dusty rose Bermuda shorts. Sherry liked the look and wished she had the adventurous spirit to take such a fashion leap.

"Hi, Orlando," Sherry said. "Are you excited?"

"I'm raring to go." When he pointed toward the beach, his hairy forearms blended in with the distant golden seagrass. "Stacy's out there keeping it real by shooing away the gulls who are trying to eat the fake watermelons resting on the picnic baskets. Follow me, I'll show you where I got my apron. You also need to check in."

"I'm right behind you," Sherry said. Her enthusiasm was bubbling over. "Looks like a grill challenge."

"That's a good guess," Orlando said. "Seems too straightforward. There must be a twist."

"You're right. What was I thinking?" Sherry said with a dry laugh.

"Today is mano a mano. No teams. Every man and woman for themselves. I hope I survive." He raised his hand skyward and signaled the powers above to grant his wish.

They reached a canopied table laden with clipboards, clapboards, security identification strung on lanyards, and folded aprons.

"Sherry, glad you could make it," Mick said as he made a loud entrance, his groans accompanying the progress of his gait through the deep sand. Raising and lowering his walker had him perspiring through his dark green Hawaiian shirt.

"Mick, Silvia had a wonderful idea. If someone can cut a hole in these two tennis balls, you could insert them onto the bottom of your front walker legs and get around in this soft sand a lot easier." Sherry showed him the tennis balls in her hand.

"That's a great idea," Mick said. "We have scissors in the crew pit. Thank you so much."

Basil sidled up to Mick. He was dressed in another version of a colorful Hawaiian shirt, light blue Bermuda shorts and a baseball cap. "Folks, if you haven't checked in with Mick, please do so now."

Stacy, attired in a floral jumpsuit and sandals, called Sherry's name. "Have you checked in? Your aprons are on the table."

Sherry was guided through the check-in process before accepting the folded cloth from Stacy. When she tied on the apron adorned with fireworks imagery, she was one step closer to being fully immersed in her afternoon of competition.

"You look ready for action," Silvia said when she reappeared.

It wasn't hard to identify the three competing cooks, each in their eye-popping aprons and laminated photo IDs hanging from their necks.

"Okay, folks," Basil called out. "Follow me over to the veranda, where we have four grills preheating. Yes, I said four. I have a surprise for you three. I'll save that for when the cameras roll."

Sherry and Orlando shared a mutual nod of acknowledgment for their accurate assessment of whether there would be a mystery twist to the contest. When the cooks assembled, Basil made his opening remarks.

"Let me set the scene for you, cooks," Basil said. "Keep this sentimental picture in mind. You're being transported in time to Labor Day, whether it's a Labor Day from your past or a Labor Day you've aspired to create. It's a day to relish. Either way, it's the every-year unofficial final weekend of summer. A celebration of sorts. A reason to ramp up the positivity and squeeze one more drop of fun out of the best season of the year. That's the energy we're looking for—sending summer off with one more memorable grilled meal. One that's worth a big prize. Now, I'd like Jason to have a few words with the cooks." Basil motioned to his left.

"Thank you, Basil. I am so honored to be hosting *Relish* on day three, the finale," Jason said.

"We will begin filming in ten minutes. Use the porta-potty and choose a water bottle to keep by your grill station. We will then take you three over to your marks and the show will begin." Jason excused himself and walked over to some crew members to watch a playback of his informal introduction.

Every cook used the port-a-potty. One never knew when the next chance would come about.

Silvia was first in line at the water table followed by Sherry. "No audience again today. I don't mind that. Not one bit. Except the lack of onlookers makes me think there's something up the production team's tricky sleeve. There are four grills and only three cooks."

"A twist? A new competitor?" Sherry asked.

"I think so. Who's stepping in?"

"Okay, everyone," Basil said. "Follow me back to where the action will begin."

"You nervous?" Orlando asked.

"I'm psyched to get this underway," Silvia said. "Anyone have any clues as to what the big twist is?"

"You think there's only one twist?" Orlando asked. His lean toward sarcasm indicated he knew the answer to his question.

Chapter 20

The veranda roof atop the grill area blocked the sun but trapped the heat, despite the lack of walls. When the grills were in use, the temperature would escalate. As far as Sherry knew, heat rose and would circulate without an escape route, creating the outdoor equivalent of a convection oven. One bottle of water wasn't going to be enough. Sherry cradled the refreshment as if it were the last source of hydration left on Earth.

As start time neared, the cooks were instructed to take their places on the markers in front of their designated prep and cook areas. As soon as the camera crews covered all angles with their cameras—high, low, overhead, and the all-important eye-level—Basil gave Jason the go-ahead to position himself facing the cooks. An unclaimed grill sat next to Orlando. Down the row of grills was Silvia, who was next to Sherry.

"Mick, do you have the clapboards handy?" Basil called out.

"I have them," Stacy called back. "Mick's back at the truck, remember? Doing something with his walker."

Basil grumbled a reply. "Does anyone stick to their assignments?" He cleared his throat and raised his voice. "Okay. Grab the intro scene slate and we're on our way."

Stacy squared herself in front of a camera and announced, "*Relish* Finale—Scene one, Introduction." She slammed the clapboard arm down. Sherry winced at the jarring noise.

"Good afternoon. Welcome to the final day of the *Relish* cook-off competition. My name is Jason Kilmartin and I'm your host. Today we're naming the *Relish* champion after our final challenge. There's a lot on the line for our cooks and a lot on their plates besides food." He transferred his gaze to each cook in turn. "How are you all feeling today? You're the last man and women standing. You should all be very proud of yourselves."

Jason held a polished smile while Sherry, Silvia, and Orlando exchanged appreciative glances.

"Today is Labor Day," Jason continued. "The unofficial end to the summer and always a great day to celebrate all summer had to offer." Jason walked off his mark and paced a few steps as the camera panned across the veranda with him. He turned back, his expression serious. "Labor Day is a day to honor all who work hard at their jobs. And that includes home cooks. To salute the day, *Relish* is going to ask the cooks to work for their prize. I'm not simply asking you to cook using the mystery ingredients we have provided today, but each one of you will be asked to forage for at least two ingredients that must be incorporated into your grilled recipe. A scavenger hunt of sorts."

The word *forage* was repeated by several cooks. Another pause in Jason's delivery gave Sherry time to consider the skill of searching for edibles in the wild. It was a skill she was interested in teaching during the middle school classroom visits she volunteered at. The problem was she had yet to research the science of foraging, let alone be dependent on the results for a large grand prize. No time like the present to learn the ropes.

"Oh, and you may have noticed we have three cooks and four grill stations. And four ingredient coolers." Jason's gaze drifted to the empty grill station. "It's time to make the numbers add up. Jada, would you please join us?"

Jada stepped out from behind the cameraman and took her place in front of the fourth grill.

"The judging panel has reviewed the cook-off's decision to eliminate Jada on day one. There were several factors that were considered at the time. Her prepared food was tremendous. No problem there. The main reason they made their judgment against Jada was they felt she may have received unfair assistance from one of the other cooks." Jason's gaze drifted in Sherry's direction.

"Oh, no," Sherry whispered. "I'm out. Is this the twist?"

Silvia's elbow brushed Sherry's side. "No way."

"We're glad to have you rejoin the finalists, Jada," Jason said. "You heard the instructions. Labor Day, foraging, grill-off. We're almost all set to begin, with four cooks. We do have a few other details to discuss."

Orlando didn't attempt to mask a groan.

Jason laughed. "You'll like this detail." Jason peered to his right and waved forward a group of four men and women, dressed in overalls and T-shirts. "We have secured a one-day permit from the Park Service Department to collect two ingredients by each cook from the cordoned-off area behind the dunes. It's a gorgeous wild meadow with native edible plants. Plant experts from our local division of the Park Service will accompany you cooks as each of you forage for enough to feed our three judges. The guides are equipped with plant identification knowledge, clippers, and sacks, assisting you as you gather foodstuffs from the wild. Your foraged bounty will accompany the ingredients in your cooler. We will be setting up a Labor Day pantry selection of additional ingredients during the thirty minutes you and your guide are foraging. You will be competing in the 'Four Who Forage for a Feast' challenge."

On cue, the Park Service guides split off and each found their assigned cook.

"As I said, you will have thirty minutes to complete foraging," Jason said. "Take a sip of your water because time starts in three, two, one . . . Go." Jason pointed to the meadow and only left enough time for Sherry to greet her guide and swallow one gulp of water.

"Okay, we'll stop filming until we begin the time on the other side of the dunes," Basil said. "Is Mick back?"

"Right here," Mick said. "My vehicle got an upgrade." He held up the front of his tennis-ball-adorned walker, only dropping the contraption when he lost his balance.

"Good job," Stacy said.

"Very nice. Mick, can you bring the second clapboard, please. Mark the scene as 'the meadow.' Stacy, extra collection sacks, clippers and the timer need to come along."

Sherry and her newly introduced guide, Reggie, followed the camera crew across a boardwalk that spanned a break in the grassy dunes. It occurred to Sherry the cooler ingredients hadn't been revealed. That added a deep dimension of unknown she would have to manage with her creativity. She would have to gather ingredients that could go with most any protein. Her nerves tingled as they neared the open space. She would do her best to pick the brain of her guide and select two plants he deemed all-purpose.

"Reggie, I'm counting on you to give me the rundown on what's available in the meadow. Are you a botanist?" Sherry asked.

"Plant scientist, botanist—I go by both titles. I can identify nearly all the plants local to this region. We were given a brief tour of what's available in the field. There's more to discover. I think you're going to be very successful. There's a maze of paths to wander and I didn't cover the entire landscape. As we search, I'll help you identify plants. You can choose what makes sense for your cook-off recipe. The producers would like you to do the foraging, using me as reference as to whether the plant is practical for your purposes."

"We don't want to poison the judges," Sherry said. She wasn't joking. That was her greatest fear. She suddenly recalled that poisoning someone was forewarned in *Juicy Bites*.

Reggie pursed his lips. "No, let's not do that. I'd like to keep my job."

"Glad you have a sense of humor."

"Sherry? Can I have a word with you?"

Sherry rotated and came face-to-face with Jada. "Hi, Jada. I'm so happy you're back." Sherry had few words to offer her opponent. She wasn't over the shock of Jada's re-entry into the cook-off. She was also wary of being seen conversing with her competitor again after what had happened on day one. She didn't want to compromise anyone's chances for a second time, especially her own. This contest was so different from others and seemed to be making up rules as it went along.

"Me, too," Jada said. "How you helped me was one of the nicest things anyone's ever done for me. My exit wasn't based on the food we cooked and that wasn't right. The organizers righted the wrong. No one was given an advantage in our exchange. Let's not even give the matter another thought."

"I like your attitude. I've never had an incident like this happen in all my years competing in cook-offs. I thought I'd seen it all. Then again, I've never had to forage for an ingredient, and I've never been in a three-day cook-off. What next?" Sherry asked with a shrug.

"Keep calm and carry on," Jada said.

The trek to the meadow was a slow one with Basil, Mick, and Stacy leading the procession. Behind them the camera operators labored through the uneven terrain with their hardware. Sherry was relieved to see detectable pathways throughout the tall grasses and shrubs when the group reached a cordoned-off meadow. She was back to being grateful she chose to wear pants instead of shorts. Ticks and poison ivy were a big concern in New England and avoiding both trumped comfort.

"Okay, folks," Basil announced. "There's never been a cook-off featuring foraging, as far as I know, so you're marking new territory. The crew needs a few minutes to test the camera's response to the natural lighting and we'll be set to start. Stacy will hand out two labeled collection bags for each cook, so check you're given the correct sacks."

Stacy put two sacks the size of small reusable grocery bags in each cook's hands. She handed the clippers to the guides. Sherry read her name tag attached to the sack's tie string.

"Okay, folks. Take your time surveying the plants. We will be filming without interruption, so the more you and your guide are engaged, the better. Jason will be adding narration after the fact. When the crew is ready Jason will film the intro to the scene and time will begin. You ready, Jason?"

Jason made his way past the cameras and wedged himself beside Sherry and Orlando. "All set."

"Mick, is the clapboard set? Cameras, are you a go? The generators are all powered up?"

A symphony of faint whirring sounds filled the air as the cameras' red lights came on.

Sherry's heart beat double time.

"We're all set." Mick held the clapboard high. "The Meadow" was written in thick black ink across the scene description box. "Three, two, one, Action." He slammed the arm down.

Jason lifted his chin and donned his signature smile. "Labor Day. A day to relish the bounty of riches that summer brings. What better day to be asked to sing for your supper? Or in the case of our cooks today, forage for your supper. Working hard makes the reward that much sweeter. Silvia, Sherry, Orlando, Jada and their four forage guides will be traversing this beautiful meadow steps away from the beach they will be grilling on. They've been asked to gather two wild ingredients to use with their mystery cooler ingredients."

Sherry nodded an affirmation she would rise to the challenge.

"I'd like to introduce the viewers to the history of foraging," Jason said. "Before organized agriculture and domesticated crops, humans lived a hunter-gatherer lifestyle. That worked if groups were nomadic. Eventually, settlers found staying in one place was often preferable and foraging evolved into farming. There is a resurgence of the foraging practice—so today we relish the connection to our roots. Soon we will find out what nature wants to feed us."

"There's a reason there are grocery stores," Orlando whispered. "That's my idea of foraging."

"The cooks have thirty minutes to complete the collection task and the time starts"—Jason paused and made eye contact with each cook in turn—"now."

Sherry and Reggie entered the meadow via a roped off passage leading to a mowed path, steps behind a cameraman walking backward. The young man was adept at juggling his camera on his shoulder, which Sherry estimated weighed an unwieldy fifty-plus pounds, despite the uneven terrain. Nonetheless, he encountered an obstacle in no time. Sherry saw an accident waiting to happen when they approached a hole in the ground.

"Watch your step."

"Thanks. Hazards of the trade. I'll follow behind." He crossed their path and trailed Sherry. His forehead was already perspiring. Sherry offered him her water. He declined.

"That's a first at a cook-off," Sherry said. "Warning a cameraman not to fall in a hole."

Greens, golden brown hues, and pops of color painted the horizon. Just ahead of Sherry were tall grasses, a few scattered shrubs, and three or four miniature trees. The meadow had no distinguishing features that resembled potentially usable ingredients.

"It might be easier if I hold the collection bags while you search." Reggie held his hand out to receive the bags.

Sherry's other hand clutched the cold bottle of water. "Thanks," she said, freeing up one hand.

"Stacy and Mick have extra bags, if need be, but we should be fine with two," Reggie said. He pointed to the duo only a few feet away conferencing with Orlando and his guide. Mick put up his thumb to confirm Reggie's comment.

"I'd like to move down the path a bit. It's kind of crowded right here. We're all going to end up with the same two plants," Sherry said.

"Good plan," Reggie said. "Where you lead, I will follow."

Sherry smiled in appreciation at the reference to an oldies song she loved. "Where do we begin?" Sherry asked in hopes of breaking the spell of indecision that was descending on her. Before Reggie could respond she took the bull by the horns. Her attention returned to the surrounding plants. She kneeled to take a closer look at what she thought was a familiar leaf shape. "This plant looks like mint," Sherry said. "Could that be?"

"You have just passed the first requirement of foraging. If you're drawn to a plant, let your curiosity shepherd you. I suggest you pick a leaf, rub it between your fingers and sniff. Don't be tempted to taste first. That could be a mistake."

Sherry did as she was told and picked a leaf.

"Not that one." Reggie's vigorous warning caused Sherry to drop the leaf she held between her fingers. "That one's toxic. Perilla mint, or Perilla frutescens, as it's known in the scientific world."

"Thanks. That was close," Sherry said. The camera operator zoomed in on Sherry's furrowed brow.

"That's the process. Watch carefully when you harvest. This isn't like your backyard organized garden. This is Mother Nature using all her wiles and creativity. One plant species next to another. The plants grow that way for a reason, so one plant variety isn't over-harvested by predators." Reggie reached down to pinch off a second leaf from a neighboring plant. "Look for the teeth on the edge of the leaves. That's the mint leaf identifier. See the difference? Subtle, but lifesaving."

Sherry gave the leaf the same rigorous inspection she reserved for produce, like sandy spinach leaves or unwashed organic apples. When she was satisfied the leaf fell into the tooth-edged category, she massaged the leaf between two fingers and sniffed. "Sure smells like mint. Can you confirm and tell me if it's okay to taste? If it is, I could infuse some oil with mint and use the combo."

"Yes, that is a wild mint plant. Mint is pervasive once it takes hold."

"How did mint get in this field?" Sherry asked. The camera panned down and closed in on the plant.

"Good question," Reggie said. "How did most of the edibles get in here? Lucky happenstance and maybe some intervention by park management if kick-starting a local plant is needed. Lucky for all of us."

"Maybe we can come back to this plant. I want to see what else is out here."

"You have a keen eye and nose. There are many more good plants to use. You're wise to browse. The landscape may appear as an untended jumble of plants, but to the observant there's treasure. Since each cook is only permitted to harvest, at the most, one-quarter of a plant, there'll be plenty for all if we decide to double-back here." Reggie smiled and adjusted his baseball cap. "I think you're catching the foraging bug."

Sherry bid the mint farewell. Within a few steps she discovered a patch of eye-catching heart-shaped leaves. "This is either clover or sorrel. They're doppelgangers. I'm too green to tell the difference, but I do know sorrel is very good in salads. In the small amount I've learned about foraging from fellow community gardeners, they rank finding wild sorrel as passing the foraging graduation test."

Reggie bent down to inspect the plant. The leaves resembled the shamrocks Sherry associated with leprechauns. "Sorrel, definitely. Plenty to go around." Reggie held up the clippers for Sherry's harvest.

"I don't think I'll take any. Fingers crossed I find something more interesting. Not that sorrel isn't delicious. I have a gut feeling there's more to see. I'll take my chances."

"I like your spirit," Reggie said.

The cameraman peered out from behind his lens and flashed Sherry an encouraging grin. He was enjoying the process as much as Sherry. She no longer saw the equipment as a distraction after three days of recording her every move. The operator with the camera on his shoulder or the mounted stationary video recorder was part of the scenery, akin to white noise. Sherry followed the meandering path a few more yards with a lift in her step. Within arm's length, Jada and her guide were stalled in front of a cluster of tall grasses.

"How ya doing, Sherry? Are you getting inspired by what you see?" Jada asked.

"Good, thanks. Getting loads of inspiration," she said. She picked up the pace until she was well beyond the others.

She came to rest in front of tufts of unassuming delicate green stalks. "Reggie, this looks like the onion grass that pops up in bunches in my backyard. Would that be a good ingredient?"

"Pull one out and let's check it out," he said. His tone challenged Sherry to pay close attention to the subtleties of what was coming out of the ground.

Sherry pinched the bright green stem at the base and gently coaxed the plant out of the sandy soil with a pull. She knew from experience that onions were fussy about coming out of the ground if pulled incorrectly. Pressure any higher on the plant might dislodge the valuable underground bulb from the more fragile upper stem. She studied the segmented bulb that emerged. "It doesn't look like my onion grass. What is this? Garlic?"

"Very good. Wild garlic, to be exact," Reggie said. "A wonderful ingredient."

"I'll bag a few of those. That's a no-brainer for any recipe." She pulled two more mini bulbs from the soil and popped them in her bag. "I'm betting the tops are useful, too."

"They sure are. You scored a two-in-one ingredient," Reggie said with a nod. "It probably was one of the first foods ever foraged. The scent alone tells you this belongs in cooking."

"One down, one to go," Sherry said. "How's our time running?"

"Stacy, do you have the remaining time?" Reggie called out.

Stacy and Mick were up ahead on the path, seeking shade under a tree not much taller than them. She addressed Mick. "Twelve more minutes, cooks."

"Would there be anything interesting growing under that fir tree?" Sherry asked. "Shade might give us a different yield."

"My role isn't to push you in a certain direction. I'm here to make sure you make a safe choice. It's up to you to choose what and where to harvest," Reggie said with no apologies.

Sherry shrugged. She was leaning on Reggie to shortcut the process in case time was running short. He wasn't having it. She walked on ahead to the tree that appeared to live alone until she studied the undergrowth thriving in the shade around the trunk. What looked from a distance like a wasteland was an abundance of life. Broken twigs, dried fir needle clusters, tiny sand formations and decomposing leaves from unknown sources lay at her feet. The microcosm of life hosted one bizarre inhabitant. Under the tree were many honeycomb-textured, irregular oval shapes protruding from the organic debris.

"Reggie," Sherry whispered. She may have found a pot of gold. She motioned for him to lean in closer. "Are those morel mushrooms?"

Reggie leaned in and studied the odd formations. "Yes."

"There are eight. You said I could only take one-quarter of the plant. How does that work for mushrooms?"

"You may take two. These are very generously sized. The likelihood the lifecycle of the mushroom has come full circle and the spores have been released is quite high. They've sown their wild oats for the next generation to carry on. Especially since we had rain showers within the last couple of days. Clip above the soil line, no digging or yanking. That way the root system will stay intact, and the plant will receive signals it needs to get to work regenerating." Reggie handed Sherry the clippers and another collection bag.

As Sherry positioned the blades of the clipper on either side of the mushroom stem, she had one more question. "You're one hundred percent sure these are morel mushrooms, not deadly impostors? I really want to use them but don't want to risk sickening the judges. Or worse."

"I am one hundred percent certain," Reggie said. His nod reassured Sherry.

"Here we go," she said as the clipper blade severed the stem and the mushroom tumbled off its perch. The second one she cut was even larger. She gently placed them in the bag and cradled the prizes as she hoisted herself out of a squat.

"I read these fir shoots can be used in salads," Sherry said as she brushed the light green ends of a branch off her face.

"Are you reconsidering the wild garlic?" Reggie asked.

"Absolutely not," Sherry said. "Just trying to impress you with the miscellaneous gardening knowledge I've accumulated over the years."

"I'm very impressed," Reggie said with a smile. "I'm certain you can teach me as much as I can teach you. It's been a pleasure working with you." He gazed over his shoulder. "Let's see if it's time. Stacy?"

Chapter 21

Sherry was hit by a wave of weariness on the walk back to the beach. She hadn't had much water during foraging and needed to remedy her thirst before full-blown lethargy set in. The uncertainties of the cook-off were taking their toll on her nerves, but she had more fight to fight. She drained her bottle of water before reaching the veranda, replenishing her energy tank. Ahead of her, Stacy and Mick were navigating the sandy patches on the boardwalk. Basil, on the other hand, raced ahead as if he were meeting a looming deadline.

Sherry wondered if the cooks would have a chance to freshen up before the next portion of the cook-off. Basil met them as they returned and gave them a brief time to use the bathroom. Sherry spotted a new addition to those waiting on all the cooks—Garrett. He held a notebook in one hand and a collection sack in the other.

"Hi, Garrett. Did you forage?" Sherry asked.

"I did. The team had an extra bag, and I have the interest, so I tagged along for research sake," he said. He held up his sack. "I didn't have a guide, so I went with the limited knowledge I have. Got some rose hips and some mint. Now I can make home-brewed meadow-foraged tea. How about you? Were you successful?"

"Sure was," Sherry said. "Many thanks to Reggie. Is that Mayor Drew?" Sherry asked as her gaze drifted over Garrett's shoulder. "And Kat? Who's manning the office?"

"Augustin may crumble at any moment," Garrett said with a sly smile. He paused until Sherry's full attention was back on him. "Did you find foraging similar to gathering clues in all the murder cases you've solved?"

"That's a funny question," Sherry said. "I wouldn't credit myself with solving any of them. Only providing a bit of additional know-how. Like how Reggie helped me in the field."

"It's no secret you have another hobby besides cooking competitions, gardening, tennis and hooked rugs. Besides, I'm a journalist, public relations specialist, and one of my dearest friends plays tennis with you." If Garrett were a cat, he'd have a canary locked in his jaws judging by the satisfaction he projected.

"The answer to your question is foraging is about clues and discovery," Sherry said. "We were asked to search through what was available, and that's how a murder investigation works. How long has it been since you knew the cooks would be foraging today?"

"Long enough," Garrett said. "And I'm not the only one."

"Hey, you two," Kat said. "You look as if you're sharing a secret."

"Hi, Kat," Sherry said. "Nice to have you and the mayor come down for the final day. Now I'm nervous."

"Don't be," Kat said. "You're in your element. Be nervous on the court, not in the kitchen."

"Cooks, would you please assemble over at the grills," Basil called out. "We're about to continue. Mick, has anyone seen Mick?"

"Right here," Mick said. He was steps away from his walker selecting a bottle of water from the water table. "Stretching my legs. Doctor's orders. I've got the clapboard ready to go."

"I'm going to borrow a Sharpie and mark my bag. Good luck," Garrett said as he headed toward the water table.

"Three minutes," Basil announced. He lowered his voice as he addressed Stacy.

"Knock 'em dead," Kat said. She trotted back to the mayor and Basil.

"Hustle up, Sherry. The grills are calling our names. The mystery baskets are waiting. Did you give Stacy your forage sacks?" Orlando asked as he came to rest next to Sherry.

"I did. Let's go," Sherry said. "On second thought, go on ahead." Sherry liked the idea of an additional bottle of water at her grill station. She brushed past Mick as she reached for the fizzy water she preferred. "You're mobile. That's great."

"No one's happier than me," Mick said. "Except maybe Basil. He blames me for some delays in the production."

"He's under a ton of pressure, I'm sure. Don't take it personally. Work is work."

"It's nothing but personal. He should be thanking me every opportunity he gets, not blaming me. Rachel was no better." The bitterness in his voice was startling. "Sorry, not sure where that came from."

"Mick? What's the holdup? Sherry, to your mark, please," Basil said.

The short walk back to the veranda gave Sherry time to take in the surroundings. It appeared set designers were busy decorating the veranda while she'd been trekking through the meadow. The scene captured the essence of summer. Fireworks props, bright tablecloths, light strings, and summery garland created an ambiance of celebration and welcome. The next step was up to the cooks; prepare a meal that the judges deemed one to relish.

Jason was positioned in front of the grills. The cooks were instructed to stand facing him. Stacy, Mick and Basil were giving the camera operators an earful accented with hand gestures. When they settled down Mick raised a clapboard. From her vantage point she was able to make out the scene's description: *Final Cook-off*.

Basil stepped forward and joined Jason. "Cooks, we are about to begin. By now you're used to receiving the guidelines of the cook-off at the last minute, so no one has the advantage of prior knowledge."

All the cooks nodded in agreement.

"Today is no different, except this is the final test of your cooking skills. Labor Day celebrates work, and your work will continue in a very short time. I will step out of the way and, when filming begins, Jason will give the on-camera instructions. Good luck to you all. Oh, and do me a favor, straighten out your aprons. And Sherry, you have some grass in your hair."

After some self-care, the cooks were presentable.

"Welcome back to *Relish*, the finale," Jason's booming voice projected. "Our cooks have foraged for two required ingredients and are about to get their first glimpse of their all-important picnic cooler ingredients."

One camera swung in the direction of the cooks and their grill tables. On each table was a medium-sized cooler. Sherry was glad to see the cooler was not big enough to hold an excessive number of items.

"Cooks, please remove the cooler items and set them on your table." Jason paused while the cooks lifted the lids of their coolers and reached inside. One by one they examined what their hands held. "You should see herb cornbread stuffing, tater tots, apple oatmeal bars, ground buffalo meat, and romaine lettuce."

If Sherry had to apply a theme to the cooler contents, she'd choose one word, all-American.

"You will also have a choice of up to ten additional ingredients you will find stocked in our provided pantry. Which, I may add, was quite a trick getting here while navigating the sand dunes, by land and by sea." Jason's laugh was as smooth as softened butter and just as rich. "None of the cooks has seen the pantry offerings and will have to think on the fly when the allotted time begins. Finally, don't forget your foraged ingredients. Use them wisely."

Sherry leaned in to make sure she heard the upcoming allotted time announced clearly. She was anxious to hear the overall theme applied to the recipe so she could come up with a plan. Jason's pauses were toying with the cooks for television drama.

"What's our theme today? The grill is heating up and the calendar reads Labor Day. The beach setting, the ingredients foraged, all of those can only add up to one logical theme."

Sherry sucked in a deep breath. She still had no idea where Jason was going.

"*Relish*. The name of this cook-off is *Relish*. To relish something is to savor it, indulge in it, fancy it, and value it. That, my friends, is the theme of this final day's cook-off. You'll be grilling and you'll be working with your cooking wits. In the ninety minutes allowed, I repeat, ninety minutes, please create for the three judges a main dish that should make sense for the time of year we are in, the location you find yourselves in, and most importantly, aim to entice the judges to relish your dish."

Who the judges were played constantly in Sherry's mind. It was historically impossible to cook specifically for a judge's personal preferences. Who knew what someone liked to eat on a particular day? Did someone like spicy, or saucy, or stark and deconstructed? She realized she couldn't read every personal food preference by someone's appearance, but she was confident she could get an inkling. She had no chance without seeing the individuals.

Even without knowing the judges' identities, cook-offs always had sponsors to please. The sponsors were more transparent than the judges. They wanted the cooks to showcase their star product, whether it be a cut of chicken or a spice blend. Sherry had confidence she could come up with a pleasing recipe to suit their preferences. Here she was on her third cook-off day and, as far as she could fathom, there was no specific sponsor other than the town of Augustin.

Sherry smoothed her apron and willed Jason to give the call to begin.

"We'd like to welcome the mayor of Augustin, our lovely host town." The camera Jason spoke to swiveled in Mayor Drew's direction.

The mayor tossed a wave before the lens swung back to Jason.

"He'll be presenting the winner's prizes when all is said and done. Stay tuned."

Sherry wondered if Mayor Drew was a judge. She scratched that thought on the grounds people would claim preferential treatment if she placed. Her mind was wandering. The cook-off needed to start.

146

"Okay, folks," Jason said. "You have your forage collection bounty at your grill and your cooler of required ingredients. There's only one more item on the agenda. That's to say, your ninety minutes starts," Jason pointed to his watch, "now."

First things first. Get to the pantry and claim what she needed from the minimal offerings before they were gone. She side-eyed the other cooks, who were both staring at their cooler ingredients. Her plan was to create a version of a ranch-style butter burger, with a grilled lettuce, tater tot, and apple salad dressed with wild garlic vinaigrette. If that was to come to fruition, she'd better giddy-up over to the pantry and round up her add-ons.

After she scoured the pantry for her ten selections, Sherry tucked steak seasoning, canned French-fried onions, butter, ranch dressing, vinegar, horseradish and pretzel buns into the crook of her folded arm. She had three additional choices hovering in her mind but decided to hold off choosing them to see how the recipe came together. As soon as she unloaded her pantry choices on her prep table a lightbulb went off in her head. She scooted back to the pantry and stocked up on smoked mozzarella. An extra shot of smoke to her ranch morel bison butter burger couldn't hurt and would serve to punctuate her ranch flavor theme. She could always swap one ingredient for another if need be.

The burgers would be a combination of ground bison, steak seasoning, and the secret meat moisturizer, butter. Sherry would combine the butter with the lean meat for a slow melt that yielded a juicy bite. The morel mushroom would be sliced thin, but not too thin, and grilled to achieve the char stripes that ensured a smoky emphasis on picnic flavors. The mozzarella would then be melted on top and served on a grilled pretzel bun bathed in just enough mustard to provide a tangy bite. As she reviewed her recipe steps, she had a revelation. Why not rename her burger for what it represented, she suddenly decided. She waved her hand over her ingredients.

"I christen you, the Wild West Labor Day Butter Burger."

Sherry's side dish had to be the perfect accompaniment, not an afterthought to use up overlooked ingredients. Grilled tater tots, chopped fried onions, flash-grilled and broken apple oatmeal bar croutons, a wild garlic horseradish ranch dressing, and an unexpected base to the potato salad—grilled romaine lettuce—would meld together as a side dish worthy of the Labor Day celebration. She hoped the meal was worthy of a big cook-off prize. It was all about the execution from here on out.

She combined the burger ingredients and placed four patties on a plate to rest. The timing of the grilling was crucial if the judges were to enjoy the burger at its peak serving temperature. The tater tot salad was more forgiving, but she would reserve the dressing until close to the final bell so as not to drown the crunch.

Sherry was so focused on the steps of her recipe she tuned everyone else out until she heard her name called.

"Sherry, how are you doing? You look as cool as a cucumber. You're in your element, that's for sure," Jason said as he approached. To one side of her grill space Orlando was frantically arranging items on his prep table. He stared blankly at the food groupings. On her other side, Silvia was dabbing at her temple with a napkin.

"So far, so good," Sherry said.

"Your fellow cooks wish they had your air of confidence," Jason said.

"They're all wonderful cooks," Sherry said. "No one has the advantage at this stage."

"No, but some have a disadvantage and then it's game over. Silvia's decided to throw in the towel." Jason's announcement came as a shock. If Sherry commented with any emotion, it may be misconstrued as a complaint against the event. If she didn't express compassion for Silvia, as she'd like, she wouldn't be happy with herself.

Sherry scanned down the line of grills. "I'm so sorry. I hope she's okay. Does she need anything?" Sherry didn't wait for a response. "Silvia, do you need anything?"

"No, thanks. Just win one for the rest of us," Silvia said as she vacated her grill station.

Sherry hunkered down and finished putting the tater tot salad together. She placed the meat on the grill, where the patties cooked to juicy perfection, thanks to the slow melt of butter inside the patties. The cheese melted just enough to provide drama to the presentation as the white gold dripped down the sides of the hot patties. She placed the toasted pretzel bun lid slightly askew on top of the cheese and the adorned burger was complete. No boring Labor Day burger for the judges. They would be treated to a multilayered taste sensation featuring a balance of protein, umami morel, added fat, melty smokey cheese and savory pretzel crunch. She artfully arranged each component of her recipe on a platter and signaled she was ready to be judged.

"Basil, we need you," Orlando called out.

Chapter 22

Basil approached Sherry's grill. "Is there a problem?" Two camera-wielding men followed him.

Throughout the cook-off Basil stopped by each of the cook's grill station and sampled their ingredients. Other than the obligatory check-ins he hadn't been in front of the camera in the last two days. Sherry was surprised at his presence. There must be a production problem too big for Jason to handle. She froze.

When the silence became deafening Basil rescued her. "Sherry, we have to stop you before you go any further." Sherry glanced over at Orlando and Jada. They were setting down whatever they had in their hands. Each turned to face Sherry and Basil. Her platter of burgers and salad was secured in her grasp.

"Did I do something wrong?" Sherry asked. The sight of Mayor Drew and Kat waving at her only added to her confusion. "What's going on?"

Jason and Basil exchanged glances before Jason spoke. "Sherry Oliveri, the three-day *Relish* cook-off hasn't been a cooking competition like the ones you've been so successful competing in."

Sherry let loose a nervous giggle. "I'm getting that impression." Why weren't Orlando and Jada speaking up? They were taking this odd disruption in stride.

"You haven't been competing against other amateur cooks," Jason said. "These are professionals."

"Ugh," Sherry said. "My worst fear."

"Not professional cooks. These are professional actors."

"What?" Sherry was stunned.

All of the original competitors from day one of the cook-off assembled behind Sherry's grill.

"I don't understand." Sherry set her food down on her prep table. Her voice softened. "Is anyone going to try my food? It's piping hot." She smiled at the faces in front of her.

"We can't wait to, but first things first," Jason said. "Sherry, this cook-off journey has been about you. It is a celebration of you as a successful cooking competitor, recipe innovator, and most importantly, a most valuable member of your hometown, Augustin. Some would go as far as to say you are the most relished citizen in Augustin."

The production crew, cooks, and any remaining soul in the area gathered around the perimeter of the veranda. Sherry's hands flew up to her face. She could barely feel her cheeks. All the blood must have drained out of them.

"Over the last few days things haven't been what they appeared to be."

"That sounds familiar," Sherry muttered. "Where did I hear those words recently?" She was having trouble sorting through her foggy thoughts.

"We've crafted scenarios to test a person's character to the limits and expose them for who they really are. You are that person, thanks to many nominations from friends and family. When *Relish* began the search for someone who consistently and selflessly displays the qualities of empathy, selflessness, recipe ingenuity, and warmth we got a vote for you. Then another and another, until we had to close nominations to count all your votes. It wasn't even close. It was a landslide."

"Is this real? Is this not a cook-off?" Sherry asked, her voice no more than a mouse squeak.

"Yes, you been competing in a real cook-off, but that was only one qualification of *Relish*. The judges had to relish your food and your community had to relish you. By community, I mean Augustin and your fellow cook-off contestants. We knew they did because they nominated you. But would a bunch of competitive strangers bring out the best in you, too?"

The camera operator swung the lens in Sherry's direction. "I don't know what to say. I had a notion there was something very different about this cook-off, but I couldn't put my finger on what it was."

Jada, Orlando and Silvia waved to Sherry from the crowd while the camera panned the gathering. The rest of the original cook-off participants, dressed in festive beachwear, made a point of pushing in close to the camera's range.

"Were any of them cooks?" Sherry pointed to the individuals she thought were fellow competitors.

"They were actors," Jason said. "They were good, weren't they?"

"Amazing. I love them all." A tear dripped from Sherry's eye.

"Your instincts to question the concept of the cook-off were correct," Jason said.

"Still, I had no idea." Sherry used the back of her hand to dab her nose.

"I'd like to introduce the viewing audience to the man next to me, Basil Sturges, the creator and executive producer for the *Relish* production," Jason said.

"Thank you, Jason. And thank you, Sherry," Basil said.

Sherry tossed her hands skyward, not knowing what else to do.

"Sherry, there is a reality show running on cable television about a man who believes he's selected for jury duty. As the show unfolds, he's put through a series of character tests. He comes through with flying colors. I took creative license with that concept and applied it to creating a three-day series shadowing you as you are put through character test after character test. Why a cook-off? We wanted to make sure you were in your most challenging environment. One where you'd be forced to dig in and compete. Maybe then you'd crack. But, no. You blossomed.

"This production celebrates a person who works tirelessly for family, community and for her own betterment. She even solves murder mysteries in her spare time. I wanted to relish the idea behind Labor Day by honoring you as Augustin's hardest-working citizen. We have the mayor of Augustin here to present you with the key to the city. And let's not forget the twenty-thousand-dollar check for you, and one in the same amount for the local charity of your choice."

"This is incredible." Three words were all Sherry could articulate. She'd helped a few cooks along the way, Silvia, Jada and Orlando included. She was certain she had broken an unwritten rule in cook-offs, aiding a fellow competitor. For that she was being honored. This was crazy. It was a good framework for a television reality show, something she never thought she'd be part of in a million years. Cook-offs fell outside the genre of reality TV, until they didn't.

Mayor Drew stepped forward and handed Sherry a golden box tied with sparkling gold ribbon. She shook his hand and stared at the box, which presumably contained the fabled key to the city.

"Will this get me out of parking tickets?" she asked.

The mayor's charismatic good looks were accentuated when he flashed a brilliant smile. "Very good. And the answer is no. Thank you for all you do for Augustin, but we still need the parking violations income. You have more than enough money now to cover any fines. Congratulations." He flicked his thick bangs back into place with a suave toss of his head before swaggering out of camera range.

"No one's really sure what lock the key fits into, but since you're known for your amateur sleuthing, among so many other hobbies, you of all folks should be able to crack the case." Basil laughed at his wit.

"I do love a good mystery," Sherry said.

"Sherry, please accept the checks for showing the strength of character to stay true to yourself, even at the cost of your beloved hobby." Jason was handed an oversized cardboard check made out to Sherry Oliveri for twenty thousand dollars. He passed it across to Sherry. She grasped the top edge and held it steady for the camera shot. "Do you have a charity in mind you'd like to forward the second check to?"

"The Augustin Community Garden," Sherry said without hesitation. "We'd like to expand the garden to a younger set of patrons to teach them how to steward the earth for the future."

Behind the squatting cameraman Kat clasped her hands together and pumped them over her head.

"Consistent with your selflessness," Basil said. "Thank you, Sherry, and thank you all for making this a wonderfully successful surprise. Actors, go home and work on the kitchen skills you learned for your roles. They'll come in handy in your lives. Look where those skills got Sherry." He paused and announced a wrap. The camera's red light faded and Sherry exhaled.

Someone patted Sherry on the back. "Nice job, Sherry. We had a blast playing the role of fellow cook-off cooks. Did we have you fooled? I took cooking lessons before I even auditioned for the role," Orlando said. "Taming the kitchen beast is hard. I envy your natural talent."

"Me, too," Jada said. She gave Sherry a hug. "I loved the premise to give a deserving person, well, what she deserves."

"Now you know how I knew you played tennis," Silvia said. "We all read your profile and it's impressive. The number of hobbies you have can't leave you much time in a day."

"I love to stay busy. I'm glad to know you didn't really quit the cook-off. You didn't, did you?"

Silvia smiled. "You guessed it. It was yet another test for you to pass and you did."

"What if I hadn't offered you guys help?" Sherry asked. "The show would be a disaster because you all were counting on me behaving a certain way."

"And weren't we right? Have you ever declined anyone in need?" Kat asked from behind Jada. "The *Relish* team didn't choose you on a whim. Now you know why the mayor has been holding back his newsletter article. He wanted to write all about this before he leaves town for vacation."

"You were acting, too?" Sherry asked.

"Not exactly. I didn't know the true premise until filming began," Kat said.

"Excuse me, everyone," Basil said. "The heat is getting to me." He stepped aside, his legs buckling as he did.

"Huh," Mick said. "Are you okay?"

"Let's get you some water," Stacy said. She ran toward the water table.

Garrett supported Basil's elbow as he led him to a folding chair. Before he sat, Basil vomited. Sherry cringed when she heard his moans.

"Working too hard," Mick said.

"Guys, we need to get Basil to a doctor. He refuses to have us call for an ambulance but he's really going downhill fast," Stacy said. "He said it was something he ate."

Chapter 23

The walk back to the beach parking lot was an effort thanks to the heat of the late afternoon. The lingering high from the cook-off's outcome kept her energy up and her stride light. Sherry took her time crossing the sun-drenched sand dunes. She was in no rush. She stayed on after the cook-off to give Garrett a departing interview and tie up some loose ends. She didn't feel the need to rush home since she wasn't permitted to notify anyone of the cook-off's twist and turns. The confidentiality agreement was in effect until the air date, which was Labor Day weekend. Keeping the outcome quiet was going to require self-censorship Sherry wondered if she was capable of. That would be the ultimate character test, she mused to herself.

Kat strode alongside Sherry as they made their way back to their cars. "Sherry, I can't thank you enough for the contribution to the children's community garden."

"My pleasure. I'm as excited as you for the project to be expanded."

Kat turned and studied Sherry. "Did you forget the key to the city?"

"I would never forget that prize. The box is in my bag." Sherry lifted her canvas summer tote. "The giant checks are going to be dropped off at my house before dinnertime Stacy told me."

"I'm glad I was able to keep the secret of the cook-off concept under wraps. At first, I was put off that I wasn't in on the entire concept of the production beyond the cook-off until filming began. In hindsight, it was for the best."

"Kat, you are the best secret keeper I know. Besides myself," Sherry said with a giggle.

"We were pressing so hard for Mayor Drew to get his article written I'm shocked he didn't tell me sooner so I would stop demanding he get the darn thing done. He had plenty of chances to spill the beans."

"I changed my mind. Mayor Drew might be the best secret keeper."

"Hah," Kat laughed. "The show was one big communal character test."

"Speaking of spilling the beans, I need to text Eileen and ask her if she wouldn't mind telling your mother I'm not able to give the results of the cook-off yet. That's not going to go over well. The two have been so supportive of my success. They'll expect an update."

"No worries there. I've already texted my mom and told her as much. She'll pass on the information, or lack thereof, to Eileen."

"Thanks. I dread the lecture I'd get if Eileen knew anything before Hazel, or vice versa," Sherry said.

"Mom is Mom. She'll find something else to feel left out about," Kat said.

"What do you make of Basil getting sick just as the cook-off wrapped?" Sherry said. "Interesting timing."

"I have an update on Basil. The mayor got a text from Mick. Basil made it to the hospital," Kat said. "When they cleared his stomach contents, they found evidence of a toxic plant, often mistaken for mint. He'll be fine and discharged very soon."

"That plant was in the meadow," Sherry said. "My guide called it a mint plant impostor. I was cautioned before I made the same mistake."

"*Juicy Bites* warned, beware of plant impostors," Kat said. "The *Juicy Bites* author has struck? He or she was here?"

"If it's true there are no coincidences, it sure seems like the case. Problem is, Basil went to each cook's station and sampled their recipes in progress. All of ours. The camera followed him."

"A plant that was foraged is the culprit," Kat said. "Has to be." Kat came to a stop. "Do you think it wasn't an accident?"

"Do you?" Sherry countered. She hoped Kat may share any nugget of information she was safeguarding.

"Maybe," Kat said. "Or a warning."

"A warning? For Basil? How did the *Juicy Bites* author know the warning would be delivered in that fashion. Could the author also be the murderer and feels the walls closing in?"

"If Basil needed to be warned, he should take it as such," Kat said. "There are other areas he's becoming overbearing in. He needs to be careful of becoming more of a bully than a boss. Stacy and Mick's patience with his style of leadership is wearing thin. I don't understand why they put up with his nonsense. Who knows who else is feeling his wrath. I thought after Rachel was gone the team's spirit would pick up. I was wrong."

"There was that much discontent on the team?" Sherry asked.

"From what I observed, yes. There was plenty of friction between Basil and Rachel. Rachel was always challenging Basil's authority, often grumbling about doing Mick's job along with her own duties. For his part, I'm amazed he put up with her negativity. It was one big dysfunctional family."

Sherry and Kat resumed their walk.

"Garrett was foraging today," Sherry said. "Without a guide. What's the chance he unwittingly poisoned Basil?"

Kat sighed. "You're really asking, what is the chance Garrett had every intention of poisoning Basil? No. Garrett was at the wrong place at the wrong time. I realize you've got some fodder for suspicion, but Garrett didn't poison Basil."

"I want to believe you. I want evidence that proves that without a shadow of a doubt. I want Detective Bease to strike both of you off his list. The problem is, Garrett's entrenched on my list. He's made himself front and center because he's always with the production team, so he knows the ins and outs. He recites *Juicy Bites* blurbs as if they are his personal vocabulary. Do you think he has a problem with Basil?"

"The more I try to put these pieces together the more there seem to be extra pieces that don't fit," Kat said. "Do I really know Garrett as well as I should? As much as I'm not agreeing with you that he is somehow involved, I have some doubts as to his innocence. Your sleuthing isn't making me feel any more comfortable around him."

The sound of quickening footsteps behind Sherry caught her attention. She turned and was met with a panting runner approaching.

"Hey, ladies. Sounds like Basil's going to be alright," Garrett said. "I feel awful about giving him what I thought was mint. He was so interested in tasting my forage harvest he devoured a handful."

"Do you still have the offending collection sack?" Sherry asked.

"No. The team was told by poison control to confiscate the sack." Garrett shook his head. "I should have heeded the warning the universe gave me not to accept Basil's interest in having a taste of my harvest."

"What do you mean?" Sherry asked.

"I had left the sack on the water table after I marked it with my name. I went back to find it and it was nowhere to be found. I searched a bit longer and finally found it on a chair. I had to go out of my way to find Basil when I should have let the moment pass."

"Sounds like a misstep on everyone's part," Kat said.

"It would have made more sense the other way around," Garrett said. "He'd love to poison me."

"Why is that?" Sherry asked. "I thought you two were working well together."

"We were until now. I've reconsidered my role. I'm sure Basil has me in his crosshairs. I've decided to tell the story of the production in all its ugly glory and I let him know before filming began today. I know that's not what he signed up for, but I have a reputation to defend."

Sherry caught Kat's eye and with a wriggle of her brows sent her a message to bookmark Garrett's statement.

"Got to go," Garrett said. "The story's second ending hasn't been written yet. Kat, I'll call you. Sherry, congratulations again."

When Garrett was out of sight the silence between Kat and Sherry ended.

"Can you explain what Garrett's talking about?" Sherry asked. "Isn't he promoting Feral Creations' work?"

Kat dragged the toe of her sandal across the boardwalk. "Garrett's been caught between a rock and a hard place. Did you know Mick came up with the idea for the cook-off program?"

"I don't think that's the case. Wasn't Basil the creator? His title as creative director says as much."

"Nope," Kat said. "Mick was the one who saw a cable television series about the man called to jury duty. He was subsequently and unknowingly put through a series of character tests and proved himself an honest to goodness role model. Mick approached Basil with the idea to find a deserving citizen in a small town to put through a series of character challenges. Mick was into the idea of putting more feel-good stories on television. The cook-off angle of your story was icing on the cake."

"I don't see why Basil wouldn't give Mick the credit. Basil could still be the executive producer."

"Ego, most likely," Kat said. "This isn't known beyond the production team. I don't even know if Rachel was aware. Basil wanted to get through the filming while maintaining his leadership post to ensure there wasn't a mutiny. Another example of his lack of quality leadership."

"Did Garrett tell you all that?" Sherry asked.

"You guessed it. He's been told not to include that nugget in any articles about the show, for obvious reasons."

"How did Garrett find out about Basil pirating Mick's idea?" Sherry asked.

"When Garrett began his article on Feral Creations Mick had recently returned from medical leave. The rebranding of the company started immediately and that depended strongly on having a sound project goal waiting for a start date. His interview with Mick, whose second chance at life would be highlighted in the yet-to-be published article, revealed Mick came up with his version of the feel-good concept and Basil praised the idea as brilliant. That was until talk in industry journals described what little they knew of the upcoming project as having multiple chances of receiving huge award recognition for its uniqueness. Basil turned on a dime and according to Mick refused him any credit whatsoever."

"Mick needs to stand up for himself. And Garrett should stand up for Mick, too," Sherry said. "Why are those two things a problem?"

"I think they both should step up. Give credit where credit's due," Kat said with a shrug. "The problem is the dog-eat-dog culture of getting ahead, as opposed to being insignificant, in the television industry. In the industry you're only as valuable as your last success. Garrett wants more than anything to help give Mick a leg up by crediting him with the concept of *Relish*, but Basil hired Garrett so that's who he's really working for."

"Basil told Pep about the dog-eat-dog culture in his business. Who knew he was talking about himself? Garrett needs to tell the truth in his article or at least get the message across to Basil he doesn't agree with his business tactics," Sherry said.

"I only told you about Mick being the rightful creator of *Relish* so you'd understand how I've needed to tiptoe around the last few weeks. If I turn one way, I'm spilling secrets and risking the future of a television project so many are depending on the success of. If I turn another way, I'm a suspect in Rachel's murder."

"The more you tell me the more complicated the story is becoming," Sherry said. "Garrett has the power to set some things straight."

"You're not giving Garrett credit for the risk he's taking," Kat said.

"He's making the right move. Mick deserves to be treated correctly. He's been taken advantage of. Why would he let this go on for so long? Mick's career will survive if Basil is outed. Basil's may not. When someone feels that level of pressure, there's no telling how they'll lash out if they have no outlet."

"Like the lid of a pressure cooker that isn't secured well. Ka-boom," Kat said.

Chapter 24

"Dad, hi! How was your trip?" Sherry made a beeline to her father and gave him a hug. "Have you been here all day? Is Amber here?" She scanned the Ruggery showroom for her coworker.

"Wow, slow down, young lady. You're all revved up and raring to go. I'm still in vacation mode."

"Dad, you're never in vacation mode. You entered work mode the day you were born. That's what Gran meant when she called you a busy bee baby."

"I did keep my dear mother frantic with all my projects. You're a chip off the old block with all your hobbies." Erno finished folding a hooked rug canvas. "I've heard dribs and drabs about the cook-off you were in. Three days long? Now that's a test of your culinary abilities. How was it? Amber couldn't provide many details."

"The cook-off's over and I'm gagged from announcing the winner. I feel like a corked bottle that someone shook up. I'm ready to blow." Sherry puffed out her cheeks.

"Please, don't. Ruth bought me this shirt in Nantucket and she'd send me packing back there if I got bits of you all over it." Erno laughed so hard he had to steady himself on the edge of the sales counter.

"Everyone needs to understand that's what television likes. All surprises. And I don't think you'll be disappointed. Tell me about your vacation with Ms. Gadabee."

"We had a very nice time, thank you. That's enough vacation for me for a while. I miss this place. Vacations are overrated and way too long if you want to know the truth. But my sweetie wanted me all to herself and who am I to say no to that."

Amber appeared from behind the stockroom door. "Sherry? The store's closing in fifteen minutes. That's the shortest shift in history, but thanks for coming in."

"Very funny. I was on my way home from the cook-off, which I can't talk about until it airs week after next, and I wanted to let you know face-to-face I'll be opening the store tomorrow and staying until closing time." Sherry gave herself a golf clap.

"I was hoping you'd say that. I have a few appointments I need to be at," Amber said. "Since you can't talk about the cook-off, are you making headway in the murder investigation?"

"Whoa, whoa, whoa," Erno commanded. "I've been back for half a day and no one bothered to mention anything about a murder. Would someone care to explain?"

"I feel like that's all we've talked about for the last week," Sherry said. "The short version of the story is one of the television production crew was murdered right after you went on vacation. Filming hadn't begun and she was replaced. The body was found at the Augustin Garage between two trucks. She'd been hit by one of those clapboards used to earmark scene footage."

"Gruesome," Erno said. "I wish you hadn't told me."

Sherry sighed and turned back to Amber. "To answer your question, Amber, maybe. Nothing concrete, yet."

"Troy said he saw you at the police station," Amber said.

"He was very helpful."

"And was *Juicy Bites* right about things not being what they seem?" Amber asked.

"Absolutely. At least when it comes to the cook-off."

"Sher, your phone is ringing," Erno said.

"Thanks, Dad." Sherry reached in her purse and answered the call. "Ray?"

"Sherry," Ray said. "I pulled the accident report. I have a question for you."

"Yes?"

"The driver of the car was killed. He was ejected when the car rolled. The car landed on its side, making it very difficult for him to be extricated. Augustin EMT did a stellar job saving lives. Rachel suffered a concussion. Basil Sturges was the luckiest, only scratches and bruises." Ray spent a moment in silence.

Sherry waited patiently in anticipation of the question.

"When you spoke to the Feral Creations team as a unit, before Rachel's death, you remarked they worked well together. I have uncovered a discrepancy in that assessment. Not everyone had the others' backs."

"I've come across the same sentiment. And what's your question?" Sherry said.

"At the time of the car accident, Troy's partner documented that Rachel Yaro stated Mick was driving the car. A statement from Basil Sturges quoted him as saying the driver was the man who was ejected. Basil would have been the most credible since Rachel was knocked out briefly and may have been disoriented. She had trouble verbalizing where she thought she was."

"I would tend to believe Basil. If Rachel had been knocked out, she'd have a cloudy memory."

"I imagine there was conflict when two versions of the story were told to the attending officer," Ray said. "The team would certainly have had some post-accident discussion about the recall."

"Was Mick unconscious, too?" Sherry asked. "Why wasn't his version in the report?"

"He was out of it. Nonverbal at the time. Pinpointing the driver at the scene was important at the time because everyone had been celebrating to excess the completion of a project except the driver. He tested sober. If anyone else had been driving they could be guilty of manslaughter if charges were brought," Ray said.

"That's a lot to consider," Sherry said.

"I did a follow-up with the medical center who treated the car passengers. Mick Snider was sitting in the front seat. He and the driver suffered the most severe injuries because of the trajectory of the car's skid. Basil was in the back left and not hurt at all. Rachel knocked her head because she wasn't wearing a seat belt," Ray said. "My question is: What did you hope to learn from the accident report? Why did you ask about it in the first place?"

"I wanted to get a picture of the scene that put Mick in such a vulnerable state for most of the year. The accident was the reason Garrett Stein entered the picture, along with Yonny. It changed a lot of dynamics for Feral Creations. I wondered if Rachel was put in a position where her role changed in terms of the team. One where she was at odds with another member."

"Basil Sturges?" Ray asked.

"Why do you say him?" Sherry asked.

"He's the boss. Rachel relayed to him she wasn't satisfied with her pay based on her responsibilities. He gave her the assignment to organize and prep the production clapboards the morning she was murdered."

"That assignment put her in the wrong place at the wrong time," Sherry said.

"Those are the facts," Ray said.

"Only one detail missing," Sherry said.

Ray answered Sherry's challenge. "The murderer."

Chapter 25

Thursday's alarm went off at such an unreasonable hour Sherry thought she was dreaming the shrill wail.

"What time is it?" Don asked.

"Five. You can go back to sleep. What time should I reset the alarm for?" Sherry asked. Her groggy state cleared as she considered the mission ahead.

"Five forty-five, thanks. Love you," Don said as he drifted back to sleep.

Sherry was meeting Kat at the coffee shop one block from the Augustin Garage. Pep had given her every indication the napkins were never delivered earlier than six fifteen and never later than six thirty. She had a very specific window of opportunity. They'd catch the deliverer in the act and identify the author of the napkins if they got to the location by six oh five.

Sherry was astounded by the large number of Coffee Buzz's clientele at such an early hour. She purchased a coffee with milk and turned to look for Kat.

"Sherry. Over here," Kat called out. She was seated in a booth by the front window sipping a steaming beverage.

"Good morning, Kat. Now I know what I've been missing by sleeping to a reasonable hour most mornings. Wow! So many early risers. What's the plan?"

"We have our phones to snap a picture," Kat said between sips. "It's going to be close to sunup but still poor lighting. We're going to have to get very close to make a definitive ID."

"We have six minutes to get over there." Sherry peered out the store window. The developing sunrise was stingy providing daylight. She could make out Pep's truck parked at the garage a block away.

"What if the person spots us, doesn't take our surveillance well and fights back? What's plan B? The one where our safety is paramount," Kat said.

Sherry placed her phone on the table. "I have 911 on speed dial. We're not going to try to win a physical battle. I figure if we catch the person red-handed, and I mean with hands full of napkins, we'll have the upper hand, so to speak. Timing will be everything."

Kat heaved an exhale. "Okay. I'm all caffeined up and ready to see what we see." She picked up her empty cup and slid out of the Naugahyde-covered bench seat.

"I'm right behind you," Sherry said. She had half a serving left in her cup but the agitation in her stomach dictated she was done.

Both women wore hooded sweatshirts for protection against the morning chill and for the anonymity a raised hood provides.

"We look like a couple of subpar burglars," Kat said with a nervous laugh. "Stay within arm's reach."

They crossed the coffee shop parking lot and stepped over a row of low-growing boxwoods. The darkened garage complex was on their right. A few cars needing body work were parked alongside the gas pumps, blocking access to the nozzles during off-hours. Two truck bodies minus the cabs held prime spots along the far property line. Toasts of the Town was parked at a ninety-degree angle in front of the truck bodies. Sherry stopped Kat before either set foot on the garage's driveway.

"Where do you think the camera is?" Sherry saw nothing resembling a security camera.

"Maybe that," Kat said. She pointed to a mirrored globe secured onto the roof of the mini-mart building. "Gotta be."

"It's far from the big trucks and Toasts of the Town. No wonder the images weren't great. I don't think it'll catch us decisively either. Pull up your hood anyway. Ready to continue?"

"Ready," Kat said.

There was one light mounted on an electrical pole struggling to maintain a flickering ray over the trucks. Visibility was difficult at best with the light variations and wavering shadows cast around the vehicles. They approached Pep's truck slowly.

"There's nothing on the windshield. What time is it?" Kat asked.

Sherry pulled her phone from her pocket. "Six twelve. We need to duck between the truck bodies. Not too far in or we won't see the person."

Sherry and Kat shimmied between Pep's truck and the front of the production trucks. They turned a right angle and wedged in between the two tractor-trailer beds. There they took up their positions, pressing their backs against the cold metal walls of the truck. Pep's truck was partially in sight.

"What's that noise?" Kat asked.

"Someone's coming already," Sherry whispered. "They're early. Get ready."

Sherry was in front of Kat and the first to attempt a better look around the corner of the truck. The crunching of shoes against the loose driveway debris grew louder. Sherry only saw an oversized shadow lit from two sides. She couldn't tell how close the person was to Pep's truck.

"We have to get closer," Sherry whispered. "I can't see from here."

The only option was to get dangerously close to Pep's truck. She clutched Kat's arm in case there was any chance of her changing her mind and hightailing it out of the area. As they relocated, Sherry ducked down lower than the food truck's fender and motioned for Kat to do the same. Crouching while watching where they were going proved a tall task, and when Sherry collided with the side mirror the jig was up.

"Who's there?"

Kat gasped.

Sherry squealed. "Hazel. What are you doing here?"

Sherry and Kat straightened up.

"Mom? What's going on?"

"I'm thinking the same thing. What are you two doing here?" Hazel was dressed for a ladies' lunch. She wore scallop-edged white pants and a flowy turquoise shirt. She would be an easy target to identify on video, even if only her silhouette was captured. Her coiffed updo alone was a dead giveaway.

"Are those *Juicy Bites* napkins in your hand? Are you the *Juicy Bites* author?" Kat's tone was incredulous. "This can't be happening. You could cost me my job."

"Me? I'd say you two being here at first light is evidence enough who the authors are."

"We can explain, Hazel."

"I'll do it for you. You two are in cahoots to find the author, admit it," Hazel scolded.

Hazel's fiery proclamation had the opposite effect on Sherry. "That's right. Did we find her?" Sherry asked with a smile. "What are those?" She eyed the papers in Hazel's hand.

One glance down and Hazel's tone lightened up. "Yes, I do have a delivery of napkins here."

"Mom, you can't involve yourself in everyone else's business. You need to let events unfold on their own, without you forcing the issue," Kat said. "You're going to get hurt."

"Are you talking about *Juicy Bites* or Garrett Stein?" Hazel said. "I've heard from everyone else but you that I've made a love connection between you and that young man." Hazel gave Kat time to comment. The moment passed in silence. "You're welcome."

"I would rather you stay out of any love connection. That's not what I'm referring to in this case."

"Message received, dear," Hazel said.

"Let me give you one piece of advice, Mom," Kat said. "Wear a hat or hood next time you're sneaking about in the predawn hours and don't want to be identified. Maybe a gray sweatsuit to blend in."

"I can't have hat hair, dear," Hazel said. "It takes all day to get the kinks out. And I look washed out in gray."

All heads jerked in reaction to a bang followed by a shuttering vibration. Any rebuttal in the mother-daughter banter was put on pause. A thin beam of light traced the edge of the truck.

"Someone's coming around the side of the truck," Sherry whispered. "Hazel, get over here."

Hazel slid in beside the women. She pinched her face tight when she peered at the dusty truck walls. "My white pants will be ruined."

Kat put her hand up to her mother's mouth to stifle any noise she might make. All Sherry could think to do was wave the others down to their knees and hope they weren't spotted. The sun was making a fast entrance and in about ten minutes they wouldn't be under the cover of semi-darkness anymore. From her low vantage point Sherry saw a shadowy figure lift itself onto the food truck's driver-side bump step. The foot was misplaced and slipped off the grooved rubber cover. A raspy curse word flew out of the hooded person's mouth as a knee whacked the corner of the truck.

"I recognize that voice. Garrett? Is that you?" Kat called out.

A second knock to the knee incited another foul word. "Who's there? Kat?"

The squatting group righted themselves while Hazel was left struggling.

"Help me up, Kat. I'm stuck," Hazel said. Kat reached forward and hoisted her mother out of her crouch.

"And Hazel and Sherry," Garrett said. "Want to explain what you're doing here?"

Garrett's flashlight lit his path as he stepped down from the bump step. He closed in on the women huddled alongside one of the two big rigs' container beds.

"What am I doing here?" Garrett echoed.

Kat shone her light on Garrett's face. He was sporting a smirk.

"I certainly didn't get the invitation to join the predawn truck parking lot party. I'm glad I had the foresight to show up. Would anyone care to explain what I almost missed?"

"I'll go first," Hazel said. "I'm here because my daughter needs help and

I want to get the message out. I'm going to put this stack of napkins under the food truck's windshield wiper, and someone's going to read the message and come forward with information about Rachel Yaro's murder. I don't know what you all are here for, but if one of you youngsters wouldn't mind providing me a leg up to reach the wipers, I'd be grateful."

"There won't be much room since my stack is going up there first," Garrett said. "The stack would be up there already if I didn't have trouble with my footing. I have a message that needs to get out in a hurry. Don't worry, Hazel. I think we're both aiming to keep Kat off of Detective Bease's suspect list. And me, too." He shone his flashlight on Kat. "Kat? Sherry? You didn't come with Hazel?"

"We didn't," Kat said. "We had no idea she'd be the *Juicy Bites* author."

Kat and Sherry held one another's gaze until Hazel broke the silence.

"And do you two gals have *Juicy Bites* napkins to add to the pile?" Hazel asked.

"No. That's not why we're here. We're on a mission to find out the identity of the *Juicy Bites* author," Sherry said. "We think it's the best route to uncovering Rachel Yaro's killer before someone else gets hurt. The author had timely insight into the *Relish* production along with warnings and veiled clues. What we found here is two people taking on the role of the *Juicy Bites* author. One or both of you don't belong here. Which one of you has been supplying the napkins since Rachel's death?"

"Mom? I have every reason to believe you're not the *Juicy Bites* author. The first being you don't like paper napkins. The second being you can't even reach the windshield wipers to place the napkins where they're always found," Kat said.

"I'm offended you don't think I have what it takes to put this puzzle together day after day," Hazel countered. "Let me read you today's passage." Hazel handed the stack of napkins over to Sherry, reserving one, which she unfolded. "Shine that flashlight over here, will you, please, dear?"

Garrett fumbled with his napkin supply as he adjusted his phone to illuminate Hazel's napkin.

"Mom, that's computer paper cut into squares. Not at all the same as a napkin. People would get paper cuts if they blotted their mouths with those.

"Dear, let me read the message."

Chapter 26

She cooks off and solves murder mysteries. She has the evidence and today is judgment day.

"Mom, you can't say that if it's not true," Kat said. "Especially if the cook you're referring to is Sherry. She doesn't have the needed evidence to pinpoint the person who killed Rachel. That's why we're here."

Hazel pursed her lips as she considered what her daughter proposed. "Think about it, honey. If I put that out there, the bad guy will surely come forward with hands raised and give up. He or she needs to know Sherry's on the case."

"Your scheme may be applicable to a movie script, but doubtful in real life. You're putting Sherry in danger by insinuating she knows the identity of someone who is capable of murder and hasn't been caught."

"I appreciate what your intentions are," Sherry said.

"Okay. I should rephrase the napkins," Hazel said.

"Or don't put them out at all?" Kat said.

"Maybe you're right," Hazel said.

"One *Juicy Bites* author impostor down, one to go," Kat said. "Garrett? Are you the real *Juicy Bites* author? You've told me over and over you're not and now here you're delivering napkins to Pep's truck. Sherry was right. You're not to be trusted."

Garrett huffed a breath. "Sherry said I wasn't to be trusted?"

Sherry shrugged. "Not exactly. I did suggest you may not be innocent of wrongdoing. You haven't done much to convince me otherwise. Now you've been caught red-handed."

"I'm wasting my breath denying what's going on here. As the napkins have said, 'things aren't what they seem,'" Garrett said.

"See what I mean?" Sherry said. "You speak their language."

"May I see a napkin, please." Kat's tone was icy.

Garrett offered Kat the entire stack.

"Ouch, you're on my foot," Kat cried out.

"Sorry, not the greatest lighting here."

Kat pinched a napkin from Garrett's hand and unfolded it.

Juicy Bites

Payback becomes murder when secrets drive someone to blackmail. You've been warned.

"Care to explain?" Kat asked.

"Honey, you're being hard on the young man," Hazel said. "He's trying to move this investigation along the same as you, Sherry, and I."

"That's alright, Hazel," Garrett said. "I understand where Kat's coming from. My message is for the person who is blackmailing Mick Snider."

"Blackmailing?" Hazel asked.

"I have every reason to believe there is a secret among the Feral Creations team that's keeping Mick paralyzed with fear and may have caused Rachel her life."

"Garrett, do you think Basil has a lock on his team by holding valuable information that could damage their reputations?" Kat asked.

"That's where the napkins come in. I thought if I set them out today before the team departs, someone may be motivated to speak up."

"Did you hear that?" Sherry whispered.

Before anyone could move, the screech of rusty hinges pierced the air.

"Someone's in the truck," Garrett said.

"Duck down," Hazel hissed.

Sherry raised her hand to stall any further conversation. "Too late."

"Is this a party I didn't get an invitation to?" A figure donning a baseball cap stepped out of the production truck. "I'm trying to get some work done and all I can hear are voices. It's usually peaceful except for mourning doves at this time of the day."

"Good morning, Basil." Sherry surveyed the scene: Four people, besides Basil, wedged between two trucks, boxed in by a food truck. What must he think? "We can explain."

"I'm all ears," Basil said. "You've got the floor, Sherry."

"The cook-off's over and the production team will be moving on soon. Some of us feel Rachel's death may be connected to someone on the crew. Someone she worked with. Someone who has either been putting out the *Juicy Bites* napkins or has an investment in the napkins helping to ferret out the murderer."

"While I'd like to find the killer to clear the stigma around the production, and of course to avenge Rachel's death, I don't think the napkins had any impact. Sorry, Rachel," Basil said. He glanced skyward. "I hope *your* plan works. Was there a need for all of you to come? Garrett, Kat, and . . . you seem very familiar. I've seen you many times in the hallway at Augustin's town hall."

"This is my mother, Hazel Riordan. Mom, this is Basil Sturges. He's producing the cook-off show."

Hazel reached up to the top of her head. "Excuse my appearance. I got up so early this morning I didn't finish my full beauty routine."

"I can see even in the dim light you're as lovely as your daughter," Basil said.

"Thank you, sir," Hazel said. "You're very kind."

"Garrett, is this adventure going in the production story?" Basil asked.

Sherry detected sarcasm in his tone.

"Only if it pertains," Garrett said.

"Are those *Juicy Bites* napkins in your hand?" Basil asked.

"My attempt at them, yes." Garrett held up his stack.

"May I see?" He reached his open palm toward Garrett.

Basil read the words. "Blackmail. Interesting." He took extra time to refold the napkin before placing it on the stack Garrett held. "Mick was emotionally blackmailing Rachel. Did you know that?"

"I believe it was the other way around," Kat said. "Rachel had Mick by the throat."

"You're wrong," Basil said. "I have every reason to believe Rachel was being taken advantage of by Mick."

"How so? It seemed to me they were a cooperative team," Sherry said.

"Rachel complained to me several times how much slack she was picking up because of Mick's injuries. She felt he held his condition over her head— emotional blackmail. She told me it doesn't pay to be nice. She meant it in a literal sense," Basil said.

"Have you considered you've created a toxic work culture at Feral Creations? One based on bullying and secrets," Garrett said. "You could have stopped Mick's behavior if it hindered the cook-off's success. Instead you seem to endorse the bad behavior by taking advantage of Mick yourself."

"Garrett, you're forcing my hand. And your *Juicy Bites* says a warning has been issued. You poisoned me. Was that a form of payback for something I did that you didn't approve of? That's a strong warning that you appear to be confessing to." Basil held a prolonged stare at Garrett.

"I'd never let you blackmail me so I would never need to warn you with poison. Give me more credit than that," Garrett said. "And if I knew your secrets I'd the first to share them if it saved a life."

"I'll no longer need your services," Basil said. "And I'm considering pressing charges against you for bodily harm. Please send me your final product up to this point. As our contract agreement specifies, if I don't approve of the content, it may not be published anywhere. My lawyers made that stipulation ironclad." He dusted off his hands. "It's getting late. Is the party over?"

Chapter 27

Juicy Bites

A winner, a key, a lock, a clue. The hammer's down.
Caution: The biggest loser now walks among us.

"How could these napkins have been delivered while we were there?" Kat asked. "It's impossible."

"Whoever was waiting for the delivery opportunity was very patient," Sherry said. "Probably amused while we hashed out which one of us was the culprit."

"Pep, what time did you pick up Toasts of the Town at the garage this morning?" Kat asked.

Pep peered down from the service window as he closed the lid of a toast container. "I'd say around seven, give or take a few minutes. Funny thing was, there were so many footprints around the truck. Something must have gone on last night over there. Maybe Feral Creations went through their trucks."

"Pep, I've decided on my order, and it wasn't easy," Kat said. "I'll have the bacon, onion jam, sheep cheese crisp and fried egg toast. Or as you so humorously named it, the Yokes on Ewe. Sherry, what do you want?"

"Choosing is getting harder and harder. You must stay up at night thinking of your next menu items." She studied the words in chalk on the menu slate. "Okay, I'll have the Seedy Side Toast with peanut butter, not almond butter, please."

"That was my second choice," Kat said. "Crunchy peanut or almond butter, warm and spread on toast topped with fresh strawberry slices and pomegranate seeds with a shower of granola dust. Maple syrup optional. Yum."

"I'll call you when your toasts are ready. Have a seat until then," Pep said.

"I'm over the moon I had my first victory against you today," Sherry said as they found an empty bench near the truck. "I'm not celebrating too hard because I know you have a sore toe from getting stepped on by Garrett this morning."

"Hey, a win is a win," Kat said. "Do you think this morning was a waste of time? Not the tennis but the truck surveillance."

"Absolutely not," Sherry said.

"Okay, then, what was the takeaway?" Kat asked.

"We learned neither Garrett nor your mom writes *Juicy Bites*, although they tried to make a one-day appearance. Do you remember what the deal was if we didn't pinpoint the author?" Sherry asked.

"I don't go back on my word. Yes, I must talk to Detective Bease and tell him what I know and answer any questions he has, if I know the answers." Kat heaved a breath. "It might be a relief."

"Hi, ladies. Fancy meeting you here."

Sherry peered up and was met with the sunny smiles of Eileen and Hazel.

"Hi, Mom," Kat said with as much enthusiasm as she could muster, which wasn't much. "I thought we were Pep's best customers, but it really is you two."

"We do love his toasts. And Angel is so sweet. The combo makes for a great start to the day. Did you gals have a good tennis game?" Eileen asked. "You must have started very early. The headlights of your car woke me up before sunrise. How do you play before sunrise? Do they have lights at the park courts?"

"It's always a good game when I play Kat. I got lucky today. Kat has a sore toe. Maybe you should pull down your shades and you won't be woken up so early," Sherry suggested.

"It's not worth it. Imagine what I'd miss," Eileen said. "Let me go read the menu." Eileen headed to the truck, leaving Hazel behind.

"I haven't told Eileen what occurred this morning, but I have a feeling she's on to us. She has a seventh sense that reads my mind anytime I'm trying to withhold information." Hazel turned and waved to Eileen. "Be right there."

"You might want to see these new napkins, dear," Eileen called out.

"What? I thought . . ." Hazel began.

"That there wouldn't be a delivery today? We all thought wrong and they're not yours or Garrett's," Kat said.

"Well, I'll be darned," Hazel said.

Sherry's gaze traveled to Garrett as he neared. She monitored Kat's reaction to seeing her boyfriend after spending an interesting morning with him hours earlier.

"Is anyone happy to see me? I have some news." Garrett waited for anyone to jump in with a greeting.

"Hi, Garrett," Kat said. "I'm assuming you won't be at the final meeting with Feral Creations this morning."

"Basil texted and invited me. Color me surprised, to say the least. He claims it's only right I finish the assignment and he apologized for acting rashly this morning."

"That's surprising," Kat said. "If he was acting angry, he deserves an Oscar. Glad he came to his senses."

"Before we meet in the mayor's office, I'd like to share some of what else I'm working on." Garrett dipped his hand into his pants pocket.

"Good morning, all," Mayor Drew said as he passed by on his way to Toasts of the Town. "Garrett, I don't understand what's going on between you and Feral Creations, but I'm very sorry to have received a text saying you have been let go. Not a half hour later I received another text saying you're back in the game." He stalled his walk and shook Garrett's hand. "Would you like me to have a word of endorsement with Basil on your behalf? Couldn't hurt. It sounds as if you might need some moral support."

"I would like that," Kat said. "Basil's treating Garrett horribly. He's making him some sort of scapegoat."

"Atta girl," Hazel said. "Stick up for your man."

Kat's cheeks bloomed a rosy red. "He's not my man. I just think there's a wrong that should be made right."

The mayor turned his attention to his office manager. "Kat, I've had to move the meeting with Feral Creations to first thing per Basil's request. I'll need you to use your best stalling talents to hold the Committee for Curb Relief at bay for half an hour in your office. A group of four citizens is representing a push to lower the size of the in-town pavement curbs because of an epidemic of flat tires. Personally, I'd rather see flat tires than citizens jumping a low curb and ending up in the Silty Pretzel River that runs alongside most of downtown."

"Of course," Kat said. "I'll be in my office in a few minutes."

"See you there. Sherry, you know what I'd say to you if I didn't have a gag order on me." Mayor Drew winked, performed a salute and continued his way to the truck.

"What did he mean by that?" Hazel asked. "Does he know who won the cook-off? Who else knows?" Her tone blossomed into desperation.

"Kat and Sherry, your orders are up," Angel called out. *"Consíguelo mientras esté caliente"*

"Saved by the toast. You heard the man," Sherry said. "Get it while it's hot."

"Are you sticking around?" Kat asked Garrett. "We'd like to hear your news. I can share my toast with you."

"Can't say no to that. I don't have to be inside until you do," Garrett said with a sheepish grin. "I'll save seats."

"By the way, did you see today's napkins?" Kat asked.

"I don't need to see them," Garrett said with an air of confidence. "I put mine on Pep's windshield after everyone left. Sorry, Hazel, but I removed yours and replaced them with mine."

"Well. I never! You are a scoundrel, young man," Hazel said.

"Mom? You put yours up on the windshield after we left you? How in the world did you climb up there? I thought we decided yours would put Sherry in jeopardy," Kat scolded.

"Where there's a will, there's a way," Hazel said. "Getting up wasn't hard, it was getting down in one piece that was challenging. I almost fell before I managed to channel my inner gymnast to stick the landing. Who do you think you inherited your athletic prowess from?"

"Then how come neither of your versions are displayed at Pep's truck?" Kat asked.

"What do you mean? I just said I replaced Hazel's so-called napkins with mine," Garrett said.

"Unless you redid the message, the *Juicy Bites* napkins at Toasts currently aren't authored by either one of you two," Kat said. She handed Garrett a printed napkin. He scanned the message.

"I can explain why Hazel's aren't there. They're in the recycle bin at the garage. The same thing must have happened to my stack. They got replaced by author number three, whoever that is," Garrett said.

Hazel groaned her frustration.

"Hazel, are you coming?" Eileen called from Toasts of the Town.

"Yes, yes. On my way," Hazel called back.

"Come on, Mom," Kat said as she limped to the truck with Sherry.

When Sherry arrived at the service window Pep stuck out his hand to receive her credit card.

"Not so fast," Sherry said. "Maybe you didn't hear the news. I won today and Kat's paying."

Pep's jaw dropped. "Sorry, old habits die hard."

"Well, I'll be," Hazel said. "Isn't that unexpected."

"Okay, everyone, calm down. It was bound to happen sometime," Sherry said. She lowered her voice to a whisper. "Look who's coming. Hope this doesn't get awkward."

Heads turned to see Basil closing in. "Good morning. Everyone looks fresh as a daisy, as if they've been up for hours."

"That's an interesting observation," Eileen said. "And you're correct. How did you know Sherry's car's headlights woke me up very early this morning? How about you, Hazel?"

"I got up at the crack of dawn. Couldn't wait to start the day," Hazel said.

"Me, too," Basil said. "It's the last full day of work for Feral Creations in Augustin. I have plenty to do. This may be my last crack at Pep's toasts and I'm sure going to miss them. Right, Yonny?"

"Yes, sir," Yonny said as he sidled up to Basil. "Thanks for treating me to breakfast. I'm used to eating in the car. This is a nice change." Yonny greeted Sherry, Kat, and Hazel.

"Stacy and Mick were going to join us but there was a mix-up back at the trucks and I'm picking up their orders. Yonny's delivering them after he enjoys his out here. Today is going to be a crazy whirlwind to beat the clock. First, I have a meeting with the mayor to dot the i's and cross the t's on all the legal paperwork. Excuse me, folks. Have a good day." Basil nodded and led Yonny over to the line to place their orders.

Sherry and Kat left Hazel and Eileen to their own devices and rejoined Garrett at the bench.

"What did Basil have to say?" Garrett asked.

"He didn't say much, except he used the phrase 'beat the clock,' which I found telling," Kat said.

"What was it you wanted to share with us, Garrett?" Sherry asked.

Garrett waved the paper he had pulled from his pocket. "I've done some homework using what I consider key phrases from the *Juicy Bites* posts. Eat while I read you the list of words that caught my eye. Bear in mind what each word makes you think of first. Go from your gut."

Sherry opened her breakfast container and marveled at Pep and Angel's creation. Her first bite brightened her mood as soon as it hit her taste buds. Before Garrett could begin, Kat waved her toast in front of his face. The invitation was accepted. He moaned with satisfaction as he chewed.

"So good," Garrett said after a swallow. "Here's my list: murder, two-faced stories, two endings, beat the clock, nothing's as it seems, stick to a theme, blame game, explosive secret, impostors, key, lock, biggest loser walks among us."

"That's just about every word and phrase," Sherry said. She sighed, venting her frustration at the list's size.

"Those are the phrases I'm focusing on. I'm motivated more than ever to expose the person who murdered Rachel, especially if it's a Feral Creations employee. No one's safe until that happens."

"But Sherry just won their production's cook-off," Kat said. "That's one of the reasons I've been so reserved about speaking to the detective. If the culprit is a Feral Creations employee, is there a chance the production will be scrapped? If it is, Sherry, Mayor Drew, and Augustin will end up being, for lack of a better term, the biggest losers."

"That's alright, Kat," Sherry said between bites. "It's more important Rachel's killer is found and you're off the hook."

"There you go again, Sher, always putting others before yourself," Kat said. "Garrett, how do you see the phrases you selected in terms of fitting together into the big picture."

Garrett reviewed his written list. "Murder, an obvious selection. That's the theme of the napkins after Rachel lost her life: solving the murder. The author wants the murderer found in a timely fashion. Agreed?"

Both Sherry and Kat nodded. Neither could speak with their mouths full.

"Two-faced story, two endings, blame game," Garrett continued.

"What's the story that's two-faced? 'He said, she said' fits the scenario," Sherry said. "How can a story have two endings?"

"One perceived, one truthful?" Garrett suggested. "Next on the list: Nothing is as it seems and the term *impostors*. I'm wracking my brain on those two. I'm looking for the obvious and it's not hitting me over the head."

"The cook-off wasn't what it seemed," Sherry said. "*That's* obvious now."

"That's true. But let's focus on Rachel. What about Rachel wasn't what it appeared to be?" Garrett asked.

"I'd say her relationship with her coworkers. She appeared a team player but I had trouble trusting her motives from the time she went after Garrett right in front of me," Kat said.

"Wow," Garrett said. "I've never heard you say that before."

"It's true," Kat said. "Beyond that, Rachel wasn't happy with how Mick was being favored after the car accident. At first, I'm sure giving him fewer job responsibilities was to be expected, but that wore thin with her. She said as much, right, Garrett? She told us both."

"Absolutely," Garrett said. "She was at Mick's beck and call and that was enforced by Basil. We've said it before. Emotional blackmail."

"Think about the timeline. One day everything flipped," Kat said. "The day before she was murdered, Rachel came into the mayor's morning meeting whistling a merry tune instead of shoulders slumped and donning a scowl."

"That day's *Juicy Bites* used the phrase 'blame game.' She was the author. The napkins were on the truck that day. She delivered them before she was murdered," Garrett said.

"I'm willing to bet Rachel learned something she may not have known the day before. Something that changed Monday's sour mood to Tuesday's euphoria," Kat said. "She displayed a kind of confidence that comes with holding a powerful secret."

"We're getting closer. I can feel it," Garrett said.

"The same day she happily told me she bought me a gift," Kat said. "She claimed it was a symbol of our good times in college. We maybe had one good time. That wasn't what the gift was about. It was a hat and had one word printed on it, and it wasn't the name of our alma mater."

"What was the word?"

"*Driven*. I think that sums up her attitude. The message can be taken in several ways," Kat said. "I'd like it to mean she sees me as a person who wants to get ahead. She was that way, for better or worse."

"Or maybe the term took on a different meaning as her memory began to return," Sherry said.

"*Drive* was used more than once in *Juicy Bites*," Garrett said. "I overlooked that. I need to redo my list. Turns out every word is important. Like in a good story. And here we are, not any closer to narrowing down the suspect field."

"Today's *Juicy Bites* says the hammer's down. That means things are speeding up," Kat said.

"A trucker's call. A truck is speeding up," Garrett said. "And with it, there might go the clue *Juicy Bites* is alluding to. I've got more work to do."

"I need to get going. You do too, Garrett," Kat said as she glanced at her phone. "I've got an important task curbing the curb protesters. And finally, the newsletter can be put to bed, minus the results of the cook-off. I'm sorry, Sherry. Turns out we can't print the mayor's article until the *Relish* series airs. Too many secrets are revealed in the article."

"After all that waiting." Sherry shook her head. "Secrets are powerful."

Chapter 28

"You really don't mind coming with me to the police station at lunchtime?" Kat asked.

"Not at all. I have something I'd like to check on while we're there," Sherry said. "Text me when you're leaving and I'll meet you outside the station." Sherry disconnected the call and set her phone down on the sales counter.

"Dad, if you can take an early lunch, I'd like to run an errand at noon for an hour," Sherry said. "I'll leave Chutney with you, if that works."

"No problem. If I ever actually ate my lunch at the proper time, you'd be seeing pigs flying up Main Street." Erno leafed through his Rolodex until he found a card to pull. "Hazel Riordan is coming today to pick up one more lavender skein. I told her it would be a different dye lot and to bring in a sample of what she used last week to compare. We can make a very close match, but a discerning eye can tell."

"If anyone has a discerning eye, it's Hazel. If I'm recalling correctly, Amber suggested she buy an extra ball of each color for that very reason. Amber is so attuned to customer needs."

"Guess what? That exact suggestion is written on Hazel's card, along with last week's date. Says she set one ball of each color from the dye lot aside in the storage closet. All in Amber's handwriting. The girl's amazing." Erno held up the well-worn Rolodex card that only had enough room left on it for one or two more comments. "The yarn is all ready to go."

"Amber's the best," Sherry said. "So is your Rolodex file management system."

The chime over the front door sounded as Hazel burst through the door. "I'm here. I only have a minute. I have an appointment that I might already be late for."

"Here you go. The yarn is all balled up and waiting on the sales counter. Did you bring the sample of your lavender yarn?" Erno asked. "We could double-check a match."

"It's all fine," Hazel said. "I'm learning to take life as it comes and that includes accepting any variation in yarn tones. Life's too short to be fussy."

"No need to worry. Amber has you covered with her forward thinking."

Sherry's eyebrows shot up as she absorbed Hazel's new philosophy. "I'll ring you up and out you go."

Hazel exited the store as quickly as she entered. Other customers shopped and browsed, and the morning sped by. At five minutes before noon Sherry was on her way to the Augustin police station. Kat was waiting outside the building as planned.

"I'm nervous," Kat said.

"Don't be." Sherry laid her hand on Kat's shoulder. "Answer his questions, clear the air, and all will be fine."

"What if something I say affects the cook-off series?"

"The cook-off's over. If something you tell the detective affects the final output that's not any of your doing." Sherry recalled Hazel's updated philosophy. "It's all fine. Take life as it comes."

Kat faced Sherry with a smile. "Have you been talking to my mother? You're spouting her new outlook on life."

Sherry opened the station door for Kat.

"Sherry, you're back. I don't see you on the schedule. Who are you here to see?" Officer Hastings was positioned behind the thick glass barrier. She ran her finger down a sheet of paper.

"I'm here with Kat Coleman, who's seeing Detective Bease at noon. Is it okay if I go in with her? I have a question for Officer Sedgeman, if he's at his desk."

Sherry was cleared to enter the precinct after Officer Hastings held a brief chat on the intercom. Ray met them at the door. Again, as he held it open the weight of the door knocked him askew. "Darn thing," he grumbled.

"Ray, I have a question for Officer Sedgeman while you and Kat talk," Sherry said. She scanned the room. "I see him. Would he mind?"

"Troy? Can Sherry have a word with you, please?" Ray asked the seated officer.

Trooper was laying down alongside Officer Sedgeman's desk. The dog raised his majestic head. Troy waved Sherry closer.

"I'll be right over here, Kat," Sherry said.

Trooper rose in an instant when his handler stood. Troy slid over an empty seat from a neighboring desk as she approached. Sherry proceeded with caution to get to the seat situated within feet of the curious canine.

"What can I do for you?" Troy said.

"I have a question about the fatal accident involving Basil Sturges, Rachel Yaro, Mick Snider, and the person who passed away, of course."

"Okay. I have the report right here on my desk if we need it."

"Not sure if we do," Sherry said. "It's more of a procedural question. Let me run it by you."

"Please," Troy said.

"When you got to the scene, I imagine you questioned the passengers to recreate the scene. Does that sound right?

"For the most part, yes."

"Was it established who was sitting where in the car immediately, or later when the reports were filled out?" Sherry asked.

"Every accident scene requires a different approach to establish the facts," the officer said. "In this case it was important I know who was seated where so I could ascertain whether all the occupants were out of the car. If someone was trapped in the car or unaccounted for, time is of the essence. With a fatality, no detail can be overlooked. At least three out of the four occupants sustained an injury that could have impaired their memory and their recollection, even concerning how many were in the car. Mr. Sturges was the most reliable witness since he was barely scratched. Rachel's memory came and went, although she had very strong recollections of certain details. Mick was in no shape to be questioned beyond the basics. He could only nod or shake his head. He had to be extricated by the EMTs."

"How did you establish the driver if all the passengers were out of the car by the time you arrived?" Sherry asked.

"Like I said, I questioned the occupants who were verbal. In this case that would be Mr. Sturges and Ms. Yaro. They had different answers, so both went on the report. One marked with an asterisk."

"What did the asterisk indicate?" Sherry asked.

"The annotation connected to the asterisk marked Ms. Yaro's identification of the driver as questionable due to her head injury," Troy said.

"There was some wiggle room as to who the driver was. I'm thinking out loud here," Sherry said.

"That can be the case, yes. But I went with Basil's recollection," Troy said. "He said he would swear under oath if need be. Very lucky for Mick, who was splayed across the front seat console. If he were driving, he'd be charged with involuntary manslaughter. Mick was legally drunk and that's documented in the hospital report. All this is in the report right here."

"Rachel Yaro did say Mick was driving. You personally gave that statement no weight?" Sherry asked. Troy's lips pinched tight. She had struck a nerve.

"The report is on record as is," Troy said. He seemed willing to repeat himself as often as it took Sherry to accept the situation. "It can be amended but that would need substantial factual review and likely the involvement of an accident attorney to go through the steps."

"You know Mick's injuries are confined to his left side," Sherry said. "You'd think if he were belted in and the car rolled over to the right as the diagram indicated, the right side of the car would be smashed in and that would be the side he was injured on. But I think the car landed on the left side, making it a lot easier for the front passenger to be ejected, sadly. The fatality was the ejected passenger."

"What are you getting at, Sherry?" Troy asked.

"Basil may have given his recall of the accident a twist to safeguard one of his employees. The one who survived."

Troy's jaw muscles began to quiver. "I had an appointment with Mr. Sturges this morning. He wanted to discuss a matter. He canceled about an hour after he booked the appointment."

"Interesting," Sherry said. "Any idea what that might have been about?"

"He asked me to have the accident report handy." He nodded in the direction of the report on his desk. "I did, then he canceled."

"I wonder why you signed off on the report based on Basil's version of the events when there were other circumstances? You could have left the report open to further investigation," Sherry said. She knew she was pushing Troy into an uncomfortable zone, but she'd done her homework on her last visit to the station and had been waiting to employ her reasoning.

"Basil was so calm in stating his perspective. At the time it was impossible to question his immediate recall of the accident. Rachel was emotional and hurting."

"She never came to you to change her answer?" Sherry asked.

"No. Excuse me, Sherry," Troy said. He rose and was shadowed by Trooper as he crossed the room. Then he began climbing the stairs to office of the chief of police.

"What did you do?" Ray asked. "He looks angry."

Sherry winced. "I think because I pointed out a different ending to the story."

"By the way, we're done here, but I'd like to have a word with you two. Is Sedgeman returning?"

"I'm not sure." Sherry pushed her chair back and rose. She made her way to Ray's desk and hovered over Kat. "Everything go well?"

"Better than between you two," Ray said. "I had a visit right before you came. From your mother, Kat."

Kat winced. "How much apologizing do I need to do?"

"On the contrary. She's a lovely person and a caring mother. Coming from someone who's lost his mother not long ago, I recommend you show her a little extra care for what her intentions were."

"Phew." Kat wiped her brow with a sweep of the back of her hand. "What were her intentions?"

"She came to see me to vouch for your character. She presented a litany of reasons you disappeared the day Rachel Yaro was murdered. One reason that stands out is your friendship with Sherry. She described the thought you put into not disrupting the cook-off for the sake of Sherry and the mayor and all the production personnel." Ray opened a small notepad to a dog-eared page. "She said, and I quote, 'my daughter has become the adult I had hoped to raise, and I take no credit for her maturity. She's innately selfless and a wonderful example of Augustin's finest citizens, much like Sherry Oliveri."

Something caught in Sherry's throat. At the same time, Kat coughed.

"Kat Coleman, thank you for your time. You're free to go," Ray said.

"Thank you, Ray," Sherry said. "Would you mind thanking Officer Sedgeman for me?" She glanced toward the stairs he'd taken.

"That was a lot," Kat said when they stepped out of the precinct building.

"A lot of motherly love," Sherry said. She gave Kat a fleeting back pat before checking the time. "I'm going to pay a visit to Basil, down at the production truck, by the end of the day."

"Sherry? What do you have in mind? Do you need some company? When Basil left the mayor's office this morning, he didn't seem in a receptive mood for anything but wrapping up his time in Augustin. You might need backup."

"I really don't think that's necessary, but I appreciate the offer. I have a matter I'd like him to clarify, that's all." Sherry smiled sheepishly. "If no one hears from me by tonight, you know where I'm headed."

Kat held up two crossed fingers. "Good luck."

Chapter 29

Sherry returned to the Ruggery and spent the afternoon showing merchandise, giving a hooking demonstration to a potential rug maker, and mapping out the appropriate rug collection to be displayed for the fall season. During a quiet stretch she walked Chutney outside, from the back door to the front, to give him the chance to relieve himself. All the while, Garrett's list of *Juicy Bites* words circulated through her thoughts.

Erno took a very late lunch and promised Sherry she could take off an hour later, when he returned. As soon as Erno left the store Sherry rummaged through her purse for the box with the gold ribbon. She carefully untied the bow and lifted the lid on the box. The red velvet liner cradled a rather average-looking key. There was no engraved reference to Augustin, no special embellishments, and upon close inspection, she detected rust blemishes on the edges. If the well-worn object was the city key that commemorated gratitude at the highest level, the mayor needed to rethink the chosen symbol.

"I'm a winner, with a key," Sherry said to Chutney. The quote from the morning's *Juicy Bites* was making more sense. Chutney cocked his head as she addressed him. When she didn't offer a treat, the Jack Russell sauntered off.

Sherry needed to get down to the Augustin Garage. Basil had some explaining to do. If Mick was the driver of the car that killed a team member Basil may be keeping the secret for blackmailing purposes. How Rachel's death factored in was complicating the matter. Sherry removed the key from the gift box. She threaded a six-inch strand of orange rug yarn through the loop on the head. She stored the adorned key back in the gift box and dropped it in her bag.

Erno brought a leftovers container back from his lunch. "I had a picnic for one at the marina and it was glorious. Frankly, I don't know why people take vacations away from Augustin in the summer, when they have all the beauty and activities right here in our backyard."

"I agree, Dad."

"While I was watching the boats come and go, I thought about our summers at Bluefish Run Beach. Weren't those the best?" Erno said. His voice trailed off as if he were being teleported back to his mid-thirties. "I wish Mom had been around longer to see how you three kids turned out so well. I could have used the help at the beach besides."

"I do, too. You made those times into great memories."

Erno was going to be thrilled when the cook-off series was released. His memory would be jogged even further when he saw Sherry compete on the sandy beach he navigated all those years ago. Here's hoping Basil hadn't done anything nefarious to compromise the production coming to fruition.

"I'll watch Chutney while you do your errand?" Erno asked.

"Thanks, but no thanks. He's my travel partner. We'll be in bright and early tomorrow, Dad. Amber's off and you can take the morning off if you need to acclimate slowly to the workaday world."

"We'll see," Erno said. "I really missed this place while I was gone. I'm an old dog who might not be willing to be taught new tricks, like time off." He kissed his daughter's forehead and held the door open for her. "We'll talk in the morning."

Sherry drove down to Coffee Buzz and parked the car in the lot farthest from the establishment. She hooked Chutney up to his leash and walked the periphery of the property to get to the edge of the Augustin Garage. She eyed the camera lens and lowered her head in case someone was manning the video in real time. The possibility was slim she was being watched, but she wanted to avoid attracting attention. She walked a wide perimeter around the trucks and discovered each had a sliding side door equipped with a collapsed set of steps. There was a good chance one of the trucks was occupied, as the rear doors were ajar. The other appeared closed tight. She put her hand in her purse and touched the yarn tied to the key.

Sherry led Chutney to a row of old-growth viburnum bushes that provided a barrier between the garage and a commercial driveway next door. She needed to formulate a plan.

"This bush is taken."

Sherry gasped when Garrett appeared from behind an especially thick growth of branches.

"What are you doing here?" Sherry hissed. "You scared the life out of me. You're here more than Juan, the owner of the garage."

"I could say the same," Garrett said. "I'm on assignment."

"Really? Who is the assignment for? *Trucker's Daily*?"

"I've assigned myself to follow up on my list of words," Garrett said.

"Down here? In the bushes?"

"I think this is the hot spot for *Juicy Bites*. *Juicy Bites* is very closely associated with Rachel's murder. I assume that's why you're here?"

"I'm here to have a word with Basil," Sherry said.

"Why don't you just knock on the trailer door?" Garrett asked.

"The same reason you haven't done that," Sherry said. "I need more than my intuition to shore up my point. Is there a specific phrase you're working on while you're in the bushes?"

Garrett brushed a leaf from his pants. "I'm concentrating on 'two-faced stories have two endings.' When I interviewed for the job of image rebranding Feral Creations, I was told a story of how a member of the Feral Creations team died under debatable circumstances. There was a story out there that shed a negative light on the company. I need details."

"We're on the same page, Garrett. I think there's a second ending to that story and it involves an impostor," Sherry said.

"And things aren't as they appear," Garrett said. "*Juicy Bites* is on a mission to change the story ending."

"Okay, who wants to explain?" Kat asked as she emerged from behind a viburnum.

"How many people can one bush hold?" Sherry asked.

"At least three," Kat said. "And a dog, too."

"I can only explain for myself," Sherry said. "I'm evidence gathering before I have a word with Basil." She squinted for impact. "Kat, I thought I said I didn't need any backup."

Kat studied her shoes. "I vetoed that idea." Her gaze shifted to Garrett. "I'm guessing you two didn't travel here together. Are you going to talk to Basil, too? I don't think that's a good idea. He's a little ticked off with you."

"Sherry and I both think he has the answer to our question about who's writing *Juicy Bites* and maybe who killed Rachel. What are you doing here?" Garrett asked.

"I know Feral Creations is pulling up stakes first thing in the morning," Kat said. "Time is running out." She threw up her hands. "Am I the only one of us three who is certain Basil's the author of *Juicy Bites*?"

"What makes you so sure?" Sherry asked.

"At the final meeting he had with the mayor this morning, Basil referred to how well Mick is doing with his recovery and how far he's come. He said Mick was walking again and was driven to recover quickly. He was sorry to see Yonny go. He didn't need him anymore. It was time for him to move on. He said he was so glad to have the incident finally behind him and that the story of the accident could have had a second ending."

"He might as well have been quoting directly from *Juicy Bites*," Garrett said.

"I agree."

"Chutney, quit pulling," Sherry commanded. She dropped her purse when the tenacious pup yanked her forward with a mighty tug. The purse caught the leash loop and Sherry couldn't maintain her grip. Chutney scooted forward and circled back to the bushes.

"I'll get him," Kat said. She pushed limbs out of her way to track the small dog. "There must be a bunny under here. Chutney, come on, I'm getting scratched." Kat was forced to sink to her knees to trail the dog under the leggy branches. "Got him." She emerged from the back of the bush with leash in hand. "What's in your mouth, boy? Sherry, look."

Sherry knelt and gently pried Chutney's mouth open. He released his treasure. "Lucky he didn't choke on that." A piece of rubber covered in yellow fuzz lay at the dog's paws.

"We're not even close to the courts," Kat said.

"Good boy, Chutney. All our hard work has paid off. I think I know how this tennis ball got here," Sherry said. "Mick used tennis balls on the bottom of his walker for stabilization."

"Unfortunately, that can't be. Mick was never at this site," Garrett said. "I know because my job entailed documenting the team's prep operations. He was originally assigned each day's clapboard organization task but decided he couldn't manage to climb into the trucks. He was barely ready for his walker at that stage. The truck steps would be too difficult for his atrophied legs. He handed the task off to the other team members and with it the prestige of overseeing clip organization. I subsequently journaled Rachel, and then Stacy, for my article when they took over the task. The shift in responsibilities was an interesting part of the production that needed to be included."

"Mick knew you were tailing him?"

"Of course," Garrett said. "They all did. Full disclosure and all that."

"The timeline makes sense. I hadn't given him the tennis balls for the legs of the walker yet. Maybe he would have handled the job if he'd known the trick," Sherry said. "There goes that theory. Now we know Mick wasn't the *Juicy Bites* author. He couldn't maneuver to Pep's truck if he couldn't get to the production trucks. One suspect down, many to go."

Sherry tucked the dregs of the tennis ball in a baggie of cough drops she found in her canvas tote.

"You're keeping that?" Garrett asked.

"It went straight into my vault," Sherry said.

"I want to get inside the locked trailer. Those cables trailing from the rear compartment are a strong signal there might be a computer plus printer setup inside," Garrett said. "I think we're going to find tomorrow's *Juicy Bites* in there. If we do, we go straight to Basil and confront him. It's time he tells all if he's the author."

"What's the chance Basil's the murderer and he's sent everyone on a wild-goose chase to buy time," Kat said.

"Maybe. That scenario can't be ruled out. How do you propose we get inside?" Garrett asked.

Sherry waved the orange-yarn-adorned key in the air. "I think this 'key to the city' could be what we're looking for. I'd put a wager down this is a duplicate key to the one Rachel was found clutching."

Garrett put out his hand and received the key from Sherry.

"That key?" Kat asked. The distaste on her face made Sherry smile.

"You don't recognize the key to the city?" Sherry asked.

"That's not the key the Augustin Mayoral Council stamps to give to worthy citizens. That key is embarrassing." Kat curled up her lip. "I can't apologize enough for the mix-up. I don't understand how that happened."

"Not a mix-up at all. There's a very good chance the swap was intentional," Sherry said. She pointed to the sliding door on the second truck. The shiny lock secured to a latch was begging for a key test.

"Basil, you devil," Kat scolded. "He had me store the gift box supposedly containing the key to the city in my desk drawer until the last day of the cook-off. He said Mayor Drew gave him the commemorative key to award to the winner. How was I to know the impostor key was in the box?"

"Sherry, let's go test your theory." Garrett led the way around one truck and came to rest in front of the thick lock on the door of the other truck. "Wish me luck." He unfolded the stair and made the lengthy step up with a groan. He inserted the key and with a twist the lock popped open. "Eureka! I've struck gold."

Sherry handed Chutney's leash and her tote to Kat. "Would you mind? I'll be a minute."

"Sure. Leave me here alone. What could go wrong?" Kat said. "Chutney, you're my guard dog. My life is in your hands."

"Come on, Sherry. Grab my hand." Garrett held out his hand, and when Sherry clasped it he hoisted her up to the sliding metal panel. "Let's be fast."

It was necessary to use phone flashlights to get a good look at what the truck contained. Cameras, cables, boxes and more boxes were stacked in well-aligned rows.

"Over there," Sherry said. She pointed to the far corner of the interior, where an oversized computer screen and printer dominated the space. To make her way to the opposite end of the truck she had to turn sideways to maneuver between crowded rows of equipment. When she reached the printer, she searched and found what she was looking for: the garbage bin. If *Juicy Bites* were being printed in the truck the throwaways were most likely not discarded in a public garbage, for discretion's sake. A massive garbage bin, able to hold large amounts of discard, sat tucked underneath the printer stand.

"This big guy could hold two weeks' worth of paper," Sherry said with a sigh. "Hope it doesn't take that long to go through it." She sifted through the top layers before unearthing a layer of brown lightweight paper. She touched the paper with shaky fingers. "That's it. The napkin." The one she lifted out of the bin was torn, clearly a casualty of a printer jam caused by lightweight paper. "Probably why only fifty napkins were printed daily. Too much hassle clearing the jammed printer." She searched for Garrett and located him still near the door. His gaze was fixed on a small cardboard box.

"I've got something here," he said.

"Me, too," Sherry replied. "I'm coming." She began to carefully walk back to Garrett. She took one step before a shiny object on the computer stand caught the beam of her phone's flashlight. She picked up a leather bracelet with a silver four-leaf clover pendant dangling from the clasp. "The same bracelet Basil wore the first day I met him at Pep's truck," Sherry whispered. She set the bracelet down and made her way to Garrett.

"What do you have there?" Sherry gazed at his hand. Garrett was holding the same variety of paper she was. "Where'd you find that? It looks in great condition, unlike this." She held up her battered sample.

Chapter 30

"Do you think that's set for release tomorrow?" Sherry asked.

"I sure do," Garrett said. "Let's prove them wrong. Let's not disappoint."

Sherry pointed to a blocky metal contraption on wheels. "There's the generator that powers the computer and printer setup. Plenty of cable length to set it up outside."

"Hey, guys. Someone's coming in." Kat's strained voice echoed through the truck.

"Hello? Is anyone in here? This looks like a piece of the famous Oliveri rug yarn. I found it attached to a key in the door lock." Basil's phone flashlight illuminated his line of sight.

"Sherry shone her light on Basil's hand. He held up the key strung on the orange yarn.

"There you are. Mind if we get out of here? I've been inside most of the day and my eyes are bleary from lack of good lighting." Basil turned and cautiously took the long step down to the ground. He offered a hand to Sherry.

She hesitated because her palms were suddenly unpleasantly clammy. She brushed the moisture against her leg and grasped his hand.

"Thanks," she said as her sneakers hit the ground with a thud.

"You figured out *Juicy Bites*. Glad to see," Basil said. "I knew you could do it."

"We haven't figured it all out," Garrett said as he navigated the huge step on his own. "Are the napkins your handiwork?"

"I should be the one asking the questions. You know I could have you all arrested for trespassing, breaking in, and robbery," Basil said. "But that might spoil the ending of *Relish*'s great story."

"If the key fits . . ." Sherry said. She pointed to the key Basil held. "By the way, that's the key that was in the beautiful gift box the mayor presented me. If I own the key, is that trespassing? And stealing garbage? That's a stretch for prosecution."

"Basil, would you like to confess anything while we're here?" Garrett asked.

"Basil? Everything okay?" Mick limped into sight from the direction of the other truck. "Hi, guys. This is a surprise."

"Mick, you're walking," Sherry said. "I'm so happy for you."

"I've been working my way up for a few days now."

"Can you make it up this step?" Sherry asked. She tipped her head toward the truck door she came out of. "That's a good test for anyone."

"If I admit I can, Basil might put me to work," he said with a laugh.

"I bet you can," Sherry said.

Mick pinched his brows together and delivered Sherry a challenging stare.

"I know he can," Basil said. "He caught me inside the truck working late last night."

"Imagine my surprise," Mick said.

"Imagine mine," Basil responded.

"Garrett, I was sorry to hear the partnership with you was terminated," Mick said. "To be honest, I'm surprised to see you here."

Garrett and Kat exchanged glances.

"Why doesn't he know Garrett's been rehired?" Sherry whispered to Kat.

"I was let go because Basil felt I was asking too much of him if I wrote the truth," Garrett said. "There's an epidemic of pressure to not be truthful at Feral Creations."

"That's a broad generalization," Mick said. "Basil knows right from wrong. He was right letting you go. Why would he sacrifice the success of Feral Creations for the sake of furthering your career by backing a sensational piece that has no merit."

"Nothing sensational at all. You came up with the concept for *Relish* and Basil snatched the credit out from under you. Is that correct?" Garrett asked. "That's an important detail to omit in the telling of the cook-off's story."

The icy exchange of glances between Basil and Mick gave Sherry goose bumps.

Basil cleared his throat. "We all contribute to the show's success. I don't recall whether Mick began the conversation about the concept at inception. If he did, I am forever grateful."

"Grateful enough to list him as creator on the rolling credits?" Garrett asked.

"Would you consider yourself the creator?" Basil asked Mick. "Or a team player."

Silence swept over the scene. One lone mourning dove called out from the power lines overhead. Sherry knew mourning doves seldom traveled alone and a feathered friend would shortly return the greeting. She was wrong. The call went unanswered.

"If you can't speak for yourself, I will," Kat said.

"I don't know if that's a good idea," Garrett said. He kept his gaze on Basil. "There's a lot on the line."

"I agree," Basil said. "Although, I'd like to hear Mick's answer."

"Mick can't stand up for himself alone," Kat said. "He's been pushed around since the accident."

"Don't worry about Mick," Basil said. "He's doing just fine."

"I'm not sure you guys are seeing this correctly. Mick's accustomed to the team culture. He had Rachel looking out for him until her death," Garrett said. "She let Mick take advantage of her, if you want my opinion."

Kat nodded. "In more ways than most are aware of. Rachel was keeping the secret of who the *Relish* creator was. She knew Mick was the brains behind the show. She sided with Mick at his lowest point, while letting Basil have his undeserved recognition. She shared her conundrum with me days before she was murdered. She said she'd be fired if she spoke up. Once I knew that secret, I was in a tough spot. The truth bothered me to no end."

"Wait a minute," Garrett said. "Rachel's mood swung from dismal to elated the day before she was murdered. What was that about?"

"It can't be from my talk about not giving her a raise she constantly rallied for," Basil said. "I didn't tell her anything she wanted to hear. I only told her to keep working hard. We all have to put in the hard yards."

Quiet swept over the group. Sherry was certain the others could hear her heart pounding. She willed Basil to share more, but to no avail.

"Since she's not here, the point is moot," Mick said. "And Garrett, this really doesn't involve you since you don't work for us anymore."

"Garrett's back on board," Basil said. "I can see his value now, more than ever."

"You were blaming Garrett for exposing the truth. I'd say you're the one who should be fired," Kat said.

Basil sucked in a deep breath. "No one's telling the truth. Nothing is as it appears. Garrett was blaming me for not giving Mick his due credit. Rachel was blaming Mick for how hard she worked to make him look valuable. I'm blaming Sherry for not solving Rachel's murder."

"What?" Sherry asked. "You're blaming me?"

"That's right. You can't tell me you're not a talented amateur sleuth. What's the holdup?"

Sherry ignored Basil's challenge. "Mick? Is this yours?" Sherry held out her hand and Kat returned her tote. She rummaged through the bag and pulled out the tennis ball fragment. Chutney jumped up Sherry's leg and snapped at the ball. "Good boy."

"No, that's not mine," Mick said.

"I thought you may have come down here to work on the clapboards at some point and this broke off your walker."

"No. Well, I mean, I thought the balls would help me get around the muck and mud down here, but the experiment wasn't successful. Basil assigned the clapboards to Rachel because the area had gotten enough rain to impede my walker the only time I tried to traverse this gunk. It was like gooey quicksand." Mick slid the toes of his shoe across the wet soil. "There was no getting through the mud. I was transitioning out of the wheelchair and wasn't too nimble yet."

"So, you tried the tennis balls on your walker before I made my suggestion to try them at Bluefish Run Beach?" Sherry asked.

"I didn't want to hurt your feelings when you made your helpful suggestion, but, yes, I had already tried the tennis ball trick on my walker. The trial run was a bust. I had to tell Basil I couldn't take on the clapboard task."

Kat pointed to the tennis ball fragment. "Sherry, that ball is . . ." Kat began.

Sherry cleared her throat, clipping Kat's thought.

"Where did you get the first set of tennis balls?" Sherry asked. "I would have happily supplied you with a second set earlier if I'd known the first set didn't hold up."

"That's very kind of you. Yonny was getting me used to the walker near the park next to the town hall early last Tuesday. A nice man and his little son offered me two of their used tennis balls to cover the my walker's legs. It wasn't long before the ball punctured and broke apart, so I gave up on the idea. That's the reason Rachel oversaw the clapboards the next morning. It could have been me murdered down here."

"Was Eli the boy's name?" Sherry asked.

"Yes. He introduced himself as Eli Washburn. Very polite young man. Do you know them?" Mick asked.

"We play near them every morning. He's getting very good for a little guy."

"Well, anyway, I appreciate you giving me the set for the walker. I'm just glad that I'm now finally out of that contraption," Mick said.

"There goes my theory," Sherry muttered. "I thought there was a possibility you witnessed something when you were down here testing your mobility. Or that you wrote *Juicy Bites*."

"Not me," Mick said. He chuckled. "I have no interest in taking on more work, thank you. I'm sure Basil wouldn't be very happy if I'd been the person spilling production secrets for the last two weeks. What knucklehead thought that was a good idea?"

Sherry choked on a swallow as she snuck a look at Basil. He bit his lower lip.

"Wait, first you said you came down here while on your walker and that was a bust, and then you said the ball broke apart in the park on Yonny's watch and that was your only trial run," Sherry said.

"Oh, yes, sorry," Mick said. He rubbed his forehead. "I'm exhausted. I can barely think straight."

"Which version is correct?" Basil asked.

"No matter which one is correct I'd say someone might be planting evidence to get Mick suspected of Rachel's murder," Garrett said. He pointed to the tennis ball scrap in Sherry's hand.

"That's okay. You don't have to defend me," Mick said. "The truth comes out in the end."

"Sherry, what were you looking for in the truck today? You figured out *Juicy Bites* was talking to you. A key, a lock, a clue. You've got the key, you found the lock. Did you find a clue?" Basil's question was oddly playful in nature.

"I found evidence you write *Juicy Bites*." She held up the crumpled paper sample she'd retrieved from the garbage. "Want to claim ownership?"

"I do," Basil said. "I'm the knucklehead."

"What?" Mick's eyebrows lifted halfway up his forehead.

"This is huge," Kat said. "But Sherry, back to the tennis balls—"

"I'm sorry I didn't find Rachel's murderer," Sherry interrupted. Kat produced a sigh of exasperation. "Unless . . ."

"It's not Basil? Basil had every reason to kill Rachel. Don't overlook the obvious," Kat said. Her voice rose an octave with her plea to be heard. "He stole poor Mick's idea and Rachel found out. The secret no one wanted her to tell. The secret *Juicy Bites* referred to as explosive. Then she was dead."

Basil sighed. "How did Augustin get so many amateur sleuths on this case?"

"It may have a lot to do with your napkin publications," Garrett said. "Can you stand there and say you didn't want this to happen? That you weren't planting seeds of the murder investigation in *Juicy Bites* so Sherry would solve the case? If she did, not only would you be absolved from turning your own employee in for the murder, but you'd have a great ending to the *Relish* story when Sherry Oliveri exhibited another of her community-minded talents, solving cooking competition murders. A murder tied to your production company. Now that's a full circle story no one can dream up."

"Do you have proof of your accusations?" Basil asked.

"I do. Basil, we were at the Augustin police station today," Kat said. "We were told you had an appointment there but canceled."

"All true," Basil said. "I wanted to set the record straight on the auto accident the team suffered last winter."

"You have a lot to set straight," Kat said. "Another example of you using someone else's mistake for your benefit. That can't make you feel good."

"This is my last day here. Things weren't budging in the murder investigation. I thought the process needed a nudge."

"You have every power to rewrite the endings to a few stories, yet you choose not to," Kat said.

"I hope you were going to tell Detective Bease that Rachel told the truth about Mick driving the car despite the fact he was well under the influence of alcohol. And that you lied to save the skin of your living employee while throwing the deceased person who couldn't defend himself, named Kyle Lemke, under the bus?" Sherry asked.

"And you're the man who fired me for wanting to tell the truth about who should be wearing the title of *Relish* creator. Shame on you, Basil. How can we not go a step further and assume you're Rachel's murderer?" Garrett asked.

"Why didn't you follow through?" Sherry asked. "Why didn't you do the right thing?"

Basil turned his back on his interrogators. He squared up to Sherry.

"Is it because if you changed the accident report to Rachel's account Mick would divulge his own truth about *Relish* to get you back? And your credibility would be down the tubes?" Sherry asked. "You've been blackmailing Mick with how the accident really played out. Admit it."

"This is all adding up. If that's the deeper secret Rachel was sitting on until she had the opportunity to use it to her advantage—by dangling the secret in front of Basil to get the raise she'd been rallying for—Basil would be plenty upset," Garrett said. "Upset enough to murder."

"Nobody reacts well to that sort of pressure," Sherry said.

"If Basil is the killer, why is he putting the *Juicy Bites* puzzle out there, trying to get Sherry to use her sleuthing talents? Seems like a lot of work if he himself is the killer," Kat remarked as if Basil weren't a few feet away.

"Basil?" Garrett said. "What do you have to say for yourself?"

"I didn't kill Rachel," Basil stated without question.

"You've been wanting me to solve this case since you got the idea to take over Rachel's newsy napkins. Was that so you'd be deemed completely ignorant of the truth? Mick was driving the car, drunk, and he killed a team member," Sherry said. "I'm so sorry, Mick, but someone must change that accident report. It's the right thing to do."

Mick lowered his head.

"Things definitely aren't as they appear," Basil said. His tone was soft. "It's time we write a new ending to the story. The missing piece of the puzzle is coming into view."

"It's becoming more than clear. You've been blackmailing Mick, and he's been blackmailing you," Kat said. "No one is innocent. And Rachel? She's involved in a big way. For lack of a better term, she was blackmailing both of you to get what she wanted. Who murdered Rachel if it wasn't Basil?"

"Don't forget, the biggest loser now walks among us." Sherry's sights darted to Mick. "Mick's now walking, but why is he the biggest loser? I have a gut feeling Mick's been able to walk longer than he says."

Mick backed up two steps. "Basil used my idea for the cook-off with a twist. Taking on *Juicy Bites* was his idea after Rachel's death. If Sherry could solve the mystery of who Rachel's killer was, he had an incredible ending to her cook-off journey. I don't see the problem there. Especially if it were Sherry who solved the mystery of who murdered Rachel. The perfect ending to *Relish*."

"Kat, what were you trying to tell me about the tennis ball fragment Chutney found?" Sherry asked.

"That's the kid's ball, the one that Eli used. See the green dot? That is a special ball for beginners. Soft and squishy. That's the ball Eli uses every morning at the park and the one he gave to Mick. No wonder it couldn't handle the weight of Mick and the walker. What's most important, that's not the type of tennis ball you provided Mick at Bluefish Run Beach a week later."

"If that's the case, there's a very good chance Mick employed Eli's tennis ball last week to get himself around the trucks to surprise Rachel and make her pay for her blackmailing, bullying, and intimidation. Any one of those words describes the bulldozing she laid on Mick after she solidly remembered him as the driver of the car that killed a teammate," Sherry said. "That knowledge changed her mood to elation. She now had a priceless bargaining chip in her pocket. She was driven to succeed."

"The secret wasn't who actually came up with the cook-off concept?" Kat asked.

"No, something much more destructive," Garrett said.

"Rachel had the power to change the ending of the accident's story and Mick needed to snuff her out before she placed the truthful blame on him," Sherry said. "By that time, he was already plenty sick and tired of being pushed around by Basil, who stole his show concept."

"How did she find out who was driving the car if she lost her memory of the accident?" Garrett asked.

Sherry nodded to Kat, who reached into her canvas bag and pulled out a cap. She placed it on her head.

"See what's written on this hat Rachel gave Kat? *Driven*," Sherry said. "The gift card attached said she worked tirelessly to regain her memory because she was driven to get ahead. Her memory was getting stronger every day. She went so far as to thank Kat for sparking her memory after she recalled their college times together. I think she finally was fully confident in her recollection of Mick driving the car that day. There's a good chance she thought using the memory of the accident creatively would be just the ticket to move her career forward. She was mistaken. The same day she pressured Mick to step aside and let her flourish, he reached the end of his rope. Is that accurate, Mick?"

"That's why Rachel came into the mayor's office happy as a clam?" Kat asked. "Her memory returned, and along with it she gained an ace up her sleeve."

"That's what the card with the hat means," Sherry said.

"Was it you who poisoned me at the beach?" Basil asked.

"Not me. It was Garrett," Mick said. "The same Garrett who is going to ruin all our careers to further his own. Don't let him convince you I did anything wrong. He's been lying since day one when he applied for a job to rebrand Feral Creations. Look at the mess he's gotten us into."

"You may be interested in the fact Augustin Poison Control tested the bag of so-called mint Garrett foraged," Basil said. "Yes, it was a plant impostor. A toxic mint impostor."

"Not true, Basil," Mick said. "That's the first of many stories that needs correcting."

"They also gave the bag over to forensics, who found your fingerprints all over the leaves inside the bag. A perfect match to the prints lifted off your walker," Basil said. "Garrett may have filled his forage collection bag with what he thought was an edible ingredient, but you refilled it with your choice of ingredients. You knew I was sampling everyone's forage collections, including Garrett's."

"Okay, I did that. It was supposed to be a funny prank," Mick said. "Who knew you'd eat a fistful of the leaves?"

"Funny prank, or a way to tell me you couldn't live with our arrangement anymore?" Basil asked.

"Someone had to give in, and it wasn't going to be me. I wanted to nudge you, as you say. You understand." Mick pinched up his mouth and his gaze darted around the landscape. His cheeks bloomed a splotchy red. "Basil and I had an understanding. He gets full credit for *Relish*, and I get to move on with my life without fear of prosecution. Rachel messed up our arrangement. She turned the tables on me. She announced she would change the police report if Basil wouldn't, unless I got out of her way at work." He backed up two more steps.

Basil groaned. "Mick, I was so afraid it was you who killed Rachel." Basil's voice was trembling. "I used *Juicy Bites* to try and flush out the truth. Ironically, Sherry was too busy with *Relish* to give the investigation the time needed. Yes, it would have been a great ending to the celebration of Sherry Oliveri, until I realized I was about to expose one of my team members for the murder of another. That's why I canceled my meeting with the police this morning. Sherry needed more time. I knew she could prove you innocent or guilty before we left town."

Mick turned and ran, as best he could, crashing through the viburnum hedge. Before anyone could respond, there was a blood-curdling scream. Everyone made their way through the row of bushes and found Mick splayed across the neighboring property's curb. "Damn thing is so high," he moaned as he kicked the curb with as much muscle as he could muster from his prone state.

Chapter 31

"Basil was the author of *Juicy Bites?*" Hazel asked. "I should have known. He was the only one who could have put the napkins on Pep's windshield the morning we were all at the garage. I need to work on my sleuthing skills."

"No, please don't, Mom. We need you safe for a long time to come," Kat said.

"That's so sweet, dear," Hazel said. "But you never know. Sherry may need me in the future."

"I appreciate the interest, Hazel," Sherry said. "I'm sure there won't be any more murders in Augustin." Sherry wiped a crumble of turkey sausage off her lips with a napkin.

"I have an update on the *Relish* cook-off," Kat said. "Mayor Drew said *Relish* will be produced and distributed, as planned. Labor Day weekend the series will play on a loop on the Kitchen Channel." She took a bite of her artichoke spinach dip toast with toasted pine nuts. "Another winner from Pep."

"Sherry, will Basil be charged with any crime?" Hazel asked. "He may not have known Mick was the murderer, but he did know with certainty Mick was driving the car that ended in a fatal accident."

"I got a detailed email last night from Feral Creations," Sherry said. "No charges are being brought against Basil for withholding the information Mick was the driver in the auto accident. The family of Kyle Lemke isn't pursuing any prosecution. Basil's lucky and I hope he's appreciative besides. The accident report is accurate now and the second ending has been officially filed."

"What about the credit Mick should get for coming up with the *Relish* concept? Will that happen even if he's behind bars?" Hazel asked.

Sherry's gaze landed on Kat. "How does she know the show's concept?"

"I'm sorry, Sherry. I had to tell my mother the true concept of *Relish*. She knows everything and has promised to sit on all the juicy details until the show comes out."

Hazel smiled. "I promise. I even saw Effi Raymond yesterday and wasn't the slightest bit tempted to spill the beans. I've turned over a new leaf. No more gossip, no more butting into Kat's love life, and no more stalking town hall, unless I truly have business down there. I've learned my lesson. Now, as for acquiring any more husbands, well, never say never."

"Mick won't be named in the credits, but the rest of the team as a whole will be credited for all aspects of the cook-off," Sherry said.

"So many second endings to so many stories," Kat said. "Basil chose the right words for *Juicy Bites*."

"And Garrett's article? Will that be published?" Sherry asked.

"In all its sensational glory, and he's thrilled," Kat said. "Feral Creations couldn't have written a script as intriguing as reality did if they tried. Basil came to his senses when he rehired Garrett. The article is the best publicity he could hope for."

"Looks like the gang's all here," Ray said as he approached. He was cradling a Toasts of the Town container. "Thank you again for all your help with the investigation. Sherry, you recruited some talented rookie sleuths."

"They recruited me," Sherry said.

"Do you all have Labor Day plans, besides binge watching the *Relish* competition?" Ray asked.

"Mom and I are having a picnic at the beach," Kat said. "Garrett hopes to join."

"Don and I will be joining Dad and Ruth at Bluefish Run Beach with a cooler of sandwiches," Sherry said. "How about you, Ray? How are you celebrating Labor Day?"

Ray puffed out his chest. "I am captaining the Augustin police unit that specializes in award-winning grill recipes and we are going head-to-head with the Augustin Firefighters and EMTs grill squad for a charity grill-off."

"Wow! Good luck! How exciting," Sherry said.

"Guns with Toasted Buns versus the Char Stars," Ray said. "Afterward is a pickleball tournament."

"You work hard and play hard," Kat said.

"Fingers crossed nothing nefarious occurs at the grill-off. Right, Sherry?" Ray raised his food container high. "Have a good day, ladies. And please, thank Garrett again for me."

"Will do. Good luck on Labor Day," Sherry called out as Ray went on his way.

Recipes from Sherry's Kitchen

Parisian Prosciutto Scramble Toast
Serves 2

2 thick slices crusty French bread, sliced on the diagonal
2 eggs, beaten
1 tablespoon milk
⅛ teaspoon sea salt
1 teaspoon butter
1 teaspoon olive oil
2 tablespoons Brie cheese
2 slices prosciutto, cut in strips
1 teaspoon fresh tarragon
Black pepper

Toast bread slices to desired crunchiness.

Whisk eggs, milk and salt to combine.

In a small fry pan warm the butter and oil over medium heat. Cook the eggs, stirring occasionally until set.

Spoon eggs onto toasts. Dot cheese across eggs.

Wipe fry pan clean and warm prosciutto over high heat until pieces begin to curl, about 2 minutes. Place prosciutto across eggs. Top with tarragon and pepper and serve.

Gold Coast Avocado Toast
Serves 2

2 thick slices multigrain toast
1 ripe avocado
1 teaspoon lemon juice, freshly squeezed
1 teaspoon honey
1 teaspoon olive oil
⅛ teaspoon red pepper flakes
⅛ teaspoon sea salt
1 hard-boiled egg, peeled and chopped
2 tablespoons smoked salmon, chopped
1 teaspoon fresh dill fronds

Toast bread slices to desired crunchiness.

Mash the avocado with lemon juice, honey, olive oil, red pepper flakes and salt. Spread on toast slices. Top avocado with egg and smoked salmon. Sprinkle dill on top and serve.

Ranch Steak Bruschetta Salad
Serves 6

¼ teaspoon sea salt
1½ teaspoons ground cumin
1½ teaspoons ancho chili powder
1½ teaspoons coffee beans, finely ground
1 tablespoon black pepper
4 (6-ounce) tenderloin beef steaks—1 inch thick, any fat trimmed
1 tablespoon cooking oil for skillet or grill pan
1 crusty French bread loaf, cut in 1-inch-thick slices, at a 45-degree angle
¼ cup roasted red peppers, chopped
¼ cup chopped basil leaves
¼ cup chopped shallots
½ cup cherry tomatoes, sliced in half
1 tablespoon fresh lemon juice
6 cups arugula leaves

In a small bowl combine the sea salt, cumin, chili powder, coffee and black pepper. Rub both sides of steaks with the spice blend. Let steaks rest on a plate for 10 minutes.

Meanwhile, preheat skillet or grill pan to medium heat. Heat 1 tablespoon cooking oil and place steaks in pan. Cook steaks for 3–6 minutes on each side, until desired doneness. Remove steaks to a plate to rest for 7 minutes.

Broil bread slices until golden, flipping once.

In a bowl combine the red peppers, basil, shallots, tomatoes and fresh lemon juice.

Slice steaks against the grain into ¼-inch-thick strips.

Assemble salad by giving each of 6 dinner plates a bed of arugula. Lay 2 grilled bread pieces on top of each arugula bed and lay a layer of steak strips across toast. Place a spoonful of tomato blend on top of steak and drizzle with horseradish ranch dressing (recipe follows).

Horseradish Ranch Dressing

1 ½ tablespoons prepared horseradish
6 tablespoons your favorite bottled ranch Dressing

Combine horseradish and ranch dressing in a serving bowl. Cover and set aside.

About the Author

Devon Delaney is lifelong resident of the Northeast and currently resides in coastal Connecticut. She is a wife, mother of three, grandmother of two, accomplished cooking contestant and a recent empty nester. She taught computer education and Lego Robotics for over ten years prior to pursuing writing.

Devon has been handsomely rewarded for her recipe innovation over the last twenty-plus years. Among the many prizes she has won are a full kitchen of major appliances, five-figure top cash prizes, and four trips to Disney World. She won the grand prize in a national writing contest for her foodie poem "Ode to Pork Passion." Combining her beloved hobby of cooking contests with her enthusiasm for writing was inevitable.

When she's is not preparing for her next cook-off, Devon may be found pursuing her other hobbies, including playing competitive USTA league tennis, gardening, needlepointing, painting, jarring her produce and hooking rugs. Her standard poodle, Rocket, is her pride and joy and keeps her on the path of sanity.

You can learn more about Devon at www.devonpdelaney.com.

Made in the USA
Coppell, TX
21 September 2024

37487909R00121